THE FAMILY CIRCLE

By ANDRÉ MAUROIS

THE FAMILY CIRCLE

By

ANDRÉ MAUROIS

Translated by
HAMISH MILES

NEW YORK

D. APPLETON AND COMPANY

MCMXXXII

PART I

I

DENISE HERPAIN's earliest memory was of a day at the seaside. For several years Madame Herpain had taken a villa every summer at Beuzeval, on the Normandy coast. "It's cheaper than Trouville," she would say. "I do it chiefly for the sake of the children." The house was called Villa Colibri, and twenty years later Denise would still recall the look of its roof, with the barge-board fretted into hearts and lacework, the half-timbering, upright and slanting, amid the brickwork, the glass-enclosed veranda, the garden gate which tinkled a little bell on being opened, and the wide metal boxes on the window-sills with their moribund geraniums smelling of earth and rotted leaves.

Denise, in her little red bathing-dress, stood leaning on her spade beside the rampart of a fort she had dug. She was looking at the sea. The wind puckered the great black shadows and sent them scurrying over the green water, which inshore took on a sandy colour. The tide was out. In front of the fort was a stretch of shingle with broken shells and razor-shells that cut bare feet. Beyond were smooth firm sand-banks, through which streamlets meandered in gleaming curves. At the bottom of these rivulets the sand lay ruffled in solid waves, and Denise was seized with a desire to feel its hard resistance under her feet. Drop-

3

ping her spade, she set off at a run. "Denise!" a voice cried. She stopped, and slowly came back.

Nurse Carrington—in France an English nursery-governess is always called "Nurse"—was in a bad temper. Before taking—goodness knows why—a situation with these Herpains, who were middle-class provincial people and did not even keep a carriage, she had looked after the children of the Comte de Thianges, who owned a château, and the Weissberger children, who spent four months of every year at Biarritz. Nurse Carrington was the daughter of a Folkestone grocer, and her ambition was to go back to England when she was about fifty and run a boarding-house. Meanwhile, over in France, she wanted to mix with either wealthy or aristocratic families.

She had not come across any fellow-countrywomen at this resort, which about 1900 was still quite unspoilt. Finding herself reduced to sitting with wet-nurses, she was filled with a grudge against the whole universe. The children's room was too small; there was only one bathroom; as usual, the children were sacrificed. Denise was becoming impossible and wouldn't lend her toys to Lolotte and Bébé. "You're a very naughty little girl . . . I'll tell your mother about you. . . ." Nurse would say. And Denise would go off and sit by herself and sulk. How could she lend Lolotte her spade when it was called Eulalie and was a real person? She had secret names for all the things about her, names it was forbidden to talk about. The leather cushion was Sebastien, and her bucket was called Monsieur

Guiborel, the same as the old gardener at Pont-de-l'Eure, who came with hundreds of little red earthenware pots to plant begonias and heliotropes. Sitting on the edge of the hole she had dug as a refuge for herself, she was now taking up big handfuls of sand and letting the fine warm grains slip through her fingers. When there was a little pebble or a piece of shell in the sand, the grip of her fingers stopped it. The tide was coming in. Denise was watching the little waves coming in from the distance. Their white froth would spread over the sand, leaving it glistening like a seal as they receded again. To the left, over by Dives and Cabourg, little boats were out fishing in a sea of light. Denise thought she would have liked to go away on board one of those big sailing-boats and that "grown-ups were unfair and wicked."

Behind her, Nurse was knitting with her back against the bathing-hut. Her head was bent over her work, and she was talking in French to the Quesnay children's "Mademoiselle."

"If I wanted to tell the things I see," Nurse was saying. "She's a bad woman, she is. . . . She spends her days writing to him. . . ."

Denise knew that Nurse was referring to her mother. She was listening as she went on dribbling the sand through the sieve of her fingers. By now there was a small heap of it beside her, finer and more golden than the rest.

About six o'clock Nurse said it was time to go home. With one hand she pushed Bébé's pram; the other she

gave to Charlotte. Denise trailed behind, letting her
spade drag, grating, over the sandy bricks of the sea-
wall. That scraping annoyed Nurse, she knew. She
had refused to have her boots put on, because she liked
the little stabbing pains the small stones gave her as
they stuck to the soles of her feet. When her bare
feet touched the front steps of the villa, the worm-
eaten wood was still warm. Denise thought of her
bath, when all the sand now sticking to her body would
come off and make a sort of little beach under the
water.

II

Madame Herpain lay reading on a chaise-longue.
Her hands were protected with gloves: she was afraid
the sea-air might hurt her skin. She wore a rose-
coloured wrap with a high waist and wide lace flounces
and leg-of-mutton sleeves. Its concertina pleats spread
fanwise over her legs. A white sunshade with embroidered openings, its design recalling the fretwork of the
roof, was propped against the back of the chair, screen-
ing her handsome face. As Denise walked up the hot
steps, she felt a wave of admiration surge up towards
this picture of coolness and comfort. Going up ahead
of the little ones, who made slow progress, having to
put both feet, one after the other, on each step, she ran
towards her mother to kiss her.

"Denise, your spade!" said Madame Herpain, torn from her novel by the metallic rasping.

She looked at the worried face of this little creature in the red bathing-suit, who had stopped dead on a level with the pink pleats.

"Your hands are full of sand," she said. "Go and wash. . . . Good evening, Nurse. I had so many letters to write, I didn't have time to go down to see you on the beach. Everything been all right?"

"Not at all right, Madame," said Nurse. "Denise . . . she again refused to lend her cushion to Lolotte."

"Denise, really, for the last few months you have been getting impossible!" said Madame Herpain.

"But, Mummy, I can't lend Sebastien to Lolotte. He hates her."

"Don't talk nonsense! You're too big for that. . . . You should set an example. . . . I do everything to make you all happy; I come to the seaside for your sakes, and you deliberately set out to vex me."

"People aren't fair," said Denise.

"What do you mean—people?" said Madame Herpain. "If you won't do it for Nurse or for your sisters, try to be good to please me."

Denise looked down at the uneven bricks of the terrace. There were ants running about on them.

"People aren't fair," she repeated with downcast eyes.

Madame Herpain sighed, shrugged her shoulders, and returned to her book. Silently Nurse and the three children went up the steep stair with its pitchpine rail,

the varnish of which stuck to one's hand. Whilst
Eugénie and Nurse were getting the bath ready for the
babies, Denise tidied up her drawers. She had not
been allowed to bring all her treasures from Pont-de-
l'Eure, but at least she had the most precious: a scrap
of gauze lined with goldleaf, a broken watch, some old
tram tickets, and her stamp-album. She always looked
over them while the babies were being bathed, because
then Nurse wasn't there to say, "Toys are meant for
everybody," and to make her lend her album to Lolotte,
who tore the pages. Soon, hearing splashings in the
bathroom, she went down to the kitchen. Victorine,
the cook, was her friend, whereas Eugénie, the maid,
who had become Nurse's confidante, would shoo Denise
out of her linen-room, with—

"Why must you always be hanging round me?"

The kitchen smelled nice. Like the fort on the
beach, it was a refuge. Its warmth wrapped one round.
Wearing a blue smock over her huge flabby bosom,
Victorine was bent over her stove. Denise adored Victorine, who taught her how to grate chocolate and grind
coffee, and sang to her "Le Petit Savoyard," "*O mon
enfant, pars pour la France. . . .*" Victorine sometimes flew into a rage, but her tempers were hot and
balmy like the steam that came out of her beautiful
copper double saucepan.

"Victorine, what are we having for dinner?"

"Will you be off!" said Victorine. "You're not din-
ing with your mamma to-night. . . . You'll be having
meat broth, spinach, and stewed fruit."

"That's not true," said Denise. "I can see inside your oven. There's strawberry tart and roast chicken."

Victorine shut the black door of the stove in a way that showed displeasure.

"Mind your own business," she said. "There's nothing there for little girls. . . . Come on, be off. You'll be getting me into trouble."

From Victorine's tone Denise realized that the tart and the chicken were signs of something mysterious and guilty going forward. At six years old, she had an uneasy sagacity, a fear of finding out. She said no more and she left the kitchen with her head down. Through the half-open door she caught a glimpse of flowers on the dining-room table. The whole house seemed to have been got ready for a party from which she was shut out. She heard Nurse's voice on the stairs.

"Denise! Where on earth is that child?"

"Nurse," cried fat Victorine, "take Denise away! With this double dinner. . . ."

She came to her kitchen door and exchanged with the Englishwoman a glance of amused contempt which the little girl in the red bathing-dress caught and never forgot.

"Hurry up!" said Nurse. "Your sisters are ready. Victorine, what is there for the children's dinner?"

"Spinach and stewed fruit," said Victorine.

"Good gracious!" said Nurse. "I'll go and speak to her."

She went towards the veranda, and Denise heard her remonstrating:

"Children must be fed. . . . I cannot starve them."

Nurse came back, and dragged Denise up to the first floor, saying to Eugénie in her faulty French:

"She is a bad mother. She thinks only of herself."

Sharp and thin and disdainful, Eugénie wore shiny black silk blouses with high collars bordered with a strip of white cambric. A threaded needle was stuck into the blouse over her bosom. Denise took off her red bathing-dress.

"Nanny," she said, "who's going to eat all that tart?"

"Don't ask questions," commanded Nurse.

And angrily she set about soaping the little girl's neck and ears.

III

THE three children were put to bed as soon as they had finished their dinner. "Because you haven't been good," said Nurse. Denise was familiar with such punishments; they coincided with the nights when Nurse wanted to go to the Casino. But Nurse was still wearing her pale blue uniform. Lying in bed with her eyes closed, Denise tried to make it out. She was thinking of the time when her mother loved her. Then, on Sunday mornings, she used to be carried into her parents' bedroom and put on their bed. Her father would get her to blow on a gold watch which flew open by itself; her mother would let her play with the plaits of her long black hair. When Eugénie had brought in the breakfast, Denise would be allowed to dip a lump of sugar in the coffee and suck it. In the daytime, too, Mummy would be like a little girl and sit on the carpet with Denise, superintending the cooking of the nursery meal. Then Lolotte had been born, then Bébé. Now she was always being scolded.

Usually Denise would sleep until Nurse came into the room with the morning sun. But that night she woke up. Through the open window a soft glow was falling on the three beds. It was a mixed light. There was the light of the moon, thin and milky, and another, stronger and whiter, which came from the veranda. Down below, someone began to sing. Denise raised herself on one elbow and listened. She adored her mother's voice. When she was only two she would go down to the drawing-room when she heard the piano and beg: "Sing, Mummy, sing." She liked best songs that made her cry, such as "Le Joueur de Vielle." When she was three she would hum tunes of Schumann and Brahms, and showed such a musical memory that her mother had made her "begin the piano." Her progress had been incredibly swift. For six months now she had been accompanying her mother in songs of which the piano part was within her power.

"Denise is very musical," Madame Herpain would say.

"How could she be otherwise, with a mother like

you?" the people of Pont-de-l'Eure would answer.

Coming forth from the silence, that voice filled the whole world. A smell of honeysuckle rose from the garden. The children slept. Tucked up in bed, Denise thought she would have liked to be alone with her mother, admiring her. The song welled out in great waves of sound. She could not understand all the words, but she heard:

"*. . . sous de vastes portiques.*"

"*Portiques.*" That word made her think of the gymnastic lessons she was taking with the Quesnay children, in the big grounds of their house. The trapeze and the rings were hung from a sort of portico. She remembered the swing of the trapeze, the creaking rings, and Antoine Quesnay, who was going to marry her when they grew up. Then she listened again. She found it so beautiful that she felt a sudden dread. For whom was her mother singing like that? Who could be accompanying her? The piano was as wonderful as the singing.

"*Les houles, en roulant les images des cieux . . .*"

From the next room, through the open door, came the sound of Nurse breathing like a person asleep. Denise listened, then resolutely flung back the bed-clothes, got out of bed, and tip-toed over to the window. The boxes of geraniums smelled of earth and rotten leaves. The sky was a wonderful black ceiling sprinkled with stars. In the distance little waves were breaking gently on the sand with a sound like the rustling of tissue paper. By leaning over the flowers, she could see the window-panes of the veranda, separated by metal frames. Her mother was standing near the piano; she wore a light-coloured dress; her shoulders were bare. On the piano-stool sat a man playing; Denise could only see his back. His thick neck was surmounted by a ring of reddish hair round a pink, shiny, bald crown. Madame Herpain had laid her hand on the man's shoulder as he bent to the piano.

"*. . . Et dont l'unique soin était d'approfondir
Le secret douloureux qui me faisait languir.*"

The strong voice seemed to rise to the very stars. Then it died away. The man took Madame Herpain's hand from his shoulder and raised it to his lips. Denise was frightened. She hurried away from the window and tip-toed back to bed again.

Who was this man whose visit nobody had mentioned? Was it for him that there had been a chicken, a strawberry tart, and violets on the table? Why had Victorine and Nurse laughed when speaking of "the double dinner"? In the moonlight she saw a shape swinging near the window. In fright she said in a low voice, "Mummy!" Then she realized that it was her red bathing-dress which Nurse had put there to dry. Below the window the piano started again. How Denise longed to play with such easy mastery! The tune was one she did not know. From her bed she could not make out any words. She turned over with a sigh, clutched her pillow in her arms, and fell asleep.

Next morning she remembered what she had seen during the night, but said nothing to Nurse and did not mention it to her mother. Sitting on the sand castle, she was thinking of the thick neck and the red curly hair, and the strange words she had heard. She sang to herself: *"Sous de vastes portiques. . . ."*

When she came back from the beach, she watched her mother to see if she was different—perhaps pleased. But as on the day before, her mother's loose wrap was spread out in a pink fan. All day Denise was disobedient, and so naughty that Madame Herpain came into her room, herself opened the sacred drawer, and took away her most particular treasure—the piece of gauze with which she used to pretend she was Cinderella ready for the ball. Denise cried for a long time. The world was beastly, wicked, hateful! After two hours of tears and sobs, Nurse washed her face and gave her back the piece of gauze. In the evening she was very good and laughed a lot.

IV

Monsieur Louis Herpain arrived at Beuzeval every Saturday to spend Sunday with his family. He was a wool merchant at Pont-de-l'Eure, and during the week he did not dare to leave a town whose ruling elders forced business people to observe strict and vain discipline. A square black beard framed his melancholy face. His head drooped a little towards his right shoulder. Madame Herpain went to meet him at the station with the little girls. To Denise it was always surprising, and rather miraculous, that out of this huge train, which seemed like another world, there should emerge the black jacket, square beard, and eye-glasses of her father. She loved him, and expected every one of his visits to bring some change to her distressful way of life. Her hope was never fulfilled.

Madame Herpain would greet her husband affectionately. He would ask:

"Have you seen anybody? Are you enjoying yourself?"

And she would answer:

"Oh! I don't bother about seeing people. . . . I am here for the children's sake; the sea-air does them good; that's all I care about. Oh! yes . . . I met Madame Quesnay on the front, but you know her way —a nod of the head and on she goes."

Then she asked about business, and the conversation became hard to grasp.

"Things are rather dead; they always are in August. But London is firm. That encourages buyers. . . . Pascal-Bouchet has taken five hundred bales of Australian from me, and I am discussing a big order from Montevideo with Schmitts' of Elbeuf."

Denise, confusing "bales" with "balls," used to wonder how Monsieur Pascal-Bouchet, who had such a fine yellow beard and whom Nurse would point out admiringly when he passed driving a pair of horses, could play with five hundred balls.   Sometimes Monsieur Herpain would try to make the little ones talk, but he was shy and made them so in turn.   What he greatly enjoyed was exchanging a few words in English with Nurse.   Several times a year he went to London for the wool sales.   That was why he had an Englishwoman in his household, though she secretly despised him.   On Sundays, if it was fine, he would take Denise to look for shrimps and sand-eels.   He would then pull up his trousers as far as the knee.   Nurse would look at his thin calves and say to the Quesnays' Mademoiselle: *"He's* not much of a sportsman."   Denise overheard and gripped her father's hand to drag him away. Trotting beside him in her red bathing-dress, she would think that she looked rather like a boy, and the notion pleased her.

On the Sunday following the night when Denise had been roused by her mother singing, the fishing expedition to the long lukewarm pools took her father and herself far from the bathing beach.   They halted close beside the Dives harbour, which smelled of mud and fish.   Monsieur Herpain said:

"We'll walk back along the sea-wall.   It'll be easier than walking on the sand."

"I'm tired," said Denise.

He took her by the elbows and lifted her up (she

liked to feel how strong he was; "Poor Monsieur is so weak," Nurse would say. Why "weak"? Denise would have liked Nurse to see how easily he carried her); he sat down on the sea-wall and looked at her with a smile, his head on one side.

"Have a rest for a few minutes," he said.

Sitting on the wall, she was on a level with his face. Never before had she seen him so well. How funny it was—his beard growing up his cheeks like grass up a bank! Once again she felt he was strong and good.

"You know, Papa," she said, "when you're not here and when we're in bed, another gentleman comes."

"Nonsense!" he said. "What are you talking about? What gentleman?"

"I don't know," she said. "I've only seen his back. But Mummy sings and the gentleman plays the piano. He plays very well. Papa, does. . . ."

He caught her by the arms so roughly that she was terrified and plumped her down on the paving of the sea-wall, then took her hand and led her quickly back towards Beuzeval. He was taking such long strides that she had to run; her net trailed behind her. She tried to talk:

"Papa, you know, I met a man who had a little monkey. He ate salad and nuts and grapes. Papa, how much does a little monkey cost?"

Her father did not answer, but as they came abreast of the villa, he suddenly turned to the right and crossed the road. The little garden gate made a bell tinkle. Madame Herpain was lying in her chair on the terrace;

she wore gloves, and her lace sunshade shielded her head; she was reading.

"Stay here," said Monsieur Herpain to Denise sternly, and threw the shrimp-basket down beside her.

She heard her father talking very loudly; then her mother laughed, and answered gently. She opened the basket; the dying shrimps were crawling and waving their arms about. There was the sound of rapid footsteps on the gravel. Nurse and her father were approaching. He had forgotten to roll down his trousers, which were still tucked up over his knees. His bare legs, his serious look, and his head on one side, all gave him a comical appearance.

"The little girl is a dreadful story-teller," said Nurse. "She ought to be punished. She is always making up stories."

Languid, but severe, her parasol carefully held between herself and the sun, Madame Herpain looked on. She caught Denise by the arm, made her drop the basket, and shook her.

"You are a very naughty girl," she said. "You've upset your father very much. You'll be shut in your room for the day. Go away at once!"

Denise screamed and cried until evening. At bath-time the two little ones looked at her curiously; they did not dare to speak to her. Nurse and Eugénie—the latter looking forbidding and haughty in her black collar with its white border—were laughing together.

V

At Pont-de-l'Eure, between 1890 and 1900, nearly every lady in the town seemed to be a paragon of virtue. It was impossible to take a walk in the streets without being watched from between curtains held back by the fingers of cunning and prying old women in their darkened drawing-rooms. A rendezvous could be arranged only at Evreux, or in Rouen or Paris; but motor-cars were hardly known, and railways journeys were watched. If chance could not account for the way in which a certain lady's visits to the dentist coincided with a certain gentleman's business visits to the Préfecture, expert female observers at once inferred the laws of such concomitant variations. Thus the whole of Pont-de-l'Eure was aware that, after Lieutenant Debucourt, Dr. Guérin had become the lover of Madame Louis Herpain.

Her conduct was the more severely condemned because Madame Herpain belonged to the industrial aristocracy of the district only by sufferance. Along with its neighbours, Elbeuf and Louviers, the pretty little town of Pont-de-l'Eure, the factories of which line the banks of the river Eure, has been one of the three capitals of the Wool Kingdom since the seventeenth century. Only by virtue of being a cloth manufacturer can one gain membership of the local nobility. Certain local families, such as the Romillys and Poittevins, still owned in 1900 factories which they had built in the days of Colbert. But great as their prestige was, it yielded to that of the Quesnay family, which had been manufacturing for three generations only, but on a larger scale. Of the five thousand workmen employed in Pont-de-l'Eure, the Quesnays were responsible for two thousand, and owned six hundred weaving looms— that is, they possessed the local equivalent of a duke- dom. For the whole of the town's inhabitants, the words *"Ces Messieurs"* referred to Monsieur Achille Quesnay and his son Fernand as plainly as, to the Duc de Saint-Simon, *"Monsieur"* meant the King's brother. The only personages in the Valley who were on equal footing with Monsieur Achille were Monsieur Pascal- Bouchet, of Louviers, and Monsieur Eugène Schmitt, an Alsatian who had set up at Elbeuf since the War of 1870, when Alsace had become German. In the Wool Valley the old nobility had been almost completely eliminated by the industrial feudality, of which those three men were the heads. A few country squires, liv- ing in broken-down châteaux, kept up among them- selves the rules of precedence of monarchical France, but as they were neither weavers nor spinners nor dyers, they were looked upon in Pont-de-l'Eure as people of small account.

Below the manufacturers, the cloth merchants, the commission agents, and the insurance brokers formed a wealthy and proud middle-class, but a middle-class which recognized the supremacy of manufacture. To their humble status the factory people allowed three honourable exceptions: the banker, Monsieur Leclerc;

the notary, Maître Pelletot; and Monsieur Aristide Herpain, wool merchant. These three formed a class of their own and occupied in Pont-de-l'Eure, side by side with the manufacturers, a position not unlike that which the judges of the French High Courts may have had in the eyes of the great liberal noblemen of the Old Regime. This prestige of the banker and the notary had quite a natural explanation: *"Ces Messieurs"* were obliged to admit them into their business secrets. Monsieur Aristide Herpain owed the esteem in which he was held by the factory people to the precious material he sold. Each morning he would bring the manufacturers packets of blue paper containing samples of wool from the Argentine, Chile, Australia, or the Cape, and in their eyes this wool was a substance comparable to nothing else. It controlled their lives; it fed their machines; in clotted layers it spread over the rollers of their combing-cards; it stretched on their spindles; it sped over their looms; it enriched and impoverished them by its unpredictable rises and falls. The man who imported it from those far, shadowy countries whose teasels and outlandish grass would scatter the tiled floors of their workrooms, the man who could tell by a glance at the black-pointed tufts of a fleece whether it came from Queensland or New Zealand, was naturally a participant in the mysteries of the craft. That was why when Monsieur Herpain came in at eleven o'clock with his blue parcels under his arm, the awe-inspiring Monsieur Achille Quesnay would mutter: "Ah, ha! Monsieur Aristide!"—and do his best to make the mutter affable. From 1890 onwards, Louis Herpain had gone round with his father and carried half of the blue parcels.

As for the most respectable families in the Valley, the Romillys, the Poittevins, and the Pascal-Bouchets, they were friendly with Monsieur Aristide, because, after a flighty youth, and indulgence in a suspect liberalism, he had, during the Dreyfus Affair, espoused that moderate republicanism which, made up of respect for Louis-Philippe and yearning regrets for the Second Empire, was the only political attitude tolerated by his class in Normandy towards the end of the nineteenth century.

VI

MONSIEUR ARISTIDE HERPAIN had made his wool business yield what the Valley of those days called "a very tidy fortune." The whole town knew the extent of that fortune, because even in those days, before income tax made concealment impossible, every inhabitant of Pont-de-l'Eure knew the exact history and financial position of all his neighbours. Thus the whole town was aware that the Herpain fortune amounted, in 1898, to 1,200,000 francs. "It's a lot for a man who professes to draw a commission of only two per cent," Monsieur Achille Quesnay would say. It was a lot especially for a man whose job was so easy that for eight hours out of ten he did not know how to kill time in his office, though he would not have deserted it without a twinge of remorse. Monsieur Aristide had two children, a daughter married to Jean Peroty, a manufacturer by birth, but on a small scale (one hundred and fifty looms), and a son, Louis Herpain, whom he had taken into his business. This son had disappointed him.

He had sent him to school, not at the Catholic College, but at the *lycée*—the State secondary school—in Rouen, which he himself had attended under the Second Empire. This had shocked people. At the *lycée* Louis Herpain had proved a brilliant pupil. The medal for history, the first prize for French composition, a "highly commended" with his baccalaureate (obtained in France at the end of the secondary-school course and not at the university), had all astonished a family with reputation enough for business and shooting but with none for literary interests. By the time he was seventeen he had become a shy, rather cultured youth who read Maupassant and Zola, and went to Rouen by the evening train once a week to attend performances of Massenet or Saint-Saëns. For Monsieur Aristide Herpain, "a fine brain" could only mean a special gift for understanding wool. On being assured that his son was a first-rate pupil, he rejoiced for the sake of his business. "If Louis keeps his weather eye lifted, he may end up with a couple of millions," he would say; and he could picture a third generation with three millions, and later on—of course he couldn't live to see it

—there might be Herpains with five, six, seven millions. A sublime vision.

To preserve intact, in hostile surroundings, qualities which enjoy no currency therein, calls for exceptional strong-mindedness. During the few years which had elapsed between his return to Pont-de-l'Eure and his military service, Louis Herpain had continued to work at night, to read, to take notes, and to exchange letters with a few of his old schoolfellows who had become professors or engineers. Then, whilst serving in the 39th Infantry Regiment at Rouen, he had fallen in love with Germaine d'Hocquinville, the daughter of a Normandy squire owning a small château midway between Pont-de-l'Eure and Louviers. In winter he lived in his town house, the Hôtel d'Hocquinville, in the Rue Damiette at Rouen. In 1882 the collapse of the Union Générale bank ruined the family and the château had to be sold. The daughter was very pretty, and her singing voice was fascinating. As Louis Herpain was understood to like music, some of his fellow-soldiers had introduced him to the house in the Rue Damiette. He sang duets with Germaine. She vanquished him with ease. When he told his father that he wished to marry her, Monsieur Herpain flew into a towering rage. The girl was poor, and had no connections in the wool world. For Baron d'Hocquinville, the misalliance promised salvation. But at Pont-de-l'Eure, to marry outside the Three Towns, even if it were marrying someone at Evreux or Rouen, was called "marrying a foreigner"; and the crime was not easily forgiven a young man. Germaine had been so beautiful and determined that the shy Louis Herpain was heartened to make a stand. He waited for three years, until he was twenty-five, and then at last obtained his parents' consent.

But this one masterful action seemed to exhaust all his powers of resistence to his surroundings. After his marriage, he sank into the uniform and cautious ways which Pont-de-l'Eure exacted from its residents. His political opinions, which had been "dangerous" in his youth (a radical professor had kindled an admiration for Jules Ferry), had become those suited to his occupation and the social success of his wife. He continued to read in secret during his long hours of idleness at the office, but he gave up talking about what he read. He got into the way of holding his head on one side and became round-shouldered. Had he been more dexterous or more of a showman, his trips to London might have endowed him with the prestige of a specialist; but he made no effort. An onlooker might have put down his meekness to a physical and conjugal failure. Before marriage his wife had seemed to love him sincerely; but a few months after their union she fell into the way of referring to him with kindly contempt. Three years later she was unfaithful to him with a subaltern. A company of the 39th Regiment was garrisoned at Pont-de-l'Eure, and in that town, whose social life was implacably viewed in terms of wool, the officers stood out like strange and dangerous beings. Their scarlet breeches made vivid splashes among the black suits of the local club, and when the Romillys gave a ball they led the girls to dance.

Lieutenant Debucourt was transferred to Eastern France and Madame Aristide Herpain hoped that her daughter-in-law would return to the strait path; but the next year a certain Dr. Guérin, fresh from walking the hospitals, bought the practice of old Dr. Petitclément, who had hitherto looked after Pont-de-l'Eure "society." It soon became known that Guérin played the piano and the violin, and that musical evenings took place at the Louis Herpains' house, when Madame Herpain accompanied. Later, Guérin had himself appointed to a public health committee which met at Rouen, and Madame Herpain showed anxiety to resume her singing lessons in that city, interrupted by childbearing. Maître Pelletot, the notary, claimed that he had met them both within twenty yards, on the pavement outside the Hôtel de Dieppe.

The women especially would not forgive Germaine Herpain for an indulgence which they did not allow themselves. Gossip about her laxity gave them a furtive, jealous satisfaction. On the very evening when Denise, standing by a moonlit window, had glimpsed through the geraniums a man sitting at the piano beside her mother, Madame Achille Quesnay and Madame Romilly, the social rulers of Pont-de-l'Eure, were discussing the doctor's trips to Beuzeval.

"It's absurd," Madame Achille Quesnay was saying. "He goes there every Friday, you know. I know because I have had to call him in twice running on a

Saturday morning, for my son Fernand. His servant told me that he would not get back from Beuzeval until ten. . . ."

"It's Louis Herpain's fault," said Madame Romilly; "he should never have allowed his wife to go off alone for the whole summer. Think of it! She went there as early as the fifteenth of June."

"Do you know what she says?" asked Madame Achille. "That her children need the sea, and of course Guérin backs her up. But a fine lot she cares about her children! Her English girl told my grandchildren's governess that she doesn't see them for days on end. . . . She pretends that noise tires her."

"Noise doesn't tire her when she's singing with Guérin," said Madame Romilly. "In any case, it's in her blood. I knew her mother at Rouen, between '72 and '75, when the father was a captain in the 7th Chasseurs. She was the joy of the whole regiment! By the way, do you have the little Herpains to the house? I've rather avoided them myself since all this."

"I see them sometimes during the day," said Madame Achille. "Their eldest daughter takes gymnastic lessons with my grandson. But I don't ask them in in the evenings—that's what matters."

From Madame Achille's garden one could see the long roofs of the Quesnay factories, with their orange-tinted tiles, the chimney-stacks from which the smoke was rising straight up, and the river edged with poplars. A train drew its wake of white steam across the plain. And the two old ladies, conscious of their own power and their own freedom from desire, looked at these things with contentment.

VII

MADAME HERPAIN and her three daughters stayed on at the seaside until the end of September. The other families had all left long before, chased away by wind and cold. The equinoctial tides had forced not only the red-and-white bathing tents but even the solid wooden cabins to retreat from the beach back to the roadway, and the last of the bathers were routed. The Quesnay children and their "Mademoiselle" had left on the fifteenth of September. One could no longer sit on the sand; it was always soaked with rain or spray. Madame Herpain, however, had resolved to remain at Beuzeval until the last day of the period for which the villa had been taken. "I don't want the children to lose a single breath of fresh air," she would say. "It's no fun for me, but I am fond of being alone and reading. If the little ones are happy, then so am I." In the kitchen, Nurse was ingeniously undermining Victorine's loyalty.

"She would let her children die of pneumonia so long as she could see her man more easily," she would say.

"There's no doubt the weather is not up to much," Victorine would reply; and there was restrained fury in the way she lifted the black cast-iron lid that covered the glowing coals.

Monsieur Herpain came to fetch his family away, a kind attention which was a sacred custom of Pont-de-l'Eure. In 1900 men took few holidays, but they did not let their wives travel by train alone. Denise found herself home again in the Rue Carnot, in the house which was the centre of her universe. All the well-to-do dwellings in Pont-de-l'Eure were alike. They had all been built by the same architect, Monsieur Coliveau, and he had never agreed to alter a single line of the only plan he had ever drawn up. They were of red brick, with dressed stone at the corners, and slated mansard roofs. The rather small gardens lay behind. When once a manufacturer or a cloth or wool merchant had amassed half a million francs, he ordered a house from Monsieur Coliveau, just as he ordered an ice-pudding and *petits fours* from Monsieur Belgiati if he were giving a big dinner. Monsieur Belgiati always supplied the same ice—a strawberry *bombe* that tasted watery; and Monsieur Coliveau always supplied the same red-brick house. This fidelity ensured their success.

The little Herpain girls did not see the house in the Rue Carnot as either beautiful or ugly. To them it was just "home." Here Denise had her own room, her own drawers, her own books. Through the window of her room she could see the combined tobacconist's and café where the workmen in caps went. Higher up, at the top of a climbing street, there was the railway line. At night she would hear the whistles of the trains.

Near the house was a boys' school, the École Bossuet, with chimes that rang at six in the morning and six in the evening. The chimes always played the same tune —a set of variations on the "Carnaval de Venise."

On the ground-floor was the small drawing-room to which the Herpains withdrew after meals; beyond that the large drawing-room, with its furniture shrouded in dust-covers. In the latter room were the piano and the music cabinet, which Denise looked on with awe. She entered the large drawing-room only to take her piano lesson with Mademoiselle Paulus or to accompany her mother. Thursday was Madame Herpain's day: in the drawing-room there would be tea and cakes, and three or four female relatives would turn up about four o'clock.

A few weeks after they had got back, Denise had an attack of bronchitis, and Dr. Guérin came to see her. In order to examine her chest he made her sit up, and through her night-dress she could feel his warm breath and his hairy ears. "Cough," he said. "Not so loud. . . . Good. . . . Now the other side. . . ." Looking down at him, she recognized the thick neck, the small red curls, and the pink baldness of the man who had sat at the piano beside her mother at Beuzeval. From that moment many conversations between Eugénie and Nurse became clear to her. She came to know that of an evening, when she was asleep and Monsieur Herpain was at the club, Dr. Guérin came for music with Mamma. Denise did not understand why it was wrong for her mother to have the doctor accompany her, but she noticed that everybody talked of it, that the Quesnays' "Mademoiselle" laughed about it with Nurse, and that owing to these evening visits her papa, her mamma, and she herself were topics for jokes and gossip in the town.

She became gloomy, and said she didn't want to see any other little girls.

At the beginning of the winter Mamma bought the three little girls each a caracal coat with an ermine collar. They wore them on Sunday mornings to go to church. Bébé could now walk by herself, and she was no longer called Bébé, but Suzanne. The Herpains' parish was that of the Immaculate Conception; but Denise always thought of it as "Immakly," which was a word at once incomprehensible and holy. Her sisters were bored by Sunday Mass, but she delighted in it: for one thing, she prayed, and always hoped that God would listen to her prayers; for another, she liked the organ music flooding the church with great waves of sound. Denise felt those waves entering into her, swinging her up, and sometimes lifting her sky-high. The organist of the Church of the Immaculate Conception was called Tournemine. He was a white-bearded old man and an excellent musician.

Papa did not often go to Mass. Every Sunday on coming out one ran into Dr. Guérin. Other people would say "Good morning" to him, but he would pretend to be rapt in contemplation of the stone figures of the porch, and did not let himself be drawn into a conversation. Denise would catch sight of his greyish-brown overcoat, his bowler hat with the red hair sticking out underneath, and his gold spectacles. He would give a start of surprise and say: "Why, hullo! It's Madame Herpain! And how are the children?" Mamma would tell them: "Say how-d'you-do to the doctor." At first the two little ones would obey, but when they saw that Denise refused and kept her hand inside her muff, they followed her example. Mamma said several times that she would punish them. "Funny little things. . . ." the doctor would say. But he did not seem upset.

One Sunday in December Dr. Guérin came to luncheon at the Rue Carnot, and afterwards Denise was called down to the drawing-room to play before him. She accompanied her mother, who sang a song from "Iphigénie." The doctor said:

"You know, she's really wonderfully gifted. You are wrong to leave her in the hands of a woman who is not in the least a musician. Would you like me to speak about her to my friend Tournemine?"

His voice was gentle and masterful. He was saying: "She must not only go on with the piano, but do solfeggio and musical dictation," and it was exactly as he might have said: "She must take a quarter of an aspirin tablet before going to sleep—no more. And three times a day before meals a dessert-spoon of this mixture." When he wrote out a prescription he always spoke it, and as he drew up the programme for her musical education, Denise was surprised not to see him sitting at a table, with paper in front of him and pen in hand:

"D'you think Tournemine would agree to take on a child of seven?" said Madame Herpain.

"She is not a child when she's at the piano," said the doctor.

From that day the feelings of Denise towards the doctor became more complex. She hated him because he was a cause of embarrassment, admired him because he could rule Madame Herpain, of whom she herself stood in awe, and was grateful to him for having changed the course of her life. At the doctor's request, old Tournemine had agreed to come to give lessons at the Herpains' house. After the lessons, as a reward, he would play Bach or Beethoven to her, or improvise on a theme chosen with her help. The doctor also supplemented the musical education of Madame Herpain herself. He introduced her to music of which she had known nothing. She was now singing Faure and Chausson, and was beginning to understand Debussy. Though naturally a lazy woman, for the sake of her lover she was able to work the whole day long.

Monsieur Herpain felt himself a stranger to all this new music, although at the time he became engaged he had been fond of music—the music fashionable at Pont-de-l'Eure about 1890—and had himself sung the *cavatina* from "Faust" and the *aubade* in "Le Roi d'Ys." He became more and more taciturn. Snug in an armchair, his head on one side, he longed to astonish his wife and the doctor by recovering his old vivacity of mind. But only remarks about business came to his lips. "The wool trade will be difficult in France this year," he kept thinking. Then he would reproach himself for his absorption in petty subjects, and strive hard to listen; and again his wits were wandering. But when his wife sang something simple and moving, like "La Bien-Aimée Absente," his eyes filled with tears.

VIII

WHEN the Abbé Faurie gave Scripture lessons to the children of the first catechism class, his solemn voice reminded Denise of an organ. The Abbé Faurie's sermons were famous in Pont-de-l'Eure. According to Madame Romilly, who was a great religious authority in the town because an uncle of hers had something to do with the charities of the Paris archbishopric, Abbé Faurie would have been a bishop if he had not been lame. Denise liked to hear the Abbé tell about the Burning Bush or the story of Abraham's sacrifice. At night in bed she would imagine her mother offering her as a burnt-offering upon a mountain. Later she delighted in the story of Jephthah's daughter, who asked to be sacrificed that her father might fulfil his vow to the Lord.

At this time, when left to herself, instead of playing with her odds and ends of stuff, she would open the "Lives of the Saints," which Grandmother d'Hocquinville had given her. The tortures terrified and fascinated her; she found extraordinary pleasure in re-reading those descriptions. She knew how St. Vincent had been bound to a rack and how the executioners had pulled his feet and hands with ropes, and how he had then been torn with iron hooks and his wounds powdered with salt to make them sting more. But she preferred the tortures of the female martyrs. She liked the stories of virgins who died to remain pure, like St. Eulalia, torn with iron rakes, burned with torches, yet never wavering in the midst of her torments; or like St. Agnes, modestly wrapping herself in her cloak when the fatal blow fell. When Madame Herpain saw her daughter lying full length on her stomach on the drawing-room carpet, a fat book in front of her, she little suspected that Denise, gazing on a picture of the Holy Penitents, led by St. Mary Magdalene, treading on the emblems of their frivolity—necklaces, jewel-cases, and perfumes—was praying that her mother too might become a penitent and a saint.

One day the Abbé Faurie spoke at length of the Holy Virgin Mary. "She is the Virgin," he said, "but she is also the Mother. . . . You should honour your mother, you should look on her lovingly and proudly, for she embodies all the family virtues. . . ."

Kneeling in the chapel, Denise tried to comply with the Abbé's direction and think of Madame Herpain with love and pride. When Eugénie came to fetch her, as she left the church, she said:

"I want to see Mummy the moment I get home."

"Just the right time!" said Eugénie sardonically.

Denise said nothing. It was six o'clock. The carillon of the École Bossuet was playing the "Carnaval de Venise." The pause between the first and the second variations was so long that one wondered if it would ever go on. When they reached home, Mademoiselle Perolaz (a young Swiss girl who had replaced Nurse) told Denise not to make a noise, as her mother was not very well. At seven Denise dined alone opposite Monsieur Herpain. He seemed sad and barely noticed her. After dinner she asked:

"May I say good night to Mummy?"

"Go in on tip-toe," said her father, "but don't stay if she's feeling tired."

She went in; the room smelled of essence of peppermint and eau-de-Cologne; her mother was lying on her side. On seeing the little girl, she raised her face; her eyes were red.

"Oh, it's you," she said in a rather gentle voice. "Who told you to come up? What d'you want?"

"Can I do anything for you, Mummy?"

"No. . . . Oh, yes! Come and put your hand on my forehead. I've such a headache."

Denise went to the bedside and placed her hand on her mother's forehead, which was burning. In a moment she said:

"Mummy, would you like me to read to you?"

"No," said Madame Herpain. "Keep quiet. The sound of your voice tires me."

A moment later she snatched away the little hand pressed to her forehead.

"You're hot," she said. "Go away. Say I'm not to be disturbed."

Denise went down to the kitchen. There she found Eugénie, Victorine, and Victorine's husband, who was called Léopold Courteheuse and was a weaver in the Quesnay factory. The Herpains kept no manservant, but Victorine's husband chopped the wood and lighted the furnace. He had huge moustaches and was always too hot, and when he sat down at the kitchen table his unbuttoned shirt showed his hairy chest. In the eyes of Denise he was a picture of strength. The executioners who used hot pincers to St. Apollonia must have looked like Victorine's husband.

"Hullo, so there you are!" said Eugénie. "I thought you were up in the mistress's room."

"Mummy is ill," said Denise. "She told me to say she was not to be disturbed."

"She would like to be disturbed all right," said Eugénie; "but not by you nor by me."

"Has the doctor been?" said Denise hesitantly.

"That's just it!" said Eugénie with a wink.

"Shut up!" said Victorine reproachfully. "Poor little girl! How can you be such a beast! Now, dearie, run off to bed," she said to Denise.

"Oh! do let me stay here," the child begged.

Victorine hugged her close to the soft warmth of her blue overall.

"All right, stay," she said. "If you have nothing else, you'll always have your Victorine."

She gave her some of the chestnuts she had been roasting for Monsieur Courteheuse. Presently the latter sang. He knew a song which Denise liked very much.

> *"Pleur' pas comm' ça ma p'tite Suzette,*
> *C'est un p'tit accident.*
> *Ça n'durera pas longtemps.*
> *Allons, voyons, fais-moi risette . . .*
> *En attendant c'joli marmot,*
> *Il faut préparer le berceau."*

Seated at the deal table, Denise sang the chorus with Victorine and Eugénie. Now she was laughing a lot. Then Victorine sang, *"Pauvre petit, pars pour la France. . . ."* A bell rang. Eugénie rose. Presently Mademoiselle Perolaz fetched Denise, who went to say good night to her father. He was alone in the small drawing-room, seated in an arm-chair, a newspaper across his knee; his expression was that of a man hurt and stunned. He kissed her forehead absent-mindedly and dropped back into his reverie.

IX

MADEMOISELLE PEROLAZ had a kinder heart than Nurse Carrington, but she made Denise suffer more than the other had. Young, enthusiastic, and warm-spirited, she stood up vigorously for justice and virtue. She was sorry for Denise, and tried to console her, and in so doing gave her a painful feeling that she was the unhappiest little girl in the world. She did not understand children, she did not realize that they either understand or distort everything they hear; from her careless talk with Eugénie in front of Denise, the child learned many details which she had not suspected in Nurse's time.

Owing to the clumsiness of Mademoiselle Perolaz, Denise came to know that her mother's illness was caused by Dr. Guérin's behaviour.

"He was taken up with a nurse at the hospital," Eugénie would say. "The mistress has made a fuss about it, and he's not the one to stand scenes, that he's not."

Madame Herpain still kept her bed. Although Monsieur Herpain was so busy and was at home only from noon until two o'clock, it was he who had to order the meals and see after the children. After luncheon, Victorine had to come to him in the small drawing-room. He would look over her books and hand her money.

"Madame is very unwell, Victorine," he would say; "give her light food. What is she fond of? What could we tempt her with?"

When Denise went down to the kitchen later, she would hear her father's words repeated by Eugénie and Monsieur Courteheuse. They laughed. She would feel ashamed and stand very close to the range so that her blushing would not be noticed.   In the black ring of iron the fire glowed as bright as that over which the executioners had roasted St. Eulalia.

One evening Denise took in Charlotte to her mother's bedside, and the younger sister provoked a fit of weeping by saying: "Oh, Mummy, why not have the *goctor?*"   As his wife refused to be seen by any local doctor, Monsieur Herpain telephoned to Professor Brunoy at Rouen and—unheard-of event!—left his office at ten in the morning in order to be at home when the professor arrived.   Madame Aristide Herpain came with her daughter, Marthe Peroty, to await "the result of the consultation."   In the drawing-rooms of the Valley both women stood up in defence of their daughter-in-law and sister-in-law; but now, alone with her daughter, Madame Aristide felt the need of relieving her feelings.

"Louis is very unhappy," she said.   "All these pains Germaine complains of are put on.   The truth is, she has lost her Guérin and hopes to get him back by exciting his pity.   As for poor Louis, she just leads him by the nose.   Just think!   He took her without a penny when he might have found a wife with a solid dowry!   And she's an absolute spendthrift; this house—neither of us has one like it—a sable coat—a pearl necklace. Yet she never says a pleasant word—always complaining and wanting things. . . ."

"Louis might get a divorce," said Marthe Peroty.

"Nonsense, girl!   No Herpain has ever divorced his wife."

Little Lolotte was on the carpet playing with a doll. She looked up.

"Mademoiselle Herpain—that's me!" she said.

"Run into the garden, darling, and look at the flowers. Bring back a nice one for Aunt Marthe."

"If she even cared for her children," said Madame Peroty.

"You know very well she lets three or four days go by without looking into the nursery!"

"Louis was not firm enough in the beginning," said Marthe.

"Louis is on his knees before her," said Madame Aristide. "He's in love with her, poor boy! After nine years of married life—can you believe it?"

Louis Herpain returned. The professor had been surprised not to find a local doctor in attendance; he was peevish, mentioned neurasthenia, described a diet, and departed. The two women looked at each other ironically. Herpain went sadly back to his office, where he picked up his Anatole France novel again. Mademoiselle Perolaz was about to go out with Denise, who had already put on her caracal coat, when Eugénie called her.

"You are both to go up to the mistress."

Denise found her mother very lively. She was sitting up in bed, a letter in her hand.

"Look, Mademoiselle," she said. "Will you take this letter to Dr. Guérin's in the Rue Saint-Etienne, and bring back a reply? Don't let the servant tell you he's not in; this is his consulting-hour. If he comes out of his consulting-room Denise can tell him that her mamma is very ill and he must come and attend her. You understand, darling?"

She drew Denise to her and kissed her tenderly. Mademoiselle Perolaz took the envelope in silence. The little girl standing beside her, running her fingers over her fur collar, knew that her governess despised her mother, and the knowledge hurt her. Downstairs, Eugénie went with them to the front door, and said:

"That crowns all, it really does! Fancy making the child do such a thing!"

With a sigh, Mademoiselle set out with Denise for the doctor's house. The streets of Pont-de-l'Eure bustled with hurrying work-people at the hours when the factories started and stopped, but for the rest of the day they were empty. The waters of the dye-works ran down to the river in swift streams, coloured blue, or yellow, or madder-red. Denise, with her head down and her hands in her muff, was walking along the pavement, very careful not to step on one of the cement joins. If she succeeded in going all the way without once touching a line, the doctor would refuse to come. She wanted him to refuse. She considered that her mother should be punished. No, she was not a penitent saint, but a great sinner like the pagan women.

Denise felt a blend of admiration and jealousy at the thought of Dr. Guérin holding in his hands the fate of the formidable woman before whom Papa trembled like a child. She pictured the doctor in his consulting-room: he was strong, bad-tempered and determined; he would tear up Madame Herpain's letter—and once again she could feel on her chest his warm breath and his hairy ears. A man brushed by Mademoiselle, walking very fast, his elbows pressed well in: it was Monsieur Lesage-Maille, a retired manufacturer. Ever since he had given up work, he had always been dashing about, a stick in his hand, a flower in his buttonhole. All Pont-de-l'Eure wondered where on earth he went.

A manservant opened the doctor's door. He was wearing a white apron and a striped yellow-and-black waistcoat.

"For a consultation?" he asked.

"No," said Mademoiselle. "It's an urgent letter for the doctor. We are to wait for a reply."

"Sit down a moment," said the servant. "I'll take it in to him when the next one comes out."

The smell of the hall reminded Denise of the medicine-cupboard. There was a wide bench below a greenish tapestry. Mademoiselle made Denise sit down on it.

"Wouldn't you rather go into the waiting-room?" asked the servant.

"No, no," said Mademoiselle.

She was uncomfortable. Denise was looking through a half-open door at a white room in which there were shining machines and tubes. Suddenly a leather door opened and Dr. Guérin appeared. He was holding Madame Herpain's letter in his hand. He seemed to be in a hurry.

"You are Mademoiselle?" he said. "Tell Madame

Herpain that, since she believes I can be of some use, I'll come to see her."

"Very good, doctor," said Mademoiselle Perolaz. "And when should I tell Madame that . . ."

"Let me see. . . ." He pulled a little book from his pocket. "This evening, six o'clock. You'd better say six-thirty, so that she won't be impatient. So"— and he turned to Denise—"your mamma is ill? And how are you? Are you playing the piano as nicely as ever?"

He chucked her under the chin. The children were afraid of his sudden gestures. Denise dropped her head and said nothing.

Next day Madame Herpain was able to get up, and two days later surprised her household by turning up in the dining-room at lunch-time wearing a white dressing-wrap. Monsieur Herpain was greatly moved. He jumped up, supported her to her chair, and said to Eugénie, who was waiting at table, "Bring up a bottle of champagne." Most of it was drunk that evening in the kitchen by Monsieur Courteheuse, and afterwards he sang more loudly than ever, "*Pleur' pas comm' ça, ma p'tite Su-ze-e-ette . . .*"

Following this episode, Denise became unmanageable.

"I can't understand it," Mademoiselle would say. "She's the most intelligent girl I have ever come across. I love her dearly; I know she likes me, and the last thing she wants to do is to upset me. Yet I can't get her to do anything. It's a kind of madness."

If Mademoiselle Perolaz had been more observant

she would have noticed that Denise's naughtiness took forms chosen to annoy or upset her mother. Always perfectly turned out herself, Madame Herpain insisted on her daughters being extremely neat. Denise made it a point of honour to be grimy. One day Mademoiselle Perolaz found her blackening her white shoes with coal-dust. The governess wept and said she could no longer take charge of such a wicked child. When the time of Denise's First Communion drew near, Monsieur and Madame Herpain had a long talk together, in the course of which it was decided that, in the following year, their eldest daughter would be sent to Saint-Jean as a boarder.

X

THE Convent of Saint-Jean is a fine group of old terraced buildings overlooking the river, between Louviers and Pont-de-l'Eure. For over a century the wool aristocracy had sent its daughters there for a Catholic education. The nuns left in 1905, driven away by the law against religious congregations, but they had been replaced by lay sisters. The headmistress, Mademoiselle d'Aubray, was a stout woman, dressed in black silk, who kept her plump white hands folded over her stomach. When she crossed a courtyard or passed through a class-room, her eyes were cast down, but from the windows of the one-storey wing she lived in, at the entrance to the main courtyard, she would keep a keen and shrewd eye on her pupils. Although she never set foot outside the walls of her convent, she was perfectly acquainted with the histories and the peculiar hierarchies of the local families. She was aware that Hélène and Françoise Pascal-Bouchet, two handsome sisters with fair hair and serene faces, belonged to a world which would be for ever closed to little Denise Herpain, whose features were hard and unpromising, and who had been brought to the convent by a too well-dressed mother. Yet she sought to restore among the children that equality in the sight of God which the vanity of their parents denied.

At five minutes to eight every morning the pupils of Saint-Jean had to line up motionless in the yard. They all wore long hair in plaits down their backs. On the first stroke of eight the headmistress came out of her little house, walked down the files of girls and chose out one whom she took by the hand. This might be a girl whose industry or piety was outstanding, or one to whom, for a reason known to herself alone, she wished to give pre-eminence in the eyes of the other pupils. Still holding the chosen girl by the hand, she led her into chapel, and, two by two, the whole convent followed. This little ceremony was not without impressiveness, and the sense of anxious expectation worked on the girls. During her first year Denise was one of those most often chosen.

The year of her First Communion was a period of

religious exaltation. She mortified herself; she denied herself chocolate or fruit of an afternoon, and conversation for two days on end. She vowed to repay evil with good, and in the holidays, when she went home to the Rue Carnot, she would share out between her astonished sisters the most jealously guarded treasures of her play-drawers. Thus she gave Suzanne the spunglass service she had won at the fair; the child broke it all almost at once; Denise wept, but went and kissed Suzanne. When Eugénie began speaking ill of her mother, she stopped her and gave her a homily on ill-natured gossip. She was upset to find that, in spite of her efforts to be saintly, the Abbé Guillemin, her director, continued to be worried about her. He was a young and very handsome priest, who blushed when he was spoken to. One day, after she had tried to tell him about her struggles and triumphs, he said: "Denise, you are like fire; you burn everything you touch."

Then she said to herself, as in bygone days on the beach, "People are not fair." When the Abbé Guillemin, blushing the while, was explaining that, under pain of suffering eternally in the flames of hell, one had to avoid impure thoughts and the sin of the flesh, she felt guilty and wretched. All round her a hundred girls in black smocks were listening with apparent placidity. Their smocks gave out an acid smell, a smell of ink and the wash-tub. Denise was thinking that her mother would spend eternity in even worse torments than those inflicted by the pagans on the martyr saints. Other girls, brought up in the country, knew a great deal about

the physical aspect of love, and expounded to her only
too clearly the nature of the sins of the flesh.   She
would imagine her mother and Dr. Guérin lying beside
one another.   Again Dr. Guérin was before her, emerging from his consulting-room into that hall with its
medicine-cupboard smell.   She almost believed the hard
impress of his fingers was still on her chin.

When her mother had brought her to Saint-Jean,
Denise's first impression, at the sight of the great white
buildings on the river bank, had been one, not of a
prison, but of a refuge.   Once behind those high walls,
with their stern sentinel towers, nobody would ever
speak to her of her home in the Rue Carnot, which to
herself she called "the house with a curse."   Within
those well-enclosed courtyards, who could know that
Dr. Guérin came to play the violin when Monsieur
Herpain was at the club in the evenings, and that
Madame Herpain made the servants laugh by the way
she carried on when the doctor took a fancy to a hospital
nurse?   But gradually Denise had found that everybody
in the convent knew her history.   It seemed as if the
whole world was interested in the house in the Rue
Carnot.   Sometimes in chapel she could imagine swift
little black devils, running from bench to bench, their
elbows well tucked in, like Monsieur Lesage-Maille,
whispering: "Denise Herpain has an adulterous mother
who is guilty of the sin of the flesh with Dr. Guérin."

Certain pupils never played with her.   Despite the
mistresses, the classes of Saint-Jean split up at play-
time into exclusive cliques.   Hélène and Françoise

Pascal-Bouchet, who ruled the most powerful of these, said "Good morning" to Denise when they met her in the passages or were next to her in file. They were quite kind and polite, but their tone discouraged any closer relation. Denise felt the sadder because she thought them both very beautiful. She would passionately have liked to gain their affection, and to astonish them by her skill at games, and by her devotion. Perhaps it was to this intensity of feeling that Abbé Guillemin referred when he said: "Denise, you are like fire."

Still, one of the leaders of the clique, Sabine Leclerc, the banker's daughter, came up to Denise before one Thursday walk and asked her if she would like to walk with her. That was miraculous joy. Picking their way between the trunks of the willows on the river bank, the two girls talked a great deal. Denise let herself go in making confidences and believed she had found a friend. Next day, at the ten-o'clock break, she sought out Sabine and asked her if she wouldn't play with her.

"No," said Sabine Leclerc with a laugh. "Why? I have my own friends."

"What about yesterday?" said Denise.

"Yesterday? Oh! that wasn't in earnest," said Sabine. "I only wanted to see what you were like because I hear so many stories about you."

Sabine Leclerc returned to her set. The favourite game at Saint-Jean that year was *la grace*, with its little sticks and hoops covered with spirals of red plush and gold braid. The plush came unstuck very quickly, and showed only a ring of common wood looking rather absurd and drab.

XI

Rebuffed by the Pascal-Bouchet clique, Denise had attached herself to another. It was one which appealed to her less, but it was more welcoming. Its centre was Berthe Pelletot, the daughter of Pont-de-l'Eure's notary. She was a fat girl endowed with genuine kindliness, and between Denise and herself a friendship developed. As the Easter holidays drew near, they could not bear the prospect of separation, and Berthe said to Denise:

"As we are both going home to Pont-de-l'Eure, I'll get Mamma to invite you to tea."

Thereupon the promised tea-party became for Denise the glowing climax of the spring.

She felt misgivings when she returned to spend a fortnight at home. At a distance, Madame Herpain had become a disturbing monster. She hated her, and blamed herself for doing so. But in contrast with a grotesque and distorted picture, she was charmed on the first day she was back to find her mother a woman so youthful and alive. Madame Herpain was wearing a new dress, of soft porcelain-blue. After the black smocks at Saint-Jean it seemed to Denise as gay as the spring. During the luncheon the mother set herself to winning her daughters and her husband. She was at once coquettish, frail, mocking, and affectionate, and in a few minutes they were all adoring her.

The house and garden seemed tiny to Denise, but to be home again gave her unexpected delight. Lying in bed on the first night, she enjoyed hearing the trains whistle in the dark. The next morning at six she was awakened by the carillon of the Ecole Bossuet playing the "Carnaval de Venise," and hesitating between the notes just like a real person. She got out of bed in the grey dawn to see the workmen in caps going into the little café over the way. When she was dressed, she went down to the kitchen. Victorine gave her a great welcome. For luncheon she was going to give them Denise's favourite dishes. There would be a macaroni pasty and a chicken with olives. Monsieur Courteheuse was shy and addressed her as "Mademoiselle Denise." The whole family went to High Mass at the Church of the Immaculate Conception, and Denise was allowed to go into the organ-loft beside Monsieur Tournemine. On coming out Monsieur Herpain walked away from his wife without a word. He went off alone, walking very fast. Dr. Guérin was looking at the stone figures of the porch, and happened to turn round just as Madame Herpain was passing with her daughters.

Then Denise understood that below the hypocritically smooth surface of family life nothing had changed. On Monday Madame Herpain said she had to go to Rouen to see her poor mother, who was ailing. Denise asked to come with her, but was cold-shouldered.

To make amends, her father took her with him to the office. She liked the sheds smelling of wool and grease, and those huge bales on top of which her father often had hoisted her as a little girl. Monsieur Aristide, asleep in an arm-chair, got up and gave his granddaughter a twenty-franc gold piece. At dinner-time Madame Herpain had not returned.

"Mummy has probably missed the five-forty-nine," said Monsieur Herpain in a way he tried to make casual. "She will be coming by the six-ten."

"The children are hungry, Monsieur," Mademoiselle Perolaz replied reproachfully. "And they must get to bed."

"Let them have their dinner," he said; "I shall wait."

Madame Herpain did not arrive until eight. Denise was hoping that her father would greet her coldly. He merely said:

"How late you are!"

She answered:

"I missed the train. It's ridiculous; they shut the gates five minutes too soon."

"Just what I thought," said Monsieur Herpain, and looked at Mademoiselle Perolaz triumphantly.

Denise wished he had shouted. She wanted to be a man, that she might knock down this smiling woman, beat her and torture her. Nothing happened. Next day Madame Herpain was more jolly and more affectionate than ever, and her husband more in love and more her slave.

By the fifth day of the holidays Denise was growing anxious at having no news from Berthe Pelletot. She mentioned the matter to Mademoiselle Perolaz, and then to her mother.

"I should be very surprised," said Madame Herpain rather bitterly, "if Madame Pelletot invited you to tea. She is friendly with your grandmother, and her husband is our notary, but she has never been on visiting terms with me, and I don't want to run after her."

"But, Mummy, Berthe asked me three times. Indeed, when she was saying good-bye at Saint-Jean she said to me: 'I'd like you to know my brother.' "

"Berthe is badly brought up: she spoke without consulting her mother."

"But Mummy, Berthe Pelletot and I are always together. Mademoiselle d'Aubray even complained about it. One day she looked at us and said she didn't care for individual friendships."

"She was quite right," said Madame Herpain. "Once again, Denise, I don't doubt Berthe is very fond of you; but if her mother had wanted to invite you, she would have done so."

"Mummy, couldn't you telephone to ask. . . ."

"I certainly can't go begging for an invitation," said Madame Herpain.

Then, noticing that the girl's eyelids were red, she added with a sudden kindness:

"What I might do at a pinch is to telephone and invite your friend to tea here."

Denise danced and leaped for joy. It would be

much nicer to have Berthe to her own home, in her own
room, where she could show off her books and toys.
Nothing of the kind was to come about. Madame
Pelletot replied "that she was very sorry, she must be
excused, but Berthe was booked up every day until the
end of the holidays." It was a bitter disappointment.

When school opened again, Mademoiselle d'Aubray
called Berthe into her study and kept her there a long
time. When she came out, Denise went up to her:

"What did she want with you?"

Berthe seemed embarrassed. She hesitated, glanced
up at the window through which the headmistress kept
an eye on the boarders, and then drew Denise into the
farthest corner of the hall.

"She told me not to tell you, but I don't want you to
think that I'm to blame. It seems that Mamma has
been to see her and complained about my having asked
you to tea. So she said to me: 'It's not for me to discuss what your mother has told me she thinks is best for
you, but it *is* my duty to say this. Your best way of
not making Denise Herpain unhappy is not to be so intimate with her.' I didn't dare to answer. It's a beastly
nuisance. . . ."

Denise did not ask why Madame Pelletot had acted
in such a way. She knew. Thenceforward she kept
herself to herself. She suspected Berthe Pelletot, the
headmistress, and her sister-pupils. To outdo them all
she determined "to be first in everything." She succeeded. Every week for three years she won the badge
of honour given for the best work. And yet she never

won the badge for conduct. She had become at Saint-Jean as much of a rebel as she had formerly been in the Rue Carnot. At thirteen she would look the headmistress straight in the face and say:

"Well, I'm not a hypocrite."

Her stage of pious exaltation had come to an abrupt end on the day Berthe repeated to her what Mademoiselle d'Aubray had said. One thing alone made her forget for an hour or two each week how wretched she was—her piano lessons with old Tournemine. It was on Mondays and Thursdays that he came. On arrival he would kiss her on the forehead and ask:

"Been working?"

"Lots," she would say.

Yet it was unusual for her to have really worked. Being very gifted, she could read anything at sight. After a few bars old Tournemine fell asleep. He would wake up at the end of the piece. Then she would beg of him:

"Play me a Prelude and Fugue."

He would play, his chubby, dexterous hands drawing glorious strains from the old piano. Denise used to weep.

"You little donkey!" he would say. "It's very fine, but you mustn't cry like that."

In front of the other girls she would not have cried.

"You are proud, Denise," Abbé Guillemin would say to her, and he eyed her sadly. "The proud have no faith in themselves, and that is why they need to be reassured. If you would abase yourself before Our

Lord you would gain confidence in His goodness. You
would feel how before Him you are on a level with all
others, and you would be freed from your worries.
'Whosoever shall exalt himself shall be abased; and he
that shall humble himself shall be exalted.' "

She had no wish to humble herself. She was pleased
to overhear the mistress saying: "Denise is remarkably
intelligent, but she is dreadful." Made restive by in-
justice, she wished to play the double part of Virtue
Persecuted and the Avenging Rebel. As she finished
her preparation before any of the others, she had time
to write surreptitious novels and plays in which the
innocent heroine sometimes exterminated her enemies
and sometimes perished on the scaffold. The headmistress confiscated one of her manuscripts. After reading
it, she summoned Madame Herpain and told her that
her daughter was too excitable to get on with other
children; she much regretted it because she was fond
of Denise, but she must ask her not to send Denise back
to Saint-Jean after the summer holidays.

XII

ALTHOUGH Monsieur Coliveau had provided the
well-to-do families of Pont-de-l'Eure with several
dozen houses, all exactly alike, he had never noticed
that all these edifices possessed a common and regret-

table feature: the fireplaces of the ground-floor and those of the first floor formed as it were the two mouth-pieces of a speaking tube. Thus in the Rue Carnot, from Denise's room one could hear what was being said below in the small drawing-room. Lying prone on the carpet, a Walter Scott novel in front of her, she was listening to the voices of her mother and Dr. Guérin coming out of the fireplace, the register of which she had pushed up. They were talking about her.

"Believe me, I'm worried about her," Madame Herpain was saying. "Goodness knows, I've made allowances for her; but really she's become a perfect little demon. You can't imagine how contrary she is! Last night, for instance, I thought she might enjoy being taken to the theatre to see the Baret Company in 'Cyrano.' She refused—and very acidly. You ought to hear her tone in answering me. I've tried gentleness, I've tried strictness. But the more she is punished, the more obstinate she gets."

"It's wrong to regard symptoms as if they were causes," came the clear tones of Dr. Guérin. "In the case of a disease, symptoms may be signs of a disorder lurking in some corner of the body very remote from the part which seems affected. A headache may result from kidney trouble. . . . The same applies in psychological illness. I have watched the girl; she has character, and probably some moral nobility, but she is suffering on account of something—perhaps on account of our affair."

"What nonsense!" said Madame Herpain. "A child

of thirteen? She must be a thousand miles from ever thinking of it. True, Mademoiselle Perolaz has said she has a tendency to gossip."

"One should be very careful and make every allowance," said the doctor. "In your place, I'd try letting her live for a few years in quite new surroundings. That would destroy her painful associations. Why not send her to the *lycée* at Rouen?"

"To the *lycée?*" came Madame Herpain's voice. "No girl of our class goes to the *lycée.*"

"All the better," said the doctor. "The change would be more complete."

For a moment no voice came from the fireplace.

"It's true," said Madame Herpain at last, "if she were at school in Rouen she could live at mother's. I should be able to see her. It wouldn't be so inconvenient."

Still lying on the carpet in her room, Denise set her teeth with rage. In this horrible world nobody told the truth. Mamma and Dr. Guérin addressed each other as "Madame" and "Monsieur" in public, but talked as intimates when alone. Calling on Grandmother Herpain on the previous day, Denise had mentioned casually how frequently the doctor came to the house, and the old lady, carried away by her hatred of her daughter-in-law, had shown that she knew everything.

"Even Eugénie, whom I myself placed at your mother's so that I should know a little about what goes on, has turned against me," she said.

Yet Grandmother Herpain was coming to dinner this

evening; she would address Mamma as "My dearest
Germaine"; she would praise the dinner, and she would
say with a favouring smile, "Good evening, Eugénie."
Every single person she had been taught to respect
behaved badly—except her father. But then he was
so weak—always silent, always tired.

Lost in these reflections, she had not heard the doctor
go. Suddenly the door of her room opened. Madame
Herpain was before her. Nothing upset Denise more
than these sudden irruptions. Nurse, and later Mademoiselle, had taught her that one should always knock
at a door before entering. Grown-ups did not apply
their own code.

"What are you doing here, Denise? I have forbidden you to lie on the floor in your newly ironed
dress. Look here, I have half an hour to spare before
going out. Would you like some music with me? We
can play a duet or you can accompany me, as you like."

Madame Herpain, freshly primed by her lover, had
come upstairs only to win her daughter over.

"No!" said Denise sulkily. "I'm reading an interesting book. If even in the holidays. . . ."

"Oh, very well!" said Madame Herpain, surprised
and keenly disappointed. "I thought you'd like it. I
can't make you out."

She inspected the room with her eye, put a vase back
in its place, repeated, "Can't make you out," and shut
the door again. A moment later Denise heard her singing, and was all attention and secretly delighted. She

recognized Schubert's "Der Wegweiser," which she loved accompanying because of the delightful rhythmic march for the piano. The rich power of the voice overwhelmed her. Her enjoyment was less when she *saw* her mother sing. Denise was too young to analyse the distinction, just though it was; but Madame Herpain when singing took on a certain mincing expression which revealed the woman herself, so inferior to the singer. She sang for half an hour, and then the piano was silent. Through the open window came the distant humming of the looms. In the street a bicycle bell rang. A train whistled. Denise went down to the garden.

Throughout the holidays she steadily set herself against her mother. Once again Madame Herpain took her daughters to the Normandy coast, but this time near Caen, to Riva Bella. Charlotte and Suzanne— Suzanne especially, for Charlotte sometimes showed jealousy towards her elder sister—had become Denise's disciples. They in turn discovered the mysteries of their home, and on the sands, with Mademoiselle out of earshot, the three girls would talk interminably of the doctor, of Madame Herpain, and of the two grandmothers. Among themselves they always referred to their mother by her Christian name, "Germaine." They would say "Germaine got out of bed on the wrong side this morning," or "Germaine is all smiles; she's had a letter smelling of the medicine-cupboard."

"Don't stay there chattering; play," Mademoiselle

Perolaz would say. "Come on now! Play, I say!"

"But we *are* playing, Mademoiselle. We're playing at talking."

Feeling outmatched, Mademoiselle Perolaz left it at that.

When the holidays were over, Madame Herpain said to her husband that as Denise was now nearly fourteen she should begin studying in earnest, and, as Saint-Jean would not have her back, she would like to send her to Rouen to the Lycée Jeanne d'Arc. She could live with Madame d'Hocquinville.

"A jolly good idea," he said. "But I insist on her coming over every week-end to spend Sunday at Pont-de-l'Eure. We mustn't lose touch with our children."

"We can't get into touch with them, no matter what we do," said Madame Herpain. "Children are not fair."

XIII

MADEMOISELLE CHRISTIANE AUBERT, one of the teachers at the Lycée Jeanne d'Arc, scanned her new class with curiosity. Being quite young, she was not yet used to the idea of herself as a teacher. On the wall behind her Denise could see a portrait of Descartes, and a blackboard on which a circle and a tangent had been drawn. As soon as Mademoiselle Aubert spoke, her voice captivated the girls. She said that she wanted to feel that she really knew them, and that for the first preparation she would ask them to confide in her.

"You are to take this title, 'A Childhood Memory,' and as you please you may either tell me of an actual memory, the one you like best, or you may invent a story. About four pages. The chief thing is to be natural. Bring the papers to me to-morrow morning."

Then, as her pupils were still without either books or lessons, she said she would take up the period by reading to them passages from Pascal.

" 'Our nature,' " read Mademoiselle Aubert, " 'is all knowing, all love; our worries and our troubles are due to the fact that our surroundings are not equal to satisfying that thirst for knowledge and that need of love.' "

"That's it," Denise thought, and her eyes were fixed brightly on Mademoiselle Aubert. "That's it; nothing can satisfy my thirst. Everything is petty and beastly, and yet I know I am all love."

" 'I know not who put me into the world, nor what the world is, nor what I myself am,' " read Mademoiselle Aubert. " 'I am in terrible ignorance of all things. I know not what my body is, nor my senses, nor my soul and that very part of me which thinks what I say, reflects on everything and on itself, and knows itself no more than the rest. I see the fearful spaces of the universe that enclose me, and find myself tied to one corner of this vast expanse, without knowing why I am put in this place rather than another, nor why the short time given me to live is assigned to me at this point, rather than at another of all the eternity that was before me, and of all that which shall come after me. I see nothing but infinites on all sides, enclosing me as if I were an atom and a shadow, enduring only for one instant without return. All that I know is that I must soon die, but what I know least about is that very death I am unable to avoid . . . !' "

Nobody had ever spoken in the hearing of Denise in such a tone of sublimity and despair. She was over-whelmed. Mademoiselle Aubert commented upon what she had read. She made her hearers see the vast ball spinning eternally in the dark, itself a mere clot of mud. She explained how modern science had only made more amazing and more mysterious those two infinites that appalled Pascal. Christiane Aubert lived alone, in a small flat near the *lycée*. With her books, the death-masks of Pascal and Beethoven were its only ornaments. As she listened, Denise gave a sidelong glance at the red-haired girl next to her, and wondered why God had put such a pretty white-skinned girl on a huge ball that spun in the dark. Then, gazing at Mademoiselle Aubert's face, and listening to the per-fect and effortless phrasing of the words she spoke, she felt a passionate desire to win the mistress's friendship.

School over, she returned to her grandmother's. Madame d'Hocquinville lived in a charming ram-shackle house midway between the Church of St. Ouen and the Church of St. Maclou. The neighbourhood had been a wealthy one in the fifteenth and sixteenth centuries, but, as always happens in the centre of a big town after many years, had become a poor, working-class quarter. But it delighted Denise. The queer names of the streets, the wooden houses, with their steep, narrow gables, the mullioned windows, all reminded her of her beloved Walter Scott. To reach her grandmother's she had to pass through a long vaulted passage. The door of the courtyard set going a cogwheel loaded with bells. Then one entered the narrow courtyard enclosed by the walls of the house, which were decorated with bas-reliefs.

Behind the house was a small garden, neglected and romantic. Weeping willows drooped over a round pool overgrown with wild iris. Between the trees rose the towers of St. Ouen. Madame d'Hocquinville lived here with but one servant, a deformed dwarfish woman named Louisa, who had been in her service for forty years. Thanks to her husband, Madame Herpain was able to support her mother, who no longer had any means of her own. So the old lady refrained from ever criticising her daughter's behaviour. In her own day, it was said, she had had a gay heart. And she was now a screen for her daughter's adventures; Madame Herpain could always say, "I'm going to see poor dear mamma," when she had an assignation in Rouen with her lover.

Denise could hardly realize that her grandmother and Louisa were human beings. She would answer them with the patronizing kindness grown-ups adopt in talking to children. On coming back from the *lycée* on that first day of October, her leather satchel under

her arm, she felt as if the little jangling bells at the
front door were striking up a hymn of deliverance.
She climbed the front steps, tossed her case onto a
couch, and called out:

"Good evening, Granny!"

"Good evening, darling," said Madame d'Hocquinville. "Well, now, I hope they've not been overtaxing
the little head, and you have no men teachers?"

"Not at all, Granny! We have a mistress who looks
quite angelic."

"Wouldn't you like to give me a little music? Why
not play me your Prelude?"

So far as Madame d'Hocquinville was concerned,
Chopin had composed only one Prelude, "Raindrops,"
and this had become "your Prelude" because she associated it with her granddaughter. She liked hearing it
because she could recognize it, and the exploit made her
feel very pleased with herself.

"Not to-day, Granny; I've got work to do."

She went up to her room. On her way back from the
lycée, passing through the Solférino Gardens where the
old women in black were looking after children in check
overalls, she had said to herself that her angelic mistress, of whom she was already so passionately fond,
must be made to understand in this very first preparation what her life had been like. "A Childhood
Memory." Straight-off she wrote the following account, which Mademoiselle Aubert read with some
surprise when she was correcting the exercises next
evening:

A MEMORY OF MY CHILDHOOD

I was ten years old. We lived in one of the big towns of Northern Europe in which my father was an ambassador. I was a thin little girl given to coughing, and spent most of the time in the nursery, which was like a hot-house. I can still picture our garden, where my brothers galloped about on black ponies with my mamma looking on. Her beauty was dazzling. (*"Vague epithet,"* wrote Mademoiselle in the margin.) Frail and fair, she would sit resting on the flowery terrace. But this did not last. Flowers and tears were showered on the grave of my poor mamma after she had been found dying in a pool of purple blood. (Mademoiselle Aubert crossed out "purple.") A furrow appeared on my father's brow which he never lost. Years passed. I myself fell gravely ill. Eventually my father introduced me to a little stepmother whose grace and youth helped me to live again. She nursed me and looked after me as if I had been a doll. I can still see us seated on the ground together for a picnic. But she tired of the childish game, and as she saw little of my father— whom heavy work kept a great deal at the embassy —she went in search of consolation in the American colony, and I imagine she found it. (*"But this is real biography,"* wrote Mademoiselle Aubert in the margin.)

When my father discovered her unfaithfulness, he was so heartbroken that for a second time he lost all desire to live. In the evenings he shut himself up for hours on end, and I saw him no more. He alone mattered in my life. To protect him was my sole purpose in living. To withstand the snares of the world unprotected by his strength seemed impossible. (*"Exaggerated,"* Mademoiselle Aubert put in the margin. "But what an odd girl!" she thought to herself.) One evening I went to sleep with this promise from him: "Daddy, you must never leave me." I had been dreaming when suddenly the sleep weighing on my aching temples was broken. I opened my eyes in terror. It was in the middle of the night. A taste of stale blood seemed to fill my mouth. (*"What a terrifying imagination!"* commented Mademoiselle Aubert.) The wind was rising. I slipped out of bed to seek the peace my father's company would give me. I opened the door of their room. The bed was empty. Mamma had not come home. . . . That horrible sensation which overcomes children who fall a prey to anxiety seized me. Where was Papa? I slipped down to his study. . . . There he was—weeping. Seated at his desk, he was clasping his brow and sighing deeply. I could see his face bent forward, his long wet eyelashes veiling his eyes (*"Commonplace,"* wrote Mademoiselle Aubert, but she sighed), and his mouth quivering between two furrowed lines of bitterness. As I entered, he raised his head, and I saw his clear, distraught eyes turn in supplication to a portrait of my fair mamma. His mouth opened and he groaned like a wounded animal. (*"Not very happy,"* wrote Mademoiselle Aubert.) And as he threw back his head I suddenly saw again my brother's features as they looked one day when he fell off his pony. They were both alike. My father was a child, a pitiable child, and nothing of a man's will remained in him. What had happened to his courage and his strength? The man whom I had made my ideal had a flaw. (*"Weak,"* wrote Mademoiselle Aubert.) I realized how he was at once immeasurable and miserable. Who could console him? Who could protect *him* in his turn? I realized that he himself was but an atom confronted by unknown powers. (*"A simpler style would be more suitable,"* wrote Mademoiselle Aubert.) And then I wished I could embrace my dear father's knees. But a sense of respect made me slip silently away. My little bed took back my chilled body. The dark power which leads men held me in thrall. I had realized now that confidence, security, and hope do not last long, that man is destined to suffer without even knowing the purpose of his sufferings. Filled with a vast scorn for the invincible powers which control human creatures, I fell into the sleep of consolation.

Mademoiselle Aubert carefully read over the whole paper, and then wrote at the head of it: *"This shows originality. Much too excited. Manner of expression very lively, but sometimes too oratorical. Too many epithets."* She hesitated before awarding marks, and finally put down "6½." But she thought that this dark girl who had taken a seat on the back form was the most interesting pupil in her new class.

When she met the headmistress in the yard, she asked:

"Do you remember, Madame, one of my pupils,

Denise Herpain?   Do you know if she has lost her mother?"

"Why?" said the headmistress.   "No. I remember perfectly well. She belongs to a family in Pont-de-l'Eure. The mother herself brought her to me, and the child is remarkably like her."

"That's very strange," said Mademoiselle Aubert.

XIV

ALTHOUGH Denise now lived with her grandmother, she was not at all intimate with her. She looked upon Madame d'Hocquinville as an automaton whose reactions could always be exactly foreseen, and would never have dreamed of confiding in her. She had found that three stories were to be expected from her: the story of how she got married—"My poor Adhéaume was a Norman; I was born in Berri, so we should never have come across one another had not Monseignor de Cabrières. . . . ."; the story of poor Adhéaume's part in the Prussian War of 1870-71; and the story of the selling of the Château de Thuitsignol, the cradle of the Hocquinville family. She also came to expect that if any old friend of her grandmother spent an evening in the house, her grandmother would send for her and say: "Now play us *your* Prelude." Several times Denise imagined she might enjoy some other piece; but she soon learned that any change only saddened and upset Madame d'Hocquinville.

Her relations with her grandmother remained affectionate, though superficial; but those years in Rouen she came under two quite different influences. There was first that of Mademoiselle Aubert, who taught her to write simply and to transpose her personal grievances into more broadly human meditations. But being a Catholic and probably a Jansenist, Christiane Aubert accepted without accounting for the disharmony between man's desires and his pettiness; Denise Herpain, on the other hand, remained a rebel, looking on the world as cruel and mean, and wishing either to shun it or transform it. Very quickly she came to reign over this *lycée;* she was always head of her class and the favourite of the teachers.

The second influence was that of a trio of boys who, like herself, left Rouen every Saturday evening by the same train, and returned every Monday morning. One of the three, Bertrand Schmitt, went to Elbeuf; the other two, Bernard Quesnay and Jacques Pelletot, travelled with her all the way to Pont-de-l'Eure. Jacques Pelletot was the notary's son, the brother of Berthe, who for one term had been Denise's friend at the convent. In 1912 he was fifteen; the others were both seventeen. All three had a taste for culture and were great readers; they introduced Denise into a world new to her.

Bertrand Schmitt was reputed to be the most remarkable of them, but Denise was more attracted by Jacques

Pelletot. She liked that rather frail body, his delicate features, and his fine brow, with its sweeping lock of brown hair. It may be, too, that she unconsciously harboured an old grudge against Madame Pelletot, who had parted her from Berthe; that made her desire to win the liking of *her* son rather than of anyone else.

For a year Bertrand Schmitt was her tutor in reading. He introduced her to Maurice Barrès and André Gide, then to Laforgue and Rimbaud. Later on, having himself been initiated to Stendhal by his philosophy teacher Royer, he made her read "Le Rouge et le Noir." It was wonderful matter for a girl in rebellion. Bertrand did not want to take over the management of the factory from his father; he wanted to go on with his studies in Paris, and then to write.

"But what sort of thing would you write, Bertrand?"

"Oh! I don't know yet. . . . Novels perhaps. . . . When I read Dickens or Tolstoy, I always long to take people I know—you, Jacques, Bernard, my parents— and throw them into the book I'm reading. Of course I say that, but I suppose that if I do take up writing, it will be horribly dull stuff."

Bertrand was a dreamer and expressed himself with some difficulty. The more brilliant and definite Jacques used to criticize Mademoiselle Aubert's Jansenism. One day he delighted Denise by saying:

"I ran into your father yesterday, and we spoke of you. He's very intelligent."

"Papa?" said Denise. "What did he say to you?"

"I can't remember. Oh! Yes: we talked about Taine and Renan. He's read a lot."

The following year Bertrand Schmitt went off to Paris to work at the Sorbonne. After obtaining his second baccalaureate, Bernard Quesnay entered a battalion of light infantry. And so on Saturday evenings Denise found herself alone in the train with Jacques Pelletot. They became very close friends. Every week he would help her with her work, and being good at mathematics, he clarified questions which seemed incomprehensible to her in school.

They were now so used to the journey that they never looked out at the splendid valley of the Seine, or at the chimneys of Elbeuf between the two bridges spanning the curve of the river, or at the forest of Louviers, with the garlands of snow on its bare branches. Nor did they hear the names of the stations, the stationmaster's whistle, or the guard's toot-toot. In their compartment, with its dirty grey upholstery, they worked under the reddish and uncertain light of the oil lamp.

"But look, Denise, I can't understand how you don't see it. What do you *want* to do? Solve an equation with an x squared in it? What *can* you do? You can manage a linear equation? Well, then. . . ."

"I can't follow, Jacques. Math just makes me stupid."

"Nonsense. You must think. What you've got to do is to change what you don't know into what you do. Look here: if this trinomial was itself a perfect square, then you could transform your quadratic equation into a linear equation?"

"Yes, but $ax^2 + bx + c$ is not a perfect square."

"Of course not. But can't we find the makings of a perfect square?"

Next to them, two men who had got in at Quévilly were discussing the presidential election.

"You can say what you like," one of them was exclaiming; "Republican discipline demands that Poincaré should retire—Pams has got more votes!"

"There can be no question of Republican discipline in the case of two Republicans," the other retorted, and he sneezed.

"So here you are," Jacques was saying, "$x = \dfrac{-b \pm \sqrt{b^2 - 4ac}}{2a}$. How's that? Do you understand now?"

"This time I have. Thanks, Jacques. You're a prodigy."

"I'm not a prodigy, but I love explaining things to you. I should like to explain things to you all my life."

"How d'you mean, Jacques?"

"I beg your pardon. It's a ridiculous thing to have said, but you understand quite well."

During the previous holidays at the seaside the boys had begun treating her as grown-up. She had become slimmer, and the fineness of her features had become manifest. People in Pont-de-l'Eure would stop in the street to look at her in surprise. "But is this your daughter, Madame Herpain? I shouldn't have recognized her. But she is delightful! She's exactly like you now." Such admiration pleased her. She had made up her mind not to marry. She had seen too much of marriage. From her childhood fears there survived strong instincts of chastity. Once, in the tunnel near Pont-de-l'Eure, Jacques was alone with her in the compartment and tried to kiss her. She thrust him away so decisively that he never tried again. After that, when the train entered the tunnel, Jacques used to clap his books into his satchel to avoid being tempted.

"I shall never marry, Jacques. But I should like to live with you and work with you. I have faith in your future. I think you'll be a great man."

"Oh! you're certainly wrong. What sort of great man?"

"I don't know. In science. . . . You will make great discoveries. Or else I'd like you to be a great politician—you talk so well. . . . As for me, I'll tell you just what I would like: I'd like to be the inspiration of a great man and help him in a life of heroism. It's dreadful to be a woman. It's so unfair."

"It would be marvellous to have you at my side."

"Listen, Jacques, I want you to promise something. . . . You must never settle down in Pont-de-l'Eure. . . . You mustn't go to sleep in that horrible place. . . . You must go to Paris and you must work."

"I can claim no credit in promising you that. I've already said as much to my father."

"What did he say?"

"He said: 'You get through your Law. Then we'll see.'"

The train was slowing down as it ran into the little station of Pont-de-l'Eure. The steam of the engine was marking the hard-trodden snow on the platform with a dark wet patch.

XV

JACQUES PELLETOT lived at a cousin's in Rouen, and so was his own master. Whenever Denise asked Madame d'Hocquinville: "Granny, may I go out with Jacques Pelletot?" the latter would invariably reply: "Pelletot? Pelletot? Isn't that the notary at Pont-de-l'Eure who drew up your mother's marriage contract?"

"It's his grandson, Granny," Denise would say.

"That's very funny," would say Madame d'Hocquinville. "Your grandfather was very angry with that notary; he was an ill-bred grumpy fellow. Just imagine! He came to our house on instructions from the Herpains to put a figure on what your mother would bring into the family, and after looking into everything, he said to poor Adhéaume, 'It's quite simple, Monsieur d'Hocquinville. Naught plus naught equals naught.' As a matter of fact, I was giving your mother half my jewels, the crested silver which came to me from Aunt Céline. . . ."

Denise listened no longer.

In the spring Jacques and Denise formed the habit of going for walks together after school. Half-way between the two *lycées*, they would meet in the Solférino Garden. If it rained, they went into the Museum together and looked at the Monet paintings and the Géricault drawings; when it was fine, they climbed up in the direction of Bihorel or Mount Saint-Aignan. They loved to look down at the lacework spires of Rouen from where they sat on a bank at the foot of a cob-wall, or leaning against an apple-tree on a hillside. The triple spires of St. Ouen gave answer to the three towers of the Cathedral, and between these topmost clusters stood the shorter tower of St. Maclou, marking with an almost imperceptible line the true centre of the view. The wind-borne smoke of the factory chimneys scored the rising river-mists with wavy, pale white parallels.

Denise had brought in her satchel some books she wanted her friend to read—Amiel's "Journal" and Tagore's poems. Jacques took them to please her, but he preferred Anatole France or Voltaire. Even above them he put Nietzsche, whom he had been reading for a year past and in whom he thought he was finding the justification of the free, sensual life which beckoned him. His vocabulary had been transformed: he talked of "a morality for the strong" and described as "artificial" whatever he did not himself feel. From his professor of philosophy, Royer, whose youthful boldness inflamed his pupils, he had acquired a new morality —that of reason. He read Denise fragments from his course:

"Cultivate the habit of acting according to reason, that is to say, of neglecting advice, conventions, and scruples.—A strong man does what he wants to do and does only what he wants to do.—Always act in such a way as to retain your self-control, no matter what constraint events place upon your sensibility."

Denise envied these calm certitudes, but could not accept them. Her convent days, and the Abbé Guillemin's sermons on Hell, had left her with a vague but invincible fear of inhuman powers. Though brave, she dreaded storms and the dark. She would not have dared to tell Jacques so, but to her thunder seemed a warning from on high. She liked Maeterlinck's early books—at that time Maeterlinck was greatly admired by the young—because they allowed for the intervention of the invisible and the infinite in life.

"No, no," Jacques would tell her, "you are far too tolerant of all that mystical, occultist stuff in Maeterlinck."

"I dare say . . . I can't help it. . . . Say what you may, Jacques, there is something terrible in life."

"I don't see it. . . . It's very simple. . . . We must get rid of pity and jealousy, and all the artificial passions, and give ourselves up to healthy egoism. Then life will become natural. . . . Only, you never let

yourself go. . . .   You're always strung-up and
quivering."

She stretched out in the grass.

"But I try to let myself go. . . . When I lie close
to the earth like this I feel, like you, that everything is
simple.   I become just an animal. . . .   Push my
satchel under my head, will you?"

"Kiss me, Denise. . . .   Or let me kiss you. . . ."

He leaned over her.   Denise shut her eyes.   She felt
an arm encircling her, and then the warm touch of lips
on her own.   She crushed down an impulse to flee, and
for a moment lay passive; then gently she pushed him
away with a murmur and a smile.   He was on his knees
beside her, in the meadow.

"Dear," he said, "you're not cross?"

"No.   I'm very pleased.   I'm only cross with myself.
I murmured only to tell myself—'You see, Denise Herpain, you're just like the rest. . . .'"

"You're *not* like the rest; you're more beautiful, and
more intelligent."

"Oh! you think so because you've just kissed me;
but that's not what I mean.   No, I'm not like the
rest. . . ."

"Why?"

She sighed, and watched a bird hovering in the sky.
Again Jacques put his arm round her; she turned away
and he put one hand on her dark head to draw her to
him.   He saw her eyes full of tears.

"What's wrong, Denise?   Have I upset you?"

She shook her head.

"I can't tell you."

Then, suddenly, she tore herself from his arms, sat up in the grass, and fumbled in her satchel; the rulers and compasses clattered noisily, and she pulled out paper and pencil. She wrote a few words, supporting the paper on his knees, and then held out the sheet. He read:

"I am ashamed of my mother. I don't want to be like her."

He looked at her in surprise. His own family was united and dull; the tragedies of married life never entered his thoughts. To him, Madame Herpain was a pretty woman, though getting on; he rather liked seeing her in the street, and she sometimes sang at concerts at the club. He had heard it said that she was unfaithful to Monsieur Herpain; but that was no concern of his. He wanted to speak. Denise laid her hand on his lips and held out the pencil.

"Don't speak. Write."

He wrote:

"Why be ashamed? You and your mother are two quite distinct beings. In any case, she is not a criminal."

She took the paper, sighed, and held out her hand for the pencil.

"Yes. Very nearly a criminal. She has spoilt my father's life, and mine, and the lives of my sisters. I have suffered horribly ever since I was six."

He was reading over her shoulder.

"Your life is only beginning," he said.

She added, still in pencil:

"It is finished."

Kneeling before her, he took her in his arms again, and pressed her to himself with painful violence. Again she murmured and smiled. She was surprised she had had no pleasure, and to find she was summing him up, and, for the first time, dominating him.

"He needs me," she thought. "I don't need him."

The moon was rising. It was going to be a splendid night. She groped for the pencil in the grass, and then, unable to see, wrote in large letters:

"I think I am going to love you."

He had to get up to make out the sentence, holding the paper up towards the moon.

After that they went out together nearly every evening. He had tried to be bolder, but Denise was pure, and he respected her. She told him now about her childhood; he had never suspected that such strange emotions could exist in real life. He was startled and fascinated.

XVI

JACQUES obtained his second baccalaureate in July 1914; his father insisted that he must start on his Law course in Paris in the following year; but Jacques wished to study medicine, and told Denise that, as Law was easy, he would take the two together. During the last days of July, at Pont-de-l'Eure, they saw a good deal of each other. They regarded themselves as an engaged couple. Their intimacy caused Madame Herpain some concern.

"What do you think you are doing with the boy? You know quite well the Pelletots will never let him marry you."

"Marry me? But I don't want to get married."

"What childish talk! Every girl gets married."

She tried to bring Monsieur Herpain to step in, but he loathed any such discussions.

"Why worry?" he kept saying.

She shrugged her shoulders. He had always denied problems in order to avoid having to solve them.

By about July 25 the inhabitants of Pont-de-l'Eure were talking of the possibility of war. They discussed it without believing in it. Entering the office where Monsieur Herpain was unwrapping his blue parcels, Antoine Quesnay, an officer in the Reserve, displayed a pair of marching boots he had just bought.

"My fighting kit," he said. "I am going to get them greased."

"Be quiet," said Monsieur Achille. "It's no subject for joking."

The killing-machine started up with pitiless smoothness. Just as the aprons of the cards slowly and steadily bore the flocks of wool to the hard-pointed rollers that gripped and tore them, so did courage and fear draw this peaceable town into war and carry out the smooth sifting of death. In one single day all the young men vanished. The red-eyed women came back alone to silent houses. Then the older men appeared in uniform. Monsieur Belgiati, the pastry-cook, became the sergeant in charge of the eight men guarding the station. Dr. Guérin was suddenly transformed into a captain wearing the velvet collar of the Medical Service. He left on the eighth day of mobilization. Louis Herpain, a warrant officer in the Territorial Army, went up for medical examination, only to come back depressed and discomfited. An Army doctor had listened to his heart and then said:

"Nothing doing. You stay at home, my friend, and watch your aorta. Put him down for auxiliary service."

At Madame Herpain's request Dr. Guérin went to see his military colleague, and explained that her husband had a very serious heart disease. Madame Herpain was full of solicitude.

"My poor Louis," she said, "you must have yourself properly examined, treated. . . ."

"By whom?" he replied in such a tone that she did not dare to press it.

At first, Pont-de-l'Eure had thought the factories would have to close. But very quickly, with northern France invaded, orders were diverted to the Three Towns. The looms were turning out miles and miles of red and blue cloth. Then, when the Ordnance adopted horizon-blue, the streams ran with a pale sky-blue water.

Denise had not gone back to the *lycée* when the new term began in October. Her grandfather was ill. Deprived of most of his staff, her father had suggested that she might lend her help. She accepted readily, glad to be useful to him and not caring about living in Rouen now that Jacques was in Paris and due to be called up on his eighteenth birthday. She came to know the wools—the Australian, short and soft, the French, rough and long, and the Moroccan. And, what was more, she came to know her father.

This proved extremely surprising to her. She had imagined that, away from home, Monsieur Herpain led a straightforward mechanical life. She had never wondered what he did all day. Now that she worked with him, she learned that after finishing his letters he would open a small cupboard under the window and take out a book. The first time he revealed this hiding-place in her presence, he smiled at her as at a fellow-conspirator. He showed her his secret library: Taine, Renan, Victor Hugo, novels by Paul Bourget, and books on spiritualism. He watched her expression as she scanned the titles. When she came to the books on spiritualism, he said shyly:

"Who knows? There may be something in it."

After that they had some talks together, and he tried to explain his views. She found him pleasantly ingenuous, with less knowledge of life than Jacques or Bertrand Schmitt; but she felt sympathetic. One interesting thing was that in his eagerness to please his rebel daughter he recovered the radicalism of his youth. She then made another discovery, still more astonishing. She returned unexpectedly one evening to the office to fetch her coat, as it was raining, and found her father embracing Mademoiselle Protat, his typist, a thin, long-nosed girl. Denise shut the door with a sense of revulsion. What a vile world! You could not look closely at anyone without finding out his rottenness! Then she decided she was being stupidly puritanical, and even found an odd pleasure in the thought that her mother too was being deceived. Besides, the girl had fine eyes. Perhaps she was intelligent? She reproached herself for never having treated her like a human being. When she next saw her father, he was very hesitant, and then apologized:

"One can't help it, you know. You have no idea what a life I've had. She is gentle and kind, and has helped me a lot to put up with—with certain things. . . . You'll understand later on."

"But I understand quite well now, Father," said Denise.

Thereupon they spoke freely about Madame Herpain. Denise asked why her father had not divorced her.

"For your sake. . . . In a small town like this a divorce would have harmed all three of you. Besides, in spite of everything, your mother and I have had some good times together. . . . If I had to go through it all over again, I should do just the same. When she married me she loved me. She waited three years for me, you know, although in Rouen she was much courted. She was so wonderful. You should have seen our musical evenings in the Rue Damiette when I was a soldier. In those days I sang too. She used to accompany me."

"What songs did you sing, Papa?"

"Oh! lots and lots! All the songs they sang in those days. The *cavatina* from "Faust," "Le Roi d'Ys," "Samson et Dalila . . ."

"I should like to hear you sing. Sing me some tonight."

"No. Your mother doesn't like singing just now."

They got back to the Rue Carnot in high spirits. Madame Herpain had a headache and was in bed. Having had no news from her lover, she was anxious, regarding the European War as a plot against her happiness. After dinner Monsieur Herpain and his three daughters slipped quietly into the large drawing-room and Denise accompanied with the soft pedal down, "*Salut, demeure chaste et pure. . . .*" Monsieur Herpain's voice quavered. He was short of breath, ingenuously ardent. He had not looked so happy for many a day. Behind his back Denise and Suzanne glanced at each other with kindly pity. Charlotte giggled.

XVII

THE soldiers' letters staked out the lines of the War. Pont-de-l'Eure had its sons scattered all along the front and all over France. Jacques Pelletot had enlisted as soon as he was able to, in October 1915. He told his parents that he was engaged to Denise Herpain, and Madame Pelletot, transformed by anxiety, cried and kissed her son. No protest was raised by the notary; but he said:

"I only ask you to wait until the War is over before discussing this formally."

Bertrand Schmitt, an interpreter with the British Army, was somewhere between Armentières and Béthune. Denise received his letters, mingling the poetic and the macabre. His brother André had been killed at Charleroi. Bernard Quesnay was a lieutenant in the infantry; for three months his battalion had been in Alsace, in the snow, and Dr. Guérin was its medical officer. Antoine Quesnay, badly wounded in Champagne, was limping about the factory yards. He was said to be engaged to Françoise Pascal-Bouchet; and to the people of the Valley that seemed a more astounding fact than Verdun.

In February 1916 a British training-camp was set up on the plateau a couple of miles from Pont-de-l'Eure, and its advent transformed the town. Officers and soldiers came to the school for special courses from the front, for instruction in new methods of bayonet-fighting, in bombing, and in building dug-outs. One of the instructors, Captain Robinson, twenty-three years old, became the cavalier of Denise. Pont-de-l'Eure acquired the habit of taking a Sunday stroll to the camp, to gaze admiringly at the neatly ranged tents, the wooden huts built in the Far West style by the Cana-

dians, and the little flower-gardens with which the
Tommies reminded themselves of home.

"I'm going to show Miss Denise a dug-out," Robinson told Monsieur Herpain, who nodded his assent
with his head on one side.

The captain led Denise across to the marvellously
spick-and-span model trenches, with their spotless sandbags and gleaming pit-props.

"Can you jump?" he would ask in halting French.

He gave her his hand. She admired the tall supple
youth, bearing himself so easily in his open-necked
tunic.

"Come and look at this officers' dug-out, Miss
Denise. . . . Careful! You'll have to bend down.
. . . There are twenty-three steps!"

To guide her in the darkness, he put his arm round
her, and held her hand. The feel of his strong palm
on hers suddenly terrified her, by the pleasure it gave
her.

"No," she said. "I feel giddy. Let's get out."

In the spring the officers at the camp arranged a
party. Captain Robinson, who was now "Robby" to the
three girls, asked Denise to come as his guest. Madame
Herpain had gone off mysteriously to Paris two days
earlier. Ever since Dr. Guérin, who was now a major,
had been put in charge of a hospital at Compiègne, she
was for ever finding pretexts for journeys. "Germaine
has got St. Vitus's dance," her daughters would say.
During dinner Denise said to her father:

"Papa, I'm going out to-night; up to the English camp."

"At night?" said Monsieur Herpain, with an anxious look. "Why? Who with?"

"Robinson is fetching me in his car, and he'll bring me back. There's a soldiers' concert."

"And hasn't he asked your sisters?"

"He couldn't. You know he has only a two-seater."

Monsieur Herpain drummed his fingers on the table-cloth. He leaned his head still more on one side and sighed. Often he seemed to get out of breath. It was painful to see.

"What's wrong, Father? Don't you like my going out with Robby? I've been out with him quite often."

"Yes, my child, but not at night."

"What difference does it make—night or day?" said Denise rather impatiently. "Well, if you don't like it, I won't go. But it's a nuisance, because it's all fixed up, and Robby is coming along in a couple of hours' time. He'll think me an awful idiot."

Monsieur Herpain sighed again.

"Oh! you may go," he said. "I shouldn't want to spoil your enjoyment. We are not having much of a time here nowadays. Only don't get back too late. I'll wait up for you."

"But that's ridiculous, Father. The concert will certainly not be over before midnight. Why sit up? What can happen to me? You've known Robby now quite a long time."

"I shouldn't be comfortable unless I knew you had got back all right."

Denise looked at her sisters in a way which seemed to say: "Poor Papa!" and the remainder of dinner was silent and depressed.

A little later the bell rang with a peal that cut through the silence of the night, and Robinson's cheerful voice was heard saying with a terrific accent:

"*Bong-swar, Youjaynee.* . . . I've come for Miss Denise."

Denise kissed her father ever so kindly—a long kiss, much longer than usual—and her sisters went out to the hall to help her to muffle up without disturbing her hair. Left alone in the drawing-room, Monsieur Herpain heard them singing to the tune of "Tipperary":

"Good-bye, Mister Robby,
Farewell, Sister Neeze . . ."

Then came Charlotte's voice, saying in English:

"Robby, you are a pig not to have asked me too."

"I wish I could," he said.

"You wish no such thing. You are delighted to have Denise to yourself in your horrid little car."

For another minute he heard them laughing, humming a snatch of song, and doing a few dance-steps.

"Look, Robby, I can do toe-dancing now as you showed me. . . . He isn't looking! He's thinking only of carrying off Denise. Good night, Mr. Lovelace! Good fun, Denise!"

The laughter and singing made Louis Herpain feel he was old, old before his time. It wasn't so long since Germaine used to sing a snatch of song at the door in the Rue Damiette with three soldiers, of whom he was the favourite! The two girls came back and said good night. They could not resist going up to their room for a long talk about Robby's passion for Denise. Monsieur Herpain was left alone. He went to the bookcase and chose a book at random. It was Balzac's "Le Lys dans la Vallée." Settling in his arm-chair, he tried to read.

"I comply with your wish. The privilege of the woman whom we love more than she loves us, is to make us constantly forget the rules of common sense."

The words left him thoughtful. . . . "The privilege of the woman whom we love more than she loves us, is to make us forget the rules of common sense." How true! How often with Germaine had he forgotten the rules of common sense! He called to mind the views on marriage he had professed when he married. In those days he considered that a husband should be strict, that it was men's lack of firmness which caused women's downfall. . . . But at the first clash of wills he had yielded.

He picked up Balzac again. "To avoid a wrinkled brow, to chase away the sulkiness of lips saddened by the least contrariness. . . ." And with incredible vividness he saw Germaine again, just as she had looked that first evening when she went out alone with Lieutenant

Debucourt. It was two years after Denise was born. He himself had caught a silly infection of mumps from the child. There was a concert at the theatre, and Debucourt had offered to escort Madame Herpain to it. She too, just like Denise this evening, had been affectionate and submissive. "If you don't like it, I won't go," she said, and he replied as he had to Denise, "I don't want to spoil your enjoyment. . . ." He had waited up for her until midnight. He was feverish. Every now and then a passing carriage threw floating ribs of light through the shutters across the ceiling. And at last she came home, looking delightful in her evening dress, and bringing in with her the cool of the night. . . . That was the first step on the path to his years of wretchedness.

He looked at the little clock facing him on the writing-table. Five minutes to nine. . . . How this evening was going to drag! He began to feel that mortal anguish which sometimes gnawed at his heart. . . . He must read on: "I have weighty memories buried in the depths of my soul, like those deep-sea growths which are visible in calm weather and are cast up in fragments on the beach by the waves of storms. . . ." With an effort he managed to read a few pages, then noticed that he did not know what he had read. He glanced at the clock. Twenty past nine. . . . The minute hand disappeared. A pile of books hid the left side of the clock-face. Now reading, now musing, he watched for the hand to reappear. . . . Five past ten. . . . A sound of distant footsteps gave him an absurd hope; the footsteps drew nearer, rang sharply under the window, then passed away again.

"After all," he thought, "they're in a car. . . . Why am I getting upset like this? It's natural to be jealous of one's wife, but not of one's daughter. My wife's behaviour has become a matter of indifference to me, and my daughter's—— What a pretty smile she gave me, apologizing for leaving me! Exactly like her mother's, twenty years ago. . . . Denise is a charming girl. . . . Intelligent, too. . . . If she were a boy, she would be what I should have liked to be. . . . And some young fool will turn up, Robinson—one of the Quesnays—goodness knows who—and take her away from me. . . ."

He opened his novel again. "All these morbidities worked upon me to such a point that even after I was twenty I remained puny, then, and pale. . . ." The minute hand emerged from behind the pile of books. Five past eleven. The sound of a car came nearer, and nearer, and hit dully against the door. A key turned. Denise's voice called out farewells and thanks. He rose, and met her in the hall.

"Oh, it's you? Already? I wasn't expecting you for another hour."

"Yes. But I saw when I left that you were worried, and so I begged Robinson to bring me home before the end. He's been a lamb."

"That was really very nice of you, Denise. But I could have waited quite patiently till midnight. I had a good book."

"What were you reading?"

" 'Le Lys dans la Vallée.' "

She pouted. When she had finished untying her scarf, she came over to kiss him. It seemed to him as if, like someone else, she had brought in with her the cool gladness of the night.

XVIII

In July Denise went to Caen to sit for her first baccalaureate, and passed. She then told her sisters that when the school-year opened she would go to live at Grandmother d'Hocquinville's, that she would go back to the *lycée* to take her philosophy course, and that nothing would deter her from this plan. There were many reasons for so firm a decision.

She was alarmed by the feelings Robinson stirred in her. "I never felt that bodily affection for Jacques," she said to herself; "that craving for his presence. . . . What mattered with Jacques was the idea. . . . Ideas. . . . Admiration for his intelligence, the picture of what our life together might be like, the certainty of making a man of him. . . . With Robby it's quite different. I only want him to *be* there; I like watching him, seeing him do things. . . . I should like to lie beside him on a beach, and stay there for whole days on end in the sun, burning, happy. . . . And when I feel like that I hate myself. . . . Robby humiliates me in my own eyes. . . . I must get away from him."

She felt that she had not treated Jacques properly, the more so because Jacques himself was querulous. In every letter he would ask: "Is Robinson still at Pont-de-l'Eure?" The youthful scorner of passion was becoming romantic and jealous. He wrote that if he could no longer believe in Denise, "everything would become a great black void, he would have no taste for anything, and he would get himself killed." She answered:

> I cannot really believe that I am all you say. Don't worry, my dear. I am not one of those changeable women. . . . But I want no more of that horrible word "jealousy" in your letters. You told me you didn't understand it. And I am always astonished by the disagreeable sensation which Robinson gives you when I mention him. It's unreasonable in a reasonable man like you.

She went on to explain why she was leaving home:

> I feel like a caged bird in this house. I go from my desk to my piano, then I return to my room. Mamma's presence is more distressing to me than I can say. She fails to realize that I am now a woman like herself. She treats me as a child. I can't put up with it.
>
> I've made a kind of start, with Papa's help, on my philosophy. . . . I am curious to know your views on Kant and Spinoza. I confess that the categorical imperative makes Kant rather uncongenial to me. In

Spinoza I like very much all he says about love, but his God bores me. I find him theoretical and abstract. When I was religious, it wasn't in his way. Thanks for the life of Nietzsche you sent me: clearly the man for you. He's a "real beauty," as we used to say. . . . But I didn't like reading the story of his madness. Stories of madmen always frighten me. Here it is raining, the sky is grey, and the drops are coming down on the roof with dull little whacks. I wish all this water would melt Germaine like a salt statue, and give her rheumatism, or such a toothache that she would be driven to taking the train to Paris, or rather to Compiègne. . . . Alas! it won't. The sun will follow on the rain and make pink patterns on the roof. Calm will succeed the storm and Germaine will remain in the best of health. I've given up struggling. I try, as you're always telling me to, to be only an onlooker. . . . But I want to get away. . . . Did you know that Bernard Quesnay had won a medal?

September 20, 1916.

No news again to-day. I've explained my wonderful plans to the Family (with a capital F!). Mamma said: "Rubbish! People don't go back to the *lycée* at eighteen." It was exactly what I expected and did not excite me. Papa upset me. He took me out into the garden and we walked round the lawn for an hour. He told me he had only myself and that he felt very ill. I replied that I'd often come to see him, but that I loved you and wanted to marry you, that when the War is over you'll go on studying in Paris, and that I wanted to be fit to go there too. You know my father; he is timid; he gave in at once. I now feel rather remorseful. Suzanne weeps. Lolotte is inclined to be glad: she will be the undisputed queen of the English camp. How wrong you were, my poor dear, to be so worried about Robinson. Last Sunday he came to tea. I told him: "You know, Robby, this is the last time you'll see me. I'm going to work in Rouen." He laughed and replied: "Are you really?" Then he talked of something else. But I think his indifference is feigned, and I hope he's sorry all the same.

Rouen, October 20, 1916.

My dear, women are monsters, but men are most unfair. It was for your sake that I wanted to get away from Pont-de-l'Eure, and now you reproach me for having done so. How can you say it will be less convenient when you're on leave? You'll come to see me at Rouen and I shall be much freer. How can you be surprised that I should want to live away from home? Don't you understand that I really suffer in the Rue Carnot? Nothing can be more awful than a hateful home. But you don't know, you can't know. If you changed places with me for a single week, you'd understand. Let me tell you that I should prefer to be unhappy anywhere, for in others' homes it's natural to be unhappy, but it isn't natural in one's own. Here, in the Rue Damiette, I am Denise Herpain; I am not a piece of furniture to be put there or moved into another room at will; I am not just somebody to be given a talking-to. People

knock at my door and wait before coming in. I can
be sure that nobody will rummage in my drawers behind my back, that nobody will open my letters, that
I shan't be told to put on a green blouse when I'm
wearing a pink one. Here I am perfectly happy. I
have to work in my chilly room and go out early in
the morning mists with my feet like ice—but it
simply doesn't matter so long as I'm left in peace.
. . . When I get too cold, I walk round and round
the garden at the back. Or else I go down and sit
with Grandma, the only person entitled to a fire in
these hard times. She has three stories to tell me:
one is about *your* grandfather's insolence regarding
my maternal family's possessions, another is about the
glorious campaign waged by *my* grandfather against
the Germans in 1871, and the third is about her own
marriage. "I was born in Berri, your grandfather
was Norman——" After I've listened to the three
stories, she says: "Now play me *your* Prelude." I
play *my* Prelude, and then I come upstairs again to
write my dissertation on "Suicide." A good subject,
don't you think? Good night! Is it true that one of
these days I shall say good night to you every night
in my own way? Do you remember Romeo?

"Good night, good night! parting is such sweet
   sorrow,
That I shall say good night till it be morrow."

                    Caen, June 13, 1917.

Hooray! I've passed. I told you how dubious I
was about the *viva*, but these good gentlemen were

very kind. In any case, I knew it all practically. History and geography: the Treaty of Frankfort and Canada. In physics, the laws of sound pipes (you remember you explained them to me on the gravel of the tennis-court!) In chemistry, CO_2. Philosophy, Stuart Mill and Utilitarianism. I didn't know a thing, so I talked about Bentham so fast that he couldn't stop me. He said nothing and marked me 13. Natural history, the blood (like you—it made me smile inwardly). English was my triumph. I had to translate some Dickens which I knew almost by heart. I think I got the maximum marks. Thank goodness, that's over! Now I shall be able to catch you up next year.

October 20, 1917.

At last. . . . I have been terrified for the past week. Even your mother had no news of you. My poor dear, I imagine you in a very white bed, as narrow as a schoolboy's. Be good. Let them bandage you without any fuss. And the size of the wound? How large? How deep? You understand, I want very exact replies, in centimetres. My poor dear, you must be quite unable to move. Why have they sent you to Brive? I grabbed the gazetteers in the Library. I got covered with dust, all in vain: no details about Brive. I'm going to Pont-de-l'Eure this evening. I want to see your father when he gets back from Brive, and also to look after Papa, who was very ill last night. Suddenly, he had a suffocating attack. To-day it seems he's better, but everybody has had a fright. Poor Papa! What a thin time he's had in life! I don't know if I shall make you very happy, my dear, but I'll be desperately faithful to you.

XIX

THE heavy door in the Rue Damiette opened and set the bell-wheel jangling. In the courtyard old Louisa was scrubbing the front-door steps.

"Make haste, Mademoiselle Denise. There's somebody waiting for you."

"Somebody for me?"

"Yes, Mademoiselle, a young officer. . . . He's very nice. . . . I wanted to take him in to Madame. He said he'd rather wait for you in the garden."

"He's in the garden?"

"Where would he be, eh? He's been walking round and round for the last hour."

Denise took the five steps at one bound, flung her case of books on the floor of the hall, and opened the garden door. Under the willows a young man in uniform was gazing into the ornamental pond. It was Jacques. She ran across and threw herself into his arms. Then she looked at him. He did not look ill, though perhaps rather pale. But how small and frail! Her memory had kept a more manly picture of him.

"Oh! Jacques, how glad I am! How did you get here? Why didn't you let me know?"

He explained that he had been given convalescent leave only the day before, and had wired to Pont-de-l'Eure that he would be there next morning so as to have this evening alone with Denise in Rouen.

"So you're not going till to-morrow?"

"Yes, I left my kit at the hotel."

"It's very nice of you to come and see me before going home to your people. . . . So I'm to have you for a whole day? Marvellous! I shan't leave you for a moment! The chemistry and natural sciences can go hang! I'm cutting the lot!"

She led him up to her room.

"You see, I have your photograph and your Nietzsche at my bedside."

He sat down on the bed and put his arm round her.

"Dearest," he was saying, deeply stirred and pressing his head on her breast. "If you only knew how I've thought of this moment for months and months."

He drew her to him, made her lie down, and leaning over her kissed her lips savagely. Feeling him so close to her whole body, she felt startled and made as if to free herself.

"Don't, don't, Denise! I've wanted you so badly. The other fellows in our squadron were always chasing women when we were in billets. But I—I wanted nobody but you. Even to-day, passing through Paris, I wouldn't—— You, only you!"

He was beseeching and gentle. Denise remembered that he was going off again in a few days, perhaps to die. She sat up, laid two cool hands against her lover's cheeks, and gazed steadily into his eyes. She was trembling.

"Look here, darling. I'm going to take you down to Granny. I shall tell her that I'm going off with you to Pont-de-l'Eure by the six-ten, and then I'll spend the night with you at your hotel."

He seemed delighted and anxious.

"That would be marvellous. But suppose your parents telephone?"

"Granny hasn't got a telephone. What could happen? And anyhow, let's chance; I like taking risks."

"Yes, no doubt, Denise, but have I the right to let you? It's awfully dangerous, your plan. . . . A girl——"

She wrenched herself out of his arms. Madame d'Hocquinville had great difficulty in grasping her explanation.

"What's that you say? Little Jacques Pelletot? Is he related to the notary who drew up your mother's marriage contract?"

"Yes, Granny. It's his grandson."

"Ah!"

Denise saw all the old grievances against Maître Pelletot reflected in her grandmother's face: "Naught plus naught equals naught." But all Madame d'Hocquinville said was:

"And so he's a soldier?"

"Yes, Granny."

"In 1870 my poor Adhéaume had a uniform very like that. Only the *képi* was higher."

Returning to her room with Jacques, Denise flung a few things into a suitcase. Jacques had glimpses of a pink nightdress and leather slippers. Half an hour later they reached his hotel together. On the way Jacques had said he would take a room for her next to his. Both were so frightened by their boldness that the situation remained vague and inexplicit. She felt a shock of surprise when she noticed the hotel was the one where Madame Herpain, according to Ponte-de-l'Eure, used to meet Dr. Guérin once a week. They ordered dinner in Jacques's room, but were scarcely able to touch anything. They looked at each other, agitated and anxious. She tried to get him to tell her how he had been wounded. When the table had been taken away, she bolted the door and came and sat on his knee. He kissed her, gently at first, and then furiously.

"You still murmur, Denise!"

"Yes, but it's pleasure. . . . The rebel happy to be vanquished. . . . Am I too heavy? I'm not hurting your wound?"

"Oh! no. That's all over and done with. . . . It didn't amount to much—my wound, I mean."

"Where was it?"

He took off his tunic, opened his shirt, and showed her a pink hollow. She kissed the scar and stood up.

"Wait here a minute," she said. "I'll call you."

A few moments later she called from the next room: "Darling!"

He flung himself beside her. With difficulty she

checked an instinct to flee; she obtained no pleasure, but a kind of moral satisfaction in having overcome an aversion.

About midnight Jacques, still enfeebled by his wound, fell asleep on her shoulder. She lay scrupulously still, breathing softly so as not to wake him. She herself was much too perturbed to sleep. After all, what she had done was no light matter. Would Jacques be true to her now that she was no longer a mystery to him? Perhaps he had been disappointed? Did he too feel this anguish and expectancy? How could he sleep so calmly after doing something that committed one for life? Towards dawn she dozed for a couple of hours and saw in her half-dream the chapel of Saint-Jean, the Abbé Guillemin, and Sabine Leclerc walking beside her along the bank of the Eure.

It was fun, in the morning, to arrive together at the station where they had met for the first time. Seated hand-in-hand, beside the window, they looked out at the landscape they knew so well. Denise talked about her work.

"Yesterday morning they gave us herrings to dissect. The heart is lovely—a tiny triangle, beautifully modelled. The air-bladder looks just like a pearl bubble. Dissecting is really great fun. . . . You are told: 'So-and-so is there'; then you search with incredible care until you find it, and it is always more beautiful and more perfect than you expect."

"Yes," said Jacques, looking tenderly at her, "always so much more beautiful and more perfect than one expected."

She blushed and squeezed his hand.

"Do you mean that?" she said.   "Are you pleased?"

"Denise," he said, "don't you think I ought to talk to your parents?   We should be wiser to marry now."

"Good heavens, no!   Certainly not!   I don't want to turn you into a married student, burdened with a household. . . .   That would be dreadful. . . .   We must first have a few years of work and freedom. . . . There's no need to bring the Pelletots and the Herpains and the whole of Normandy into it."

They had no difficulty in passing off the story they had invented to explain their arrival together.   Denise stayed at Pont-de-l'Eure throughout Jacques's leave, and was received by the Pelletots as their son's fiancée, although the word was never mentioned.   Then she returned to Rouen.

XX

MONSIEUR HERPAIN died suddenly in December 1918, a few weeks after the Armistice.   He had a seizure in the night.   His wife was at Compiègne, paying a last visit to Dr. Guérin, who would be demobilized in January after the last wounded were evacuated from the hospital.   Eugénie and Victorine hastened to him when they heard his bell, but he was already suffocating. Dr. Bosredon, Guérin's *locum*, arrived, and said that perhaps if Monsieur Herpain had been bled he might possibly have got over it once more, but in any case he could not have lived much longer.

A warning telegram brought Denise from Rouen in the course of the morning. Charlotte and Suzanne met her at the station; they were in a state of fright. Denise felt strong and firm; she had loved her father very much, but felt that death was a deliverance for him, and also that one had to keep a stiff upper-lip. She astonished the servants by the resolute way in which she walked into the bedroom and kissed the cold forehead.

Madame Pelletot called about eleven to ask if she could be of any help. "Poor girls! Poor girls!" she kept repeating. She dared not question the children about their mother, but in the hall exchanged lengthy whispered confidences with Eugénie, who was the sister of her own cook.

"Poor girls!" she said again. "What will become of them? It would be best for them to go to live with their Grandmother Herpain."

"Oh! I don't think so," said Eugénie. "Mademoiselle Denise has never got on with Madame Aristide. Far more likely at the Baroness's, for she is easy-going."

Nobody knew where to wire to Madame Herpain. She had left, as so often lately, carrying only a small bag. "I shall be back on Wednesday," she had said, and left no address.

"Really?" exclaimed Madame Pelletot. "But surely she can't have gone without giving some excuse to her poor husband . . . without telling him where she was going?"

"Well," said Eugénie, "perhaps she said something to the poor master, but he's no longer here to tell us what it was. . . . In any case, she won't be long now. She'll be here about midday. She always comes by the eleven-forty-six. Monsieur Bouctot has been ordered to meet her at the station."

She arrived about lunch-time in Monsieur Bouctot's taxi. Eugénie was sobbing when she opened the door to her.

"Ah, Madame!"

"What's the matter?" exclaimed Madame Herpain. She had realized at once what must have happened, but her natural sense of drama made her insist that scenes of pathos should be handled in accordance with the rules.

"Ah, Madame!" said Eugénie, knowing quite well that her mistress knew, but being likewise fond of traditional developments. "Ah, Madame! The poor master!"

"The master?" said Madame Herpain. "What's the matter with him? Has he had another attack?"

"Worse than that, Madame. . . . He's in a very bad way."

"Good heavens!" said Madame Herpain, leaning against the door.

"A very bad way—very bad," said Eugénie.

"Is he—dead?" said Madame Herpain, this time really moved.

"Yes, Madame," said Eugénie.

Madame Herpain wanted the whole story. Eugénie had already composed an official account, which was almost true. Victorine and she had heard cries, then choking groans. As the master had already had attacks, they realized what was wrong and hurried to his side. The poor master was clutching at his chest and saying: "It's the end . . . I can't breathe . . . Germaine!" Then he had dropped back. Mademoiselle Lolotte and Mademoiselle Suzanne had come along in their little nightdresses, but had not been allowed in, as it would have been too frightening for children to see the body lying sideways across the bed with open mouth and staring eyes.

"We laid him back on the pillow, Madame. . . . And we telephoned to Dr. Bosredon. . . . But the exchange didn't answer. . . . So Victorine's husband, whom we had waked up, rushed over, and in less than a quarter of an hour, Madame, the doctor was here. But he said at once that nothing could be done; if he had been there when the attack came he might have bled him, but now it was too late . . . and that perhaps it was all for the best."

"Yes, perhaps, Eugénie. He suffered so dreadfully in those attacks. . . . O Lord! O Lord!"

Now she was crying, and Eugénie took her arm.

"I can't go up like this, in light blue. Eugénie, bring me down my black dress here, in the small drawing-room—not the *crêpe-de-Chine*, but the serge one. Then I can go up. . . . Are the children upstairs?"

"Yes, Madame. . . . Poor little souls—they're very unhappy. . . . Mademoiselle Denise has been very brave. . . . I don't understand why they haven't come down. Shall I call them?"

"No," said Madame Herpain. "I'm so overcome. . . . I'd rather have a moment or two to nerve myself."

Five minutes later, robed in black, she went upstairs, at once sincerely grief-stricken and concerned about the appropriate demeanour. On reaching the top of the stairs, she saw her three daughters standing outside the bedroom. She advanced to kiss them, a handkerchief in her hand.

"Oh! my poor dears! my poor dears!" she exclaimed.

She was dumbfounded to see the three children stretch out their arms and bar the way.

"You are not to go in," said Denise.

XXI

WHEN her daughters thus stopped her with outstretched arms from entering the death-chamber of her husband, Madame Herpain was so astounded that she failed at first to grasp the meaning of their behaviour;

she imagined they wished to spare her a painful spectacle.

"Don't be afraid," she said. "I shall be as brave as you were."

She tried gently to break the frail barrier.

"It's useless," said Denise coldly. "You shall not go in. You made him suffer all his life; leave him in peace now he is dead."

"What? What are you saying?" stammered Madame Herpain.

She glanced anxiously behind her with a look that her daughters understood.

"You needn't fear; they're in the kitchen," said Denise contemptuously. "And us also—you've made us suffer enough. Go away."

There was terror in Madame Herpain's eyes as she faced these three child furies with their twisting curls of black hair.

"You are mad," she said.

"No, we are not mad," said Denise. "We are unhappy, and we're telling you the truth for the first time."

Germaine Herpain burst into sobs. She was frightened; her daughters seemed monstrously unjust. After all, she had always tried to show affection towards the poor man. It was many years since he had been anything more to her than a friend, but a friend whom she had tended and hardly ever left. It was certainly a pity she had been away when he died, but that was merely a deplorable coincidence. She had deserted him only for two days; and in any case, hadn't she a duty also to the other man who loved her? She wiped her eyes.

"My children," she said, "I beg you. . . . Don't start a quarrel at such a time; it's dreadful. . . . You're too young to realize how horribly you're behaving. . . . Some day you'll be sorry, and then it will be too late. . . . Now let me go and kneel beside your poor father. To-morrow we can talk things over. But no scenes beside a death-bed. Poor Louis! How he hated any quarrelling! What must he be thinking?"

With a sense of bitterness Denise observed how the authority of their father—poor gentle man!—was invoked for the first time in his own house, on the very day when it held only the cold, stiff shell of his body.

"There will be no scene in the bedroom," she said in cold, implacable tones. "And don't be afraid: there will be no scene in front of anyone. We know that Papa did not like them. But you are not to go in. We shall take it in turns to watch him. You can stay downstairs and receive the visitors. . . . There will be plenty of them."

"You unnatural creature!" exclaimed Madame Herpain.

She had realized that she could not bend these slender, stubborn furies to her will. Sobbing, she went down to the small drawing-room, and there, facing the arm-chair in which her husband had so often anxiously waited for her, listening for any sound and watching every hour, she sat thinking about the future. No doubt she would marry Georges Guérin. Not at once, but in a year, perhaps two years. Public opinion had to be allowed for; Georges would need all the support he could get. Eugénie announced old Madame Aristide. She kissed her daughter-in-law and wept. In the shadow of death, she thought, quarrels should be made up. But she could not help saying:

"You weren't here?"

"No," answered Madame Herpain, dabbing her eyes. "I was at Rouen at my poor mamma's. She, too, is far from well. I shall never forgive myself for being away."

And again she wept. Madame Aristide said she would like to see her granddaughters, and rather nervously, fearing a refusal, their mother sent Eugénie to ask them to come downstairs.

"They won't leave him," she said. "It's touching. . . . I am obliged to stay down here myself. One of us must sacrifice herself to visitors."

Denise and Suzanne came down, leaving Charlotte beside their father. At the same moment Madame Achille Quesnay arrived. Holding a royal status in the neighbourhood, she had unconsciously acquired all the outward semblance of aged ladies of the blood royal, with their simplicity of dress, their old-fashioned hats, their kind, aloof questionings.

"I have come immediately," she said. "Achille is dreadfully upset. He was *so* fond of your husband."

In point of fact, when his son-in-law Lecourbe told him that Monsieur Herpain was dead, he only replied:

"Really?   I wonder who'll take over the business."
But it was one of Madame Achille's social duties to
transpose into humane terms the barbarous, wool-
minded reactions of her husband.

"Did he suffer much?" she said to Madame Herpain.
"You were with him at the fatal moment?"

"Alas! no," said Madame Herpain.   "I was at
Rouen with my poor mamma."

She avoided the eye of Denise, who left the room
without a word; and then, with a sense of more freedom, Madame Herpain continued her story.   She had
adopted Eugénie's version.

"The two maids heard him calling.   They rushed
up to him.   Poor Louis was clutching his chest and
saying: 'It's the end . . . I'm choking.'   His last word
was my own name, 'Germaine.' . . .   That's a great
consolation. . . .   But what a loss!   He was such a
guide, such a prop to me!"

When she finished, there was a silent pause; and then
the two old ladies found themselves irresistibly turning
to another topic, one which just then was exercising the
minds of Pont-de-l'Eure.

"You know that young Madame Romilly is getting
a divorce?" Madame Achille Quesnay murmured shyly.

"Oh! yes," replied the elder Madame Herpain, not
without some incongruity between the funereal tone of
her voice and the sprightly inquisitiveness of her topic.
. . . "Oh! yes.   It's incredible.   It seems that during
the War——"

So animated did their chat become that they soon

forgot to lower their voices and the widow was joining in. All three were almost laughing when Eugénie announced Madame Pelletot. And simultaneously, but independently, the faces of all three resumed a fittingly doleful expression. Madame Herpain rose and Madame Pelletot gave her a prolonged embrace.

"I've been already this morning," she said. "It's terribly sad. . . . You weren't here?"

"Alas!" said Madame Herpain. "I was at Rouen with my poor mamma. . . ."

She repeated the official account of the death, and Madame Pelletot, who had heard it already from Eugénie, noticed with secret satisfaction that the two versions were identical. After a few minutes the talk reverted to the Romilly divorce. When Madame Pelletot rose, Madame Herpain said in a quite casual undertone that she would like to see Maître Pelletot after the funeral.

Leaving Charlotte at her father's bedside, Denise wrote to Jacques: "There are days when one touches bedrock, and struggles vainly against everything base and vile. This has been one of those days for me. I am in despair. Apart from you, I have no longer anybody in the world. I am really, as Mademoiselle Aubert used to say, 'an atom dropped in a corner of the expanse,' a poor little atom, overwhelmed, battered, wounded by people and things. I should never have believed one could be so utterly, so wretchedly alone. . . ." At that moment Eugénie knocked at the door, saying that her mother wished to know if she would come down and say how-do-you-do to her Aunt Marthe.

XXII

For three days Louis Herpain had been lying at rest in the cemetery; the earth over his grave was still broken and fresh.   Under her widow's weeds Madame Herpain was gently plaintive.   Pont-de-l'Eure appreciated the way in which she had performed the rites of grief, and was viewing her with sympathy.   She carefully shunned all occasion for dispute with her daughters, and to prevent conversation from taking any unpleasant turn, she had invited Madame d'Hocquinville over from Rouen.   Unrelenting though they were, the girls could not speak freely in her presence; and she, on her side, bridged awkward moments with the stories of Adhéaume's campaigns or the sale of Thuitsignol. On the sixth day, about ten in the morning, Germaine Herpain was having her bath when there was a knock at the door.

"What is it?" she said.

"It's me—Denise."

"I'm having my bath.   What d'you want?   Is it urgent?"

"Yes."

"Oh! all right.   Come in."

Very pale in her black frock, Denise remained standing a few paces from the bath. During a moment of silence she noticed the shape of her mother's shoulders. How youthful she still was!

"What do you want?" said Madame Herpain, rather perturbed.

"Mother, for three days I have been trying to talk to you. Every time you slip away. You place somebody between you and me. You shun this talk. Why? It must take place; I must know. My sisters and I have got to come to certain decisions."

Mechanically Madame Herpain was soaping her neck and arms.

"What decisions?" she said. "I don't understand."

"Yes, you do, Mamma. Of course—you will be marrying Dr. Guérin?"

Madame Herpain dropped the soap. This abrupt directness appalled her. She belonged to a generation which did not like things to be said right out.

"Well, really, Denise! I simply don't know you nowadays! You used to be so tactful. . . . How can you ask such questions at such a time? My thoughts would hardly turn to marrying when your father has hardly been taken from us, I assure you. . . ."

"Then you are never going to marry Dr. Guérin?"

"I don't say that. . . . Certainly, as you've raised the subject, it would be to the advantage of all of you to have a man in the house again some day. . . . Your poor papa guided me in everything, and so I'm not used to dealing with business matters. We shall need a man, and a man whom we can trust, to look after our interests. But there can be no question of that for a long time—two years, or three years."

"I agree," said Denise. "But as neither my sisters nor myself wish to live in Monsieur Guérin's house, we shall leave home."

"Denise, you're mad. . . . Georges—I mean, Dr. Guérin, is very fond of you all; if ever he comes to live with us, he will be a father to you——"

"Quite possibly. I have no grudge against Monsieur Guérin. I simply don't want to live in his house. I presume I'm entitled to feel like that. In any case, so far as I am concerned, I must be in Paris to continue my studies. So I shall go there as soon as I know what income I can count on. My sisters will wait a little while."

"You won't live alone in Paris. I forbid that, absolutely."

"I've been of age for a month now, Mamma."

"Denise, your attitude is shameful. I have nothing to reproach myself with. I have lavished care and affection on you all. I have sacrificed for you far more than you can understand or even imagine. I may have had a disturbed life; that is not for you to judge. Your father was more indulgent, or rather more just. He loved me tenderly, to the very last."

"Don't suppose that," exclaimed Denise. "He had a mistress."

She fled, trembling. On the landing she stopped outside the empty bedroom, and imagined with startling vividness Dr. Guérin, with his red curls and his pink bald scalp, on her father's pillow.

"What's wrong with me?" she wondered. "Why get myself into such a state since I'm going? I went too far. . . . But I couldn't control myself. I *had* to crush the woman."

Going down to the garden, she paced round and round the lawn for a long time, soothed by deep breaths of the cool air. Then, re-entering the house, she went into the drawing-room and unconsciously opened the piano. Her fingers sketched the *cavatina* from "Faust." "*Salut, demeure chaste et pure. . . .*" Poor papa. . . . No doubt in his young days he sang that air thinking of the house he would have with a woman he loved. . . . "*Salut, demeure chaste et pure.*" Once again she saw the square beard, the drooping head. . . . She tried to catch again the tone of that halting breathless voice which yet had its throb of artless passion. . . . She wondered how well her father had been known to that thin-faced Mademoiselle Protat who had wept so much on the day of the funeral. "*Salut, demeure——*" Quietly the door opened. . . . Madame Herpain entered, surprised and shocked. In her black dress, its collar bordered with white, she was more beautiful than ever.

"It's you!" she said. "Your grandmother and I could not believe it! So, six days after your father's death you are playing the piano. . . . You are utterly heartless, wretched girl—everything points to it. . . ."

In the afternoon, Madame Herpain received a call

from Maître Pelletot. She showed him the will, which had been kept in her wardrobe. It was entirely in her favour. She inherited half of the property, one quarter outright and one quarter in trust; in addition Monsieur Herpain requested that the house in the Rue Carnot should not be reckoned in the estate, but left to her during her lifetime, to live in with her daughters. There were no other legacies. She made a few calculations with the notary. She would have about eight hundred thousand francs. On returning home, the notary said to his wife:

"It's very odd. . . . The husband whom she deceived all his life has not favoured his daughters. . . . The lucky man in the whole thing is Guérin. . . ."

"Do you think she'll marry him?" said Madame Pelletot.

He shrugged his shoulders.

"Come now, really!" he said. "What is more on my mind is our Jacques. . . . So long as Monsieur Aristide lives, the girls won't be well off. . . . And even then——"

"Well, the marriage can't be allowed!"

"Gently," said the notary. . . . "Whatever you do, say nothing. This new generation needs understanding. . . . If you don't want this marriage, be careful not to mention it."

Then, entering his study, he resumed his examination of the Romilly papers, and reflected that for this changeable new generation he would henceforth be drawing up only agreements for separation of property.

PART II

I

Denise Herpain to Suzanne Herpain

Paris, November 15, 1919.

My darling—— Since getting that sad, disheartened letter of yours, I haven't been able to think of anything but you. I picture you seeking refuge in your room on the second floor of that accursed house. Oh! how I'd like to get you here and let you share my happiness! But I mustn't get lyrical. . . . (*"Still rather declamatory,"* Mademoiselle Aubert would have noted in the margin.) I am going to try to give you an accurate and plain summary of my life. (*"Make a plan, Mademoiselle Herpain, make a plan!"*)

1.—*Living Arrangements.*—Maître Pelletot told me I should get about eight hundred francs from him every month. After much searching I have found this Pension Vigeolas in the Rue de Vaugirard, where I get board and lodging for five hundred. This leaves me three hundred for books, concerts, and clothes (in any case, I'm already set up with dresses for the winter). It seems reasonable. *Advantages of the Pension Vigeolas.*—My room is on the fifth floor, with a balcony overlooking the Luxembourg Gardens; Madame Vigeolas is a good soul; it is near the Sorbonne, and four times a day I get the lovely walk through the Gardens; finally, it is near

Jacques, who has a room in the Rue d'Assas. *Disadvantages of the Pension Vigeolas.*—The furniture is appalling, the food monotonous; Madame Vigeolas is loquacious. Having once been a teacher, and having many foreign students staying in the place, she feels obliged to get up at every meal an "instructive" conversation.

2.—*Study.*—I have paid my fees. I am naturally taking all the courses for my degree—English, French, Latin, etc. I also take Victor Basch's æsthetics course, for one thing because the subject is Wagner, and for another because Basch is reputed to be revolutionary, and to be his pupil is a token of holding advanced ideas oneself. And you know my political views: "Up with anything against the established order! Down with everything!" As for philosophy, on Monday I went to Janet's lecture and was delighted. He startled the girl next to me by saying that thought is only slowed-up action. I thought that excellent!

3.—*Human Beings.*—First, of course, there is Jacques. I don't see him quite as much as I should like, because he is at the Law School and I am at the Sorbonne. But I spend every Sunday with him, and last night we went to the Opéra-Comique to see "Pelléas" (Jacques wanted to disapprove; as usual I was enthusiastic). In the Pension there are lots of Rumanian girls, with one of whom I have made friends, some Canadians, and two Frenchmen:

(*a*) Edmond Holmann. He introduced himself by saying that his father knew some of our friends—the Quesnays, the Leclercs, etc. He is the son of a big Nancy banker. "A tremendous fortune," Madame Vigeolas says respectfully. The father insists that the son should lead a student's life—absolute plain living. The lad is shy, thin, and short-sighted, but he can be graceful (there's something of Jacques about him, but his features are less good). Overdresses rather. Wears grey spats. Double-breasted waistcoats. You won't see quite what I mean. He comes to my room in the evenings to talk. A certain Aunt Fanny in Nancy sends him wonderful parcels of macaroons and other food for the flesh. Like Jacques, Holmann is taking law and political science.

(*b*) Pierre Ménicault. He has a scholarship; according to Holmann, the son of a tax-collector in Périgord. Flowing tie. Rumpled collars. Hair too long because he can't afford a barber. He is a little bull with a real chest to him. Holmann declares he is remarkably intelligent. So far has not deigned to speak to me. Told Holmann I must be of the amateur student type. That annoyed me. I wish I could get to know him.

4.—*Relations with Germaine.*—Incredibly cordial. You were right. She is so determined to believe in her virtue that she suppresses and honestly forgets everything that might spoil the conventional, rather pathetic, portrait she has made of herself. Her letter this morning runs: "I am so pleased you are happy. As for me, I am the scapegoat. I no longer count on being happy, and if I did not live for the three of you, death would be the only thing I could desire. . . . Suzanne still addresses me in that sharp and offended tone that always hurts me. I think she needs a year away from her family. She would then appreciate better what family love means, and understand that in dealing with one's fellow-beings one has to make more allowances and be more agreeable." You should take her at her word, and ask to spend a year in England either with a family or in a school. You would be freer and you'd get to speak English better.

5.—*Paris.*—The walks in the Luxembourg, vaults of black trees. Their branching tops vanish into that pinkish-grey mist of Paris which I find enchanting. The Paris houses, so individual, so nineteenth-century, with their blue-slate roofs against a rain-filled sky. The towers of St. Sulpice, so round after our pointed Rouen. Rain on the trees of the boulevards. Pavements gleaming like the wet sand at Beuzeval. Book-shops as long as liners. Girls hurrying by with satchels under their arms. Young men, bare-headed or wearing berets. The rush of Paris. Whistling of traffic-policemen. Streams of cars. Bells of trams. I'm happy.

DENISE.

A letter written on the same day by Pierre Ménicault to his friend René Tocheport, at Bordeaux, contained these remarks: "There's a short-haired girl here who is very beautiful. I am in love with her. I have not yet spoken a single word to her. Boarding-school made me romantic; which I deplore, but can't help. I make the wildest plans: to enter her room at night and amaze her by my flow of speech. The annoying thing is that this love binds me to the Pension Vigeolas, which is too ex-

pensive for me. When I have paid my bill and settled
for my books, I am left with two francs, ten centimes.
I don't care. I shall borrow from Holmann to go to
the Vieux-Colombier and to concerts. The black-haired
girl is called Denise Herpain."

II

INTRODUCED to Denise by Holmann, Ménicault soon
became friends with her. She was a rebel, but, as with
most women, her revolt had come more from the heart
than from the head; and this moody and brilliant lad
provided her with political ideas, a doctrine.

The youth of that time were passing the consequences
of the War under a stern scrutiny. Victory had roused
great hopes; the best of the young men believed it
would transform the world. The victors, as masters of
the State, would make honour its basis. The League
of Nations, presided over by Wilson, prophet and professor, would impose perpetual peace. A republican
and disillusioned Germany would become the friend of
France and her spiritual complement. American methods would ensure the happiness of the poor through
abundance instead of revolution. For a few months
working-class and middle-class youths were united in
admiration of the heroes.

The disappointment seemed all the more unfair

because expectations had been so generous. The ex-soldiers were not in power. Selfishness and ignorance were digging new trenches between the classes. The very methods which were to establish happiness were fostering chaos and unemployment. France of the Right and France of the Left again confronted each other as foes. At the Sorbonne a small group of Social Revolutionaries defied an all-powerful opposition, and organized meetings in honour of Wilson and then in memory of Jaurès. Pierre Ménicault was one of this group. The surprising thing was that Edmond Holmann, a banker's son, and of very quiet temperament, stood by him in street riots—out of friendship. They emerged from the fray with their clothes torn, and Ménicault, who was a good Rugby player, would charge through the police barriers to retrieve Holmann's grey felt hat.

Denise became their inseparable companion, and went with them to public meetings. She was reaching the age when the negative pessimism of adolescence is succeeded, through natural reaction, by an attitude of very positive affirmation. The excellence of the causes defended was of less import to her than the vigour of the defence and the youth of the defenders. Although Ménicault thought well of her, it was with some misgiving that he took her into working-class quarters. In workmen's meeting-halls she was shy and seemed ill at ease. "Don't stare at people," he would whisper. "You say you like them, but you don't know how to mingle with them. You look them over too much. Be natural." Gradually she took to seating herself at the back of the hall, in a corner, and not moving.

Ménicault, like Holmann, was resolutely respectful of her. For some time they wondered whether they could allow her to come with them in the evenings to the Montparnasse cafés. Then they got used to treating her straightforwardly as a friend. This chaste comradeship pleased her. Her very different relations with Jacques they were hardly aware of.

Every afternoon about five, when she came out of the library, she went to his room. She would turn the key which was in the door, light the paraffin stove, and then she would hear Jacques's step in the passage. He would bring a bag of cakes, her favourites; they were called "potatoes," and smelled of kirsch and chocolate. When the bag was soaked by the rain and the cakes were nearly frozen, Jacques would hold them over the stove for a time to warm them. After tea, they lay down on the bed. On Sundays Denise arrived about noon, and they lunched together in a brasserie, or, in summer-time, outside a modest restaurant on the pavement, screened by laurels in tubs. Then they would go on to the theatre or a concert, or, if no entertainment attracted them, they would return to the Rue d'Assas.

During that first year they were very happy. Freedom, youth, love—it all seemed wonderful. When the new term of the year opened in 1920 quarrels began to spoil their enjoyment. Jacques claimed that Ménicault's influence was "spoiling" Denise. He would say "spoiling" in a very disagreeable way. Denise would retort that Jacques was growing "bourgeois and respectable." He dined every evening at the home of an uncle, a barrister, and also paid visits to the Thianges, who gave drawing-room parties, and whom he had met in Normandy (Hélène de Thianges was one of the Pascal-Bouchet sisters). He had dropped medicine, and was taking things very easily in his law course. In impartial moods Denise decided that he was not so intelligent as Ménicault, but she was still fond of him. She liked wandering with him through Sunday Paris, with its empty streets and shuttered shops, and telling him, as husband and wife might chat, of the hours of her life which he had not shared.

"This morning," Denise was saying, "I went to the Russian Church with Holmann. . . . You ought to come some day. . . . You can't imagine how splendid it was. A small gilded mosque, and the most heavenly singing, unaccompanied chants, for four voices——"

Jacques was not listening. "Where are we lunching?" he asked.

"Let's go to the Chinese restaurant. . . . It's rather fun. What was I saying? Oh! yes, the Russian Church. . . . I had to make an effort not to prostrate myself like the others. I wanted to cry, to cry at human wretchedness."

"So you're a mystic to-day, are you?" said Jacques.

Ménicault had made Denise more careful in the choice and sense of words.

"Why mystic? Sensitive to something beautiful, that's all. When I listened to that music I felt that this world was not made for petty sentiments. I thought of you, as you used to be when we climbed in the moonlight to the orchards above Rouen. . . . You had ideas in those days. . . ."

"I have no ideas now, I suppose?"

"Of course you have, dear. . . . But still you had a kind of dash and enthusiasm that you've lost now. . . ."

"I was a child," said Jacques. "Nowadays I try to want only what can be had. 'I have made it my usage to conquer my desires rather than the order of the universe.' "

"The order of the universe! How impressed you are by the order of the universe!"

"It's better than being a parlour anarchist. . . . One must know what one's after, Denise; one must decide on the life one leads. I'm sorry, I can't see anything fine in that."

They had sat down. On the table a manifesto called upon intellectual youth to support China, the ill-used victim of the great Powers. This provided a fresh topic for disagreement, Denise at once becoming excited on behalf of China and the protection of the oppressed countries.

"But what do you know about China, Denise? You believe anything. . . . You've lost all critical sense."

"It's better than believing nothing."

He shrugged his shoulders, and began talking of his approaching examination.

"And when you are a doctor of laws," she said, looking him full in the face, "what will you do then?"

He passed his hand over his forehead with a tired look.

"I don't know yet. . . . I haven't made up my mind. . . ."

"Does your father insist on your returning to Pont-de-l'Eure?"

"Yes, but I've made no promises. . . . At the same time, of course, it does seem rather idiotic to go hunting in Paris for a job at a beggarly wage as a solicitor's clerk or counsel's devil, whereas if I went home——"

"Do just as you like, Jacques, but remember—I shall never go back to Pont-de-l'Eure to be your wife. . . . Never. . . . I'm not being obstinate; I'm being sensible. . . . I was too wretched in that place. It's full of ghosts for me. . . . The prospect of spending my life in those streets and meeting those same faces, now that I know what it is to be free—I couldn't face it. . . . Poverty with you, here in Paris, as much as you like——"

"That's what you say. But you don't know what poverty means. . . . It's true I don't either, but I don't think it helps love. . . . But after all, what *is* this romantic freedom you dream of, Denise? Lunching in cheap restaurants, concerts in the three-franc seats, going about in a man's hat—is that your ideal? But, you know, it's quite possible to be just as wise and just as intelligent while leading a comfortable middle-class life. . . ."

She turned aggressive:

"I don't think so. Anything looks silly if you talk of it in a particular way. . . . The life of a saint would seem ridiculous if you described it in that way. . . . To me the cheap restaurants, the three-franc seats, the flight from Pont-de-l'Eure, are symbols. . . . Symbols of rebellion, of resistance. One begins by dressing like others; then one agrees to think like others; and then one is lost. . . ."

"Lost! Why lost? The truth is that you don't love me any more. . . . If you loved me, the places you had to live in wouldn't matter to you in the least."

On that day, for the first time and as if by common accord, they parted after lunch instead of returning together to the Rue d'Assas.

III

On Sunday afternoons the Pension Vigeolas was deserted. When she got back, Denise had a fire lit in her room and attempted a letter to Jacques.

I am alone, Jacques, and I'm horribly depressed. . . . I suddenly feel I've lost hope. I was crossing the Luxembourg just now, bereft of you, and I could feel my heart beating when I thought how sanguine a child I had been. Yes, two years ago I hoped you would do great things. It would be dreadful not to believe in you any more. Don't be content to become *a good boy*, as your parents say with a smile that hurts me. . . . Listen to me without getting angry, Jacques: I'm not blaming you. But I insist you shall live. Do you understand? *Live!* Just now you are going down among the dead men all unawares. Why don't you want any longer to be one of the strong? What have you done with your splendid daring? Am I talking into the void? Take heart again. Don't give up the fight at twenty-three. You said to me just now, "You don't love me any longer." What rubbish, Jacques! Of course I love you, and I want to go on loving you; but I'm scared of the moral torpor I see you sliding into. Your pleasures are no longer real pleasures, your enjoyment is no longer real enjoyment, and I cannot believe that your careless resignation is true wisdom. . . . No!

She had written the final "No" emphatically. She was saying "No" not merely to Jacques, but to Pont-de-l'Eure, to her mother, and to make-believe virtue.

"On with the fight!" she was thinking. " 'The fight with whom?' Jacques would say. Well, the fight with the powers that made my childhood such misery. . . ."

Just then she heard a door shut and a firm step in the passage.

"Is that you Méni?" she exclaimed.

"Yes. Hullo, you here on a Sunday, Denise?"

He appeared in the doorway.

"Come in and smoke a cigarette, Méni. . . . Why shouldn't I be here on a Sunday?"

"Because your Sunday eclipse is a known and regular phenomenon, calculable like the occultations of Venus or the precession of the equinoxes. . . . The sudden variation observed to-day will compel the astronomers to alter their formulæ."

"Don't be so ironical, Méni! And, anyhow, shut up for a moment. . . . Give me a moment to finish this letter. . . ."

He smoked for a little while in silence. She stuck down the envelope and wrote the address.

"There. Now, look here, I'd like you to take me—— Well, anywhere. To the Dôme or the Rotonde."

He said aggressively:

"I have no money."

"Well, I have a little. . . . Don't bully me to-day. . . . I'm in the dumps."

He recited:

"Do not give form to the idea of your depression. Do not define it. Depression is already a weakness."

"Stop being funny, Méni. You're depressed yourself. So why put on side? What miracle accounts for your not being with Edmond to-day?"

"Edmond is in the Rue Alfred de Vigny, in the palace of his ancestors, which is a Renaissance manor built in 1880 and bought by the high and mighty noble, Prosper Holmann of Nancy, his father, in 1905. A family gathering—aunts, uncles, and cousins."

"Poor Edmond!"

On their way to the Dôme they spoke of Edmond.

Both were fond of him, and looked on him as a child who understood much less about life than they did themselves.

"Really, you know," Ménicault said, "I should never have believed that anybody rich could be such a decent fellow. . . . But he'll be awkward with his riches. . . . He hasn't got that wholehearted love of money-bags that keeps them plump and makes the banks happy. . . . I—I, the proletarian—must explain to him what a wonderful adventure it is, in the year of grace, 1920, to be born the only son of the great Holmann."

"Is his father really a very powerful man?"

"Oh, come, Denise! One of the only powerful men, now that politicians depend on big newspapers and big newspapers depend on big business. . . . Clemenceau himself, in the midst of the War, had to reckon with Holmann. . . . One of the books I should like to write later on is a book on the real springs of power, about the men unknown to the people who actually rule the world under cover of parliamentary democracy."

They reached the Dôme.

"Are we going in?" he said. "I'm sorry, Denise; but it's quite true, what I told you just now: I haven't a sou."

"I know. Well, I haven't got much—in fact, not enough to dine out. . . . But I've enough for two cups of tea and two slices of cake. . . . After that, we'll have to go back to the pension."

They sat down on a leather bench. The tables around them were thronged with young men, all of them writing. On their right a couple, looking like Slavs and poorly dressed, attracted their attention; the man and woman gazed into each other's eyes without speaking, with an expression of fondness and despair. Every five minutes, without having exchanged one word, they drew close and kissed on the lips—long kisses. Then once more they stared silently at each other.

"It is beautiful," whispered Denise; "that indifference to their surroundings."

"They behave like characters out of Dostoievski," said Ménicault.

"Yes, absolutely. . . . Look at that little negro in the check overcoat. What lovely eyes!"

After spending an hour and more on that seat, soothed by the proximity of so many young people, they returned to the Pension Vigeolas through the Rue Auguste Comte. Darkness had fallen and the sky was laden with stars. Taking her arm, Ménicault named the constellations:

"The Great Bear, Little Bear—you know them. Starting from the Pole Star, there is the Swan, the Dolphin, and lower down Orion. . . . Where? You see that great parallelogram? No? Of course you do—very much drawn out, with three stars in the short cross-line. That powdery twinkling is the Pleiades. . . ."

To view the sky better, Denise leaned backwards against her friend.

"And you, Ménicault," she said, "how do you explain this wonderful order, the regular movements—in fact, the whole thing?"

"Why wonderful, Denise? That order has nothing wonderful about it. It is . . . and that's all about it. . . . I'll have to make you a Spinozaist. Take care, if you look up in the air, you'll step off the pavement. The philosopher in the well. . . . Listen. In this universe there are gracious and harmonious things—the sky, music, women like yourself; there are also harmful, discordant things—disease, bad prose, wars. . . . Why notice some and not the others? The world order has a meaning for man, not for God. . . . To be amazed at God's having given the world an order, and say that 'the music of the spheres is pleasing to God,' is attributing to God a limited intelligence to which the simple is more immediately intelligible than the complex. . . . That is a human, not a divine idea. . . . For a God who is perfect by definition, discord cannot be less harmonious than pure sound. . . . Everything that is is in God, evil just as much as good, as is proved in the Ethics, Part One, Proposition XV—or XIII, I don't remember. . . ."

"So you're a Spinozaist, Ménicault, are you?"

"Sometimes."

It was such a fine evening that, each of their own accord, they walked together past the pension and strolled about until dinner-time. Denise leaned pleasurably on a taut, muscular arm. At seven o'clock they returned to the Pension Vigeolas. As they were going in, she said to him further:

"Why are you nearly always so ironic? It makes me shy and chills me."

"If I were not ironical, I should be telling you that I loved you. The word is ill defined and it would be a fine mess. . . . So——"

At dinner Madame Vigeolas explained French politics to the Rumanians and Canadians. Afterwards Ménicault and Denise went to her room. Ménicault dropped into the big leather arm-chair, near the fire, and lit a cigarette. Denise came and sat on the arm of the chair. After a little while he took her hand; she let him keep it, and they stayed like that, absolutely silent, gazing at the nuts of coal, in the bright red glow of which stabs of black were now appearing. About midnight the fire died out. They had not said a word. Denise gently slipped her hand out of Ménicault's, smiled at him, and opened the door; and he left without having spoken.

IV

In February, 1921, Madame Herpain married Dr. Guérin. She announced this in an affectionate letter, informing Denise of "all the financial arrangements, which have been the work of Maître Pelletot," said how happy she was, added a suitable mournful remark about "poor Louis," and ended up: "You see, I tell you everything, because I regard you not only as my dear child, but also as my best friend. Georges shares my sentiments. He asks me to tell you that he understands yours, and will try hard by his affection to make you realize that he has entered our family solely to help and love you all. . . ." In conclusion, she begged Denise to attend the wedding and thus to prove to "the people of Pont-de-l'Eure" that the family remained united. "The ceremony will be so much nicer if you're there, all three of you." The word "nicer" exasperated Denise, and politely but firmly she refused. A few days before the wedding Suzanne left for England, where she had found a situation *au pair*. Charlotte alone gave in. The wedding was quiet, but perfect. Old Tournemine, who had had a long and learned conference with Madame Herpain and her betrothed, played César Franck and a Toccata of Bach, and improvised a stirring march at the end which he continued for his own enjoyment long after the church was empty. The Prefect of the Eure Department and Monsieur Achille Quesnay were the witnesses for the happy pair.

After her eldest daughter's refusal to come to the wedding, Madame Herpain's letters became a trifle bitter, but her reproaches were still streaked with effusive sentiment. She could not admit that Denise really intended never to return to Pont-de-l'Eure. "Can such indifference towards your mother be really desirable, and can you really merit your own indulgence? You may come when you like and stay for months or for years: you will find me always the same. . . . But I am not like the owl of the fable, and I see my young as they are. You don't seem to be very happy or very satisfied. Yet you chose the life that appealed to you. You will find out one of these days that nothing can take the place of the bond of blood." Then she complained about her income. Bad times were setting in. The franc was going down. "But the cost of living is not dropping; on the contrary. Despite the slump, I am having my room done up. It needed it and Georges found it gloomy. I shall put up a light cretonne, as they do now. Thanks to a friend of Georges, I've got hold of a delightful design, and I shall get the material on the best terms."

At the end of the university year, all of the little group were very successful in the examinations. Ménicault, having taken his degree brilliantly, went off to work in the mountains. Jacques Pelletot and Edmond Holmann became doctors of laws. Having taken her degree—notwithstanding a poor Latin paper—Denise decided to visit Suzanne in England, and in September to start taking an English degree in London. It was understood that Jacques would join her over there, after spending August at the seaside with his family. Towards the end of the year their quarrels had become less frequent, yet as soon as he was at Pont-de-l'Eure Denise began to receive rather embarrassed letters from him. He talked about "material difficulties." Then something more serious was revealed:

What I've got to tell you about, Denise, is painful, or at least it will seem painful to you. But it is always best to be quite frank. My father wants me to make up my mind, and to do so at once. He had me into his office and said to me: "My boy, I'm feeling old and worn out. I must know whether you are going to take over from me—a plain yes or no. Because if it is no, I shall have to find your sister Berthe a husband who can take my place. Needless to say, my ideal would be to have my son succeed me. But in default of a son, and if he stands down of his own accord, I'd rather have a son-in-law than a stranger." I can hear you at this distance, Denise: laughing—or crying . . . or both . . . such a fuss over the future of a notary's practice must seem absurd to you. But life is made up of such absurd incidents. Suppose I refuse. What shall I do? Become a barrister's clerk? Even then, the barrister would have to be found. Suppose that settled. What is to happen next? How shall I make a career? At the bar? Have I any gift for it? I have a clear mind, but no gift of speech. Become a deputy? Have I any political opinions? You know very well I haven't; for you have often enough reproached me for being so sceptical. Go into a laboratory? That was the dream of ignorant children. I understand the sciences, but I am not inventive and never shall be. So what then? Shall we moulder in Paris on straitened means which you will soon come to hate? Why should we, when we can be one of the five or six leading households in a pleasant small town? Does the word "pleasant" make you jump? You hate this town, Denise. But are you right in so doing? You were wretched at home with your mother? All right, but once we were married it would be a different story. We should have our own home, and if we liked we should see nobody. We should found a family, and order its existence as we thought best. I assure you that since returning to Pont-de-l'Eure I have been astonished and charmed by the quality of the people who live here. In Balzac's day the provinces may have been a world apart; that is not so to-day. The women who live here read the same books, see the same plays, and go to the same concerts as those who live in Paris. You despise bourgeois snobbery, but what could be more snobbish and more vulgar than contempt for provincial life? "Yes," you may say, "but I am afraid of my mother and my stepfather." Well, look here! I have been to see them too. You cannot imagine the way in which they speak of you. Don't forget that Georges Guérin is quite a remarkable man, very superior to your mother. He is upright and easy-going. So what about it, Denise? The decision lies with you. If you insist, I'll give it all up in order to go to Paris and engage in a foredoomed struggle. But I couldn't help feeling, if you did insist, that you must care very little for me.

Denise's answer was an invitation to come over and see her. He wired that he could not go as far as London and begged her to return to Paris. The anxious waiting blighted the last part of a stay in England which at first she had found delightful. Seated with a pile of books at one of those studious, padded tables which form the giant wheel-spokes of the British Museum Reading Room, Denise had stopped working. She let her gaze wander round that vast circle laden with wisdom and fame. She saw the names in the window-openings—Shelley, Byron, Milton, Shakespeare. Girl students and negroes were walking cautiously on the silent rubber flooring. Would she be beaten by that hateful town? No, it wasn't life in Paris that she demanded: she would have followed Jacques to Chateauroux or Mortagne, to Morocco or China; but she would not accept the feigned friendships, the moneybag comedies, the spiteful old people like Madame Romilly and Madame Pelletot. . . .

Alongside her a ray of sunlight glinted on bright gilded bindings of the "Fortnightly Review." Why was she dissatisfied with herself? "Am I sincere? Am I really seeking spiritual salvation? Isn't it rather a victory I want? Isn't it merely pride that stops me from going back to the Rue Carnot and being, if not repentant, at least appeased?" Beside her a little Hindu was eagerly turning the pages of a big book and taking notes. "He is getting ready to do without the English," she thought. "He is learning law to get rid of the English judges, ballistics to beat the English artillerymen. . . . He's reading that treatise on aerodynamics so as to fly higher than the English pilots. . . . Am I being proud?" She could feel in her heart something as stiff as a steel bar, something that she herself could not bend.

V

ALTHOUGH the Sorbonne term did not begin until early in November, Denise was in Paris by October 15. Jacques had said he would be there on the following Saturday, and then, at the last moment, sent a telegram: *"Terribly disappointed. Family matter prevents. Coming without fail next week. Best love."* For Denise, the next few days were days of anger, fear, and despair. Early on the Thursday, Madame Vigeolas brought her a letter from Pont-de-l'Eure.

"Don't be annoyed," Jacques said in it. "I realize you will be, but you cannot imagine what difficulties I am meeting at every step. My father's illness, your parents' influence, and my own common sense, are all being used as weapons against me. We must get married at once, Denise. It is the only way to stop manœuvres which in the end will get the better of us if they are not checked. I have seen your mother. She is on our side, and has grasped the situation wonderfully. She will run up to Paris on Saturday and tell you what is going on. I am terribly disappointed not to see you myself, but my seeming surrender will advance our cause better than open resistance. I love you and I wish you were with me."

"I knew you would not come," Denise replied bitterly. "I realize that henceforth you are to be at Ponte-de-l'Eure and I am to be in Paris, and that, if I agree, I shall have a hasty glimpse of you once a fortnight. Oh, Jacques! why are you going back on life so soon? What do you expect that dead world to give you? Are you in such a hurry to die yourself? And why say you are disappointed. That simply does not fit in with your behaviour. Really I cannot feel sorry for you. . . . I shall see Mamma and hear what she may have to say on your behalf. But I have nearly lost hope. Who would have dreamed that one day she would become the 'messenger' between us?"

Madame Guérin arrived on Saturday about eleven in the morning, and went straight from the Gare St. Lazare to the Pension Vigeolas. Madame Vigeolas knocked at the door.

"Mademoiselle Denise! Mademoiselle Denise! Your mother to see you."

When Denise opened the door, she said in a low voice:

"How young your mother is! And how pretty!"

Behind her was Madame Guérin, smiling and making affectionate signals. She evidently wanted things to happen as if they had parted only the day before after an idyllic family scene. Unwittingly, but in quite a good-natured way, she said:

"Goodness! Your room is in a mess! A real student's room!"

Then she sat down in Ménicault's arm-chair near the fireplace, the tiles of which were littered with cigarette ends; throughout the conversation she kept poking these back into the hearth with the tip of her umbrella.

"I've been asked to see you about a rather pleasant matter. . . . I hesitated to accept, for I know that—mistakenly, but I take you as you are—you dislike my interfering in your affairs; but Georges said it was my duty to come, and as a matter of fact the idea came from your fiancé himself."

The word "fiancé" annoyed Denise, but she lit a cigarette and said nothing.

"Well, I'll come to the point," Madame Guérin continued. "Last Wednesday Jacques Pelletot came to see me. I had been aware for some weeks that he was hovering round us. Well, he came, and told me that he loved you. . . . Oh, you may pride yourself on a conquest! You are a kind of goddess in his eyes! It all reminded me of how your poor dear father spoke of me in the days when we were engaged. . . . However, he had to confess that his parents don't want this marriage. Mind you, they've nothing against us. On the contrary, they admit that our family is a perfectly honourable one, as I come from a good family and your father was of good bourgeois stock, and besides, my marrying Georges puts us right in the front. . . . Only, as you may guess, the trouble is money. They are very well off. Everybody knows that, and their son might reasonably expect a dowry twice, or even three times, the size of yours. . . . However, they're not making too much of that. . . . As Maître Pelletot says, these things matter less than they used to. Nowadays you can't tell who will be rich in a week's time, and young people are not so dutiful as they were, and, anyhow, you have expectations for later on—the later the better, of course—there's your Herpain grand-parents—and even your mother. . . . I must put the whole thing before you. . . . In short, they recognize that their son is bent on marrying you and nobody else, and so here is the good news I bring—they're willing to have you as their daughter-in-law. . . . You see, it's a wonderful chance. . . . And there's only one stipulation."

"What do you mean—a stipulation?" said Denise, bristling.

"Oh! it's all right. Nothing serious. . . . Merely that you shall help them to convince Jacques that the best thing for him is to take over his father's practice. . . . Really, the boy is convinced already. . . . I've had several talks with him, and so has Georges, and Georges says he is very sensible. . . . But he's got it into his head that you won't agree to live in Pont-de-l'Eure, and he thinks it his duty, if you really refuse, to go off with you and face poverty. I told him the idea was positively childish; that if you loved him, you would live with him wherever his work might take him; and that I could vouch for your good sense. . . ."

"But really, Mamma, what right have you to inter-fere in interpreting my feelings? No, I shall never go to live at Pont-de-l'Eure."

"Take care, Denise! If you tug too hard, the rope will break and you'll be very, very sorry. . . ."

She watched her daughter closely. With hostile face

and tightly pressed lips, Denise stared into the fire. Then Madame Guérin went on, with less certainty in her tone.

"There's one point which I didn't want to mention, because I know you well enough to be certain that it is mere gossip. . . . But somebody has told the Pelletots that you were Jacques's mistress. . . . You can imagine their amazement. . . . I laughed like anything!"

"You're wrong. It's true."

Madame Guérin stood up.

"Denise, do you realize what you are saying?"

"And you?"

"Denise, really. . . ."

Then she controlled herself. She had promised her husband to keep calm. After all, what could it matter to her if her daughter wanted to be obstinate? Her own life was now settled again. Georges Guérin was making her perfectly happy. She had done her duty by coming and giving sensible advice. If Denise was foolishly bent on playing a losing hand, then let her please herself. Possibly—who could tell—in the deep unconscious recesses of her mind, Madame Guérin rejoiced at the refusal. For a woman still young, and only a few months married, was it really desirable to be a grandmother and have her own grandchildren in the same town and only a few houses away?

"My poor child," she said, "you're preparing a sorry life for yourself. It's your own look-out."

After a moment of silence, she wanted to relieve the rather painful tension and suggested they should spend the afternoon at a concert. Welcoming the diversion, Denise scanned the programmes. Gabriel Pierné was playing the "Unfinished Symphony."

"Do you remember, Denise?" said Madame Guérin. "I took you to hear it when you were seven or eight. Tournemine's orchestra were playing it in Rouen. You were tiny then, but you listened like a little woman."

Denise did remember. The concert had been one of the most loveliest hours of her life. That afternoon, at the Théâtre du Châtelet, when the conductor raised his baton after two sharp taps, she closed her eyes to summon back her memories. Aloof and distracted, she found it hard, during the first bars, to escape from the wreckage of her private universe. What a failure! And what would her next step be? She told herself that she would not stay in Paris, where Jacques might perhaps come after her, and where she would be tempted to give in. She would go away. Ménicault had once mentioned a mountain inn in the Swiss Jura, at a place called Verrières. He spent his own holidays there, living for next to nothing. Suddenly, when she was listening no longer, a glad, friendly melody rose soaring from the quelled orchestra. Why did these notes, flying high above the symphony like a carefree bird, waft her spirit into happiness? For a moment only did the melody hover, and then, unended, it floated down to rest on the orchestral waves. And

Denise's sole thought then was to watch for it to reappear with its lightness and charm. Once or twice since the days of her uneasy adolescence, in an orchard with a view of spires and smoke and the lovely curve of a river, in a Paris street one Sunday night with her head thrown back to see the stars, once or twice she had heard, rising high over a stormy and sorrowful symphony, those notes of hope, those first bars of peaceful melody. Then life, like the orchestra, had drowned it. Would it rise again? After the first movement, Madame Guérin said:

"The strings are good. . . . Did you know that Georges played in that orchestra when he was a student? Queer, isn't it?"

The same evening her mother went back to Pont-de-l'Eure.

VI

Denise Herpain to Jacques Pelletot

Verrières, Switzerland.

November 15, 1921.

MY DEAREST,—I hesitated about starting my letter as fondly as I used to; so many things have changed between us. Then I realized that in spite of everything, in spite of myself, my lips, less wise than my mind, still call you "Dearest," and it seems hypocritical and unnatural to feign an indifference which doesn't exist.

I am writing from an inn in the mountains, a few yards from the frontier. You know that I intended this winter to go on with my English at the Sorbonne so as to get my diploma and go to the Schola Cantorum. Alas! I couldn't bring myself to face a life suddenly so changed from what I had pictured. My work interested me, you used to call me "the passionate student," but it was so for your sake and whilst with you that I was so. When I saw after Mamma's visit that there was no hope of seeing you again as I had loved you, I realized that my only chance of salvation was to escape from my memories and my temptations. Here, living in this little frontier hotel, in a bare room, on a snowclad tableland, and alone, absolutely alone, for the last three weeks, I have recovered a certain indescribable serenity of mind, and that bare, pitifully invulnerable security of those who no longer possess anything but themselves.

I am beaten, Jacques, and beaten through you, whereas I'd expected to win, and to win through you. At first I just wanted to die. Then to give in. Now, thanks to the solitude, I have mastered both these weaknesses. I have not given up the struggle. I am becoming a rebel again. For how long? What is to become of me? I don't know. I'm not working any more. I read. I am reading Epictetus, "Jean Barois," and Sils Maria's "Nietzsche," which goes well with this strong icy air. I go for long walks along the road which rises in loops up the snow-fields. At the first bend there is a half-frozen spring bearded with stalactites; at the last bend is the grave of a lad who was killed up in the mountains. As I walk I see my life go past like the characters in a film. It seems to me a very petty affair. I believe that my real youth, that in which one still believes in the reality of a fairy universe, is over. How swiftly it has flown! The convent and my period of piety; the black smocks at Saint-Jean smelling of ink and the washtub; my years at the *lycée* with Mademoiselle Aubert reading out Pascal; those train journeys by the light of a smoky lamp when my chief joy was my admiration of yourself; the white and blue houses of Paris reaching half up to the sky; the black and coppery trees of the Luxembourg, and the cakes you used to bring me for tea, all drenched in rain and chilliness. How happy we were, dearest, and how I knew it! I can even recall my reveries, so free of self-interest or calculation, and those evenings when I was learning philosophy from Ménicault's lips and believing in philosophy. Now I believe only in the beauty of the snow-clad firs.

Yesterday, walking alone thus along my white road I once more surveyed our situation, wishing hard that I could find that you were right. I cannot see it. I shall never go back to Pont-de-l'Eure. It is beyond my strength. Do not hope for me to become your wife now that you have chosen the path which must part us. I have no idea what sort of life your choice will lead to for either of us, but I want you to look on yourself as freed of any obligation towards me, save that of friendship. You were meant, my poor darling, for a sensible life, all smooth and straight. Even when I begged you to, you would not dare to "lose your life to save it." I tried to go on believing in you all last year. I realize that it has always been in a dream that I have loved you. Don't misunderstand, I don't mean a dream of the present—for the actuality was truly lovely—but a dream of the future. In spite of what was obvious, I persisted in hoping for a miracle. Right up to the vacation I thought I should win in the fight between your comfort and our love. I was wrong, I am beaten, I am left alone in the dark. But I know that one thing, one choice, remains impossible: I will not be buried alive.

My dearest, you will marry some simple girl who will expect no more than an easy happiness, an empty existence, and nice children. As for me, I shall mount Rosinante again and go on ever seeking a pure freedom, which perhaps does not exist. A few years more will pass, and then we shall both drop into eternal sleep or into a world more dreadful even than this one. The die is cast. Don't reply to me any more. Don't try to see me again. I have made my sacrifice. Don't rob me of my courage. It's all you have left me.

When she had read over this letter, she asked herself, as she had done so often in the last few months: "Is it courage, or is it pride?" So closely entwined were the two sentiments that she could not distinguish one from the other.

VII

SHE stayed at Verrières, quite alone, until Christmas. Jacques wrote to her several times; she did not allow herself to reply. From Ménicault had come two beautiful letters signed, "From the student who used to enjoy crossing the Luxembourg with you." He told her that he had loved her, and still loved her, but refused to let this unrequited love be a reason for grieving or complaint. "I speak to you with a firm heart and beg your pardon. Most women know no sweeter music than the plaints of those they have brushed aside. But I am a child on the threshold of its career, a determined child whom you have filled with courage and who is bent on going straight ahead. My love for you must be thoroughly healthy; it must not press on me like a dead-weight. . . ." Farther on, he spoke of his studies. . . . "This morning, in the course of my reading, I came upon a passage in the philosopher Lagneau which so fired my enthusiasm that once again, as so often before, I wanted you to share my feeling.— 'Certitude is a profound region where thought can be maintained only by action. What action? There is but one: the action which contends with nature and creates it, the action which shapes the self whilst crushing it. Should one make one's life instead of merely suffering it? To answer "No" is to declare that both the world and oneself are unintelligible, to call for chaos. And chaos is nothing. To be or not to be. The choice must be made.' "

A choice? Well, she had chosen. She had agreed to fight, she had resolved to make her life instead of merely suffering it. What would the next chapter be? Home was closed to her by dictates of pride. The man whom she had hoped to have as her comrade-in-arms had also made his choice, and had chosen chaos. There were evenings when the profundity of her solitude, which at first had calmed her, overwhelmed her.

A few days before Christmas, coming downstairs as usual about eleven for her walk, she was surprised to see in the hall a fine brown leather travelling-bag. Standing with his back to her before the open door, through which the freezing air blew in, was a young man in climbing kit, breeches, and stockings. He was superintending the unloading of other luggage. At the sound of footsteps on the stair, he turned round: it was Edmond Holmann. He raised his arms and exclaimed:

"Hooray! Hullo, Denise!"

She was so delighted that she almost kissed him. He looked at her shortsightedly, with gay fondness in his eyes. Denise took both his hands.

"How did you get here, Holmann? What extraordinary chance——"

He laughed.

"It isn't chance! Ménicault told me everything— how you ran away, how you've been living all alone— and I decided to come. Only I'm working with my father now, you know. He is very strict; he wouldn't have let me go. I had to wait until Christmas, and I didn't let you know I was coming so as to give you a surprise."

"A delightful surprise. . . . You can't imagine what a joy your arrival is for me. I've been so lonely, at such a loose end for two months now."

The next hour was devoted to getting Edmond settled. She helped him to unpack and put away his shirts and clothes in the rustic firwood cupboards.

"How funny, Edmond! You've brought evening things! Oh, these rich people! My dear fellow, there's not a soul here—not a soul, do you hear—except the villagers who drop in at night for a glass of coffee and a game of cards, and dance once a week. You're going to be alone with me, all alone. . . ."

"That's just what I wished. . . . I didn't quite dare to hope. . . ."

When they had finished unpacking, Denise took Holmann out along her road through the snow. How jolly to be walking in this keen air, beside a man! His climbing kit gave Edmond Holmann an air of manliness which he had lacked in Paris. As they walked, he described his new life, which was not very happy. His father thought only of business, and apparently did not want to discuss it with him.

"He gives me the merest clerking to do. . . . My father is old, you know: nearly seventy. He married very late. . . . The youngest men in his confidence are at least thirty years older than myself. I live hedged around by greybeards. . . . And I'm bored!

I'm sometimes so fed up I wonder if I shall be able to stick it."

"But the question shouldn't arise. . . . You *must* stick it, Edmond. . . . Think of the tremendous influence you can wield some day. . . . I remember a talk I had about that with Ménicault one evening, walking through the Luxembourg. . . . He envied you. . . . 'With the world in such a mess,' he said, 'only a great revolutionary or a big banker like Holmann can still achieve a great adventure in life.' And that's quite true. I don't know much about life, but I can guess things. . . . In your place, I'd want to study Europe and the hidden workings of governments. I'd want to make mankind a little less wretched and a little less clumsy. I'd want to own newspapers and influence public opinion. And to think that you've only to be patient for a few years to have all that without any effort, just because you are born a Holmann, and yet you hesitate before life. . . ."

"I hesitate because I am lonely, Denise. You can't understand how lonely I am. I have no faith in myself. Sometimes I think that I'm just as intelligent as all these men who work with my father; I don't find them very remarkable, but they talk big and are positive, whereas I am doubtful. . . . If I had someone beside me ready to accept the period of waiting as sensibly as you've just described it, it would all be different."

Denise suddenly changed the conversation.

"Look at those firs on the slope, Edmond—how

curious! They start to grow on a slant and then straighten up and rise towards the sky just as if they were growing on level ground."

"Yes, it's a mechanical effect of light and growth."

"Of course, but it seems to me a comforting image."

They came back hungry and happy. In the afternoon Edmond hired some skis and they made their first attempts. Denise, who was very nimble, was soon able to take easy slopes. Edmond, more awkward, would fall and lose his skis in the snow, but he took his tumbles gaily. In the evening they read aloud. On Christmas Eve they decided to go to the midnight Mass in the little church of Verrières. The village lay below the inn down in the valley, and most of the peasants came to church on skis. Denise and Edmond, not yet adepts, were content with heavy iron-spiked boots. The worthy Swiss innkeeper lent them a lantern. As they came out of the hotel, they could see moving lines of lights on all the opposite slopes, all gliding down like themselves towards a still invisible goal.

"Isn't it lovely?" said Denise, delighted. . . . "In essence every human soul is like that. . . . A faint light making its way to some divine shelter, imagined, and sought, and unseen."

Edmond had his hand on her arm. Along the difficult path, covered with frozen snow, he sometimes lost his balance, and then clung to her. The village Mass moved them both. Denise joined with the peasants around her in singing the Christmas carols. Edmond could see her in profile and admired her beauty, and still more the freedom with which she yielded to her emotions.

"Thank you, Edmond," she said, when they were out in the moonlight again.

"Why? I haven't done anything. . . . On the contrary, I was just thinking that I haven't even brought you a Christmas present."

"You have brought me the best of Christmas presents: a faithful friendship. . . . And you've given me this evening. You can't imagine what a lot of good it has done me to join in this real Christmas with simple country folk."

After that they were silent for quite a time. As they were coming to the hotel, Edmond said:

"Denise, there's something I have come here to ask you. Would you be willing to be my wife?"

She had felt the question coming ever since his arrival, and dreaded it.

"Thank you for that too," she said, "but it's impossible."

"Denise, I know quite well you don't love me; I don't ask you to love me, but I have heard from Méni-cault that things have altered for you. Why not . . . ?"

"You are very kind, Holmann, but again I say: it's impossible. . . . I have not only been engaged to Jacques Pelletot. For three years I have been his mistress."

"I knew that, Denise. I'm not jealous of your past; it's your future I want."

They were at the door.

"Look here," she said very quickly, "let me go up to my room. To-morrow we can talk."

She fled.

VIII

THE stair rail of the inn at Verrières was of varnished pitch-pine, rather resinous and sticky, and whenever Denise touched it she was reminded of the Villa Colibri at Beuzeval. And often, going up or coming down those stairs, she would hear inwardly a song linked with that period of her life, Duparc's "Vie antérieure": "*J'ai longtemps habité sous de vastes portiques. . . .*" But when she left Edmond Holmann in the early hours of Christmas morning and ran up to her room, the air which ran in her mind, which she was even humming aloud, was that melody of the "Unfinished Symphony," so friendly and trusting and fond.

Once in her room, she sat on the bed and asked herself why she felt so happy. She repeated Edmond's words: "Denise, there's something I have come here to ask you. . . ." She could see his tired eyes, his tender, anxious smile. "Why am I so happy?" she thought again. "I don't love him. . . . Might I come to love him?" She took off her dress. She could hear the sound of Edmond's iron-spiked boots in the next room. A thin partition separated them. She could hear his breath, and water being poured out. "I must try to be honest," she thought. "I am happy because it's a revenge. I was hurt by being sacrificed to a commonplace career. This man is ready to sacrifice a family for me. After all, that is a bold step for a shy boy who is ruled by his father."

Knotting the cord of her pyjamas, she pictured a plan of life: to make Edmond a great man of affairs. She saw herself as his quiet and unsuspected partner, rallying hostile or indifferent men to her husband's schemes, and preparing with him for a supreme examination, the scope of which would be knowledge of the world, and the award, power. She got into bed, picked up a book, but didn't open it. Why was she drawing up a plan of married life, as if she had already decided to accept Holmann's proposal? Was she entitled to marry without loving? Possibly, provided she were to forgo love, and also provided that she loyally made her sentiments clear to Edmond. Was she entitled to marry a wealthy man? Yes, provided she made wealth no more than a means. "Clever sophistry dictated by a desire for revenge," Ménicault would have told her. But he was far away, but by coming to see her Edmond had ensured for himself the glamour of surprise, and the power of an unfamiliar setting.

"Oh, well," she thought as she lay down, "I can talk to him to-morrow morning about everything. Now I must sleep." But she could not halt the procession of pictures crowding through her mind. She had hardly lain down before she seemed to hear all the sounds of the past: the "Carnaval de Venise" and the whistles of the trains in the Rue Carnot, the wheel hung with little bells in the courtyard at Grandmother's, the sound of Jacques's key in the door of the Rue d'Assas . . . Jacques. . . . The empty and interminable Sundays and cigarettes in corner cafés. . . . And Pont-de-l'Eure, her father's home life, his evenings of waiting, his sad eyes. . . . Inwardly she vowed that if she did marry Edmond Holmann she would be faithful to him until death. "I am entitled not to marry. I am not entitled to spoil the life of a man who loves me."

About three o'clock, concerned by the prospects of a sleepless night before such a serious conversation, she took a little tablet from a glass tube beside her bed, and at last fell asleep. She had a dream which had often recurred since she had been at Verrières on nights when she slept badly. She was in a wintry forest with black tree-trunks and bushes at its edge. She was a doe hunted by hounds. One, the strongest, was taking tremendous leaps and was about to overtake her, but just when she had given herself up for lost he made a final leap and rolled over in the grass, exhausted. She went on running, but more slowly.

Waking early, she heard Edmond already moving in the next room, and got up. The window-panes were covered with ferns of hoar-frost. She called through the partition:

"Good morning! Slept well?"

"Not a wink," he said through the partition.   "Are you coming down?"

"In twenty minutes."

A little later they met in the little dining-room, its walls hung with photographs of gymnasts and choir-singers.   Facing each other over bowls of coffee and pots of honey, they talked in low and friendly tones. She spoke the phrases she had prepared.   She didn't love him, but she had a very friendly feeling for him. She rather liked the idea of a life of joint work, but she wondered if it would be fair to him. . . .   He interrupted her:

"Denise, I never hoped for more!   What you offer me is exactly what I've come to ask you for.   I have trust in you.   We have discussed marriage often enough in the last two years for me to know what you think. If you agree to marry me, you are not the woman to fail to see the thing through to the end and put all your heart into it.   I can't help thinking that life together and my fondness. . . ."

She was looking at him, animated but perturbed.

"Shall I be able to love him?" she was thinking again. She asked him if he might not find grave obstacles in his family.

"Oh, I don't think so," he said.   "My father won't set up obstacles. . . .   A dowry means nothing to him. . . . He himself married for love. . . .   No, the kind of wife he wants me to have is precisely one who will make me work and who will accept the plain life he likes.   Unless I'm mistaken, he'll be very pleased. . . .

My aunts, and especially my Aunt Fanny, may object because they are snobs. They would like me to marry a duke's daughter. . . . But what can they matter if you and I are agreed and my father approves?"

They discussed it all morning. Denise felt herself already growing used to his company and his features. She found in his short-sighted eyes something wounded and hurt which appealed to her. About eleven she suggested a walk. The snowy path led towards the sun. She took Edmond's arm with a movement that he found charmingly natural.

"Now," she said, "I'm going to ask you to make me a promise. You must let me think things over for the rest of your stay and I'll give my answer only when you go."

"Certainly, Denise, of course."

They returned to the hotel, and when she was alone in her room, she wrote to Jacques Pelletot:

"I have something I must tell you, Jacques, and I feel very awkward about it. In the past three months I have been through some very bad times. More than once I almost gave in, almost answered your letters, almost came home to see you. Now, on the contrary, I have to tell you that I am perhaps going to get married. You will be surprised, but, you see marriage and love have become so different in my eyes. Don't reproach me: you yourself have made me sceptical and resigned. As *our* dream has failed, I want no other; or rather, I want something quite different. My enthusiastic youth has been spoilt. Never again shall I be altogether happy. You, my dearest, have had all that was finest, noblest, and most sincere in me. When I say that, I am thinking of someone else. He has come to me because you had left me lonely. You know him. I've always been attracted to him by a deep sympathy, and by a certain curiosity about a different life and a new power. He wants to marry me. What shall I do? If I were the one who loved, I should have no hesitation. But I am the one who does not love. And you? Tell me whom you love?"

Just then Edmond's cheerful voice came through the partition:

"Denise! What about lunch? I'm famished."

"Just coming, dear," she answered.

And it struck her that for the first time she had called him "dear," that she had done so unconsciously, and that perhaps it was a good omen.

IX

Denise Holmann always looked back on the first three years of her married life as dull, but their dullness was not unkindly. She passed those years partly in Nancy, partly in Paris, alone with her husband and her father-in-law. It was she who had wanted to live with old Prosper Holmann in the family house in the Rue Alfred de Vigny. Both families had thought her wrong. Edmond himself said more than once that he was afraid of the boredom of such a quiet house for a young woman. Denise held out. The plan she had sketched required that Edmond should be on close enough terms with his father for him to learn not only the technique, but also the secrets and subtleties of the business in which she was determined he should be master.

Monsieur Prosper Holmann had allotted one wing of the house to the young couple. He was a taciturn and ponderous man. With his short-cut bristling hair and his old-fashioned sweeping mustachios, he reminded Denise of the old Russian generals in Tolstoy's novels. The only sentimental event of his life had been his marriage with a foreigner, whom he had met in Poland whilst inspecting the French factories at Lodz. She had died in 1902, a few years after Edmond's birth. He lived surrounded by portraits of this woman. He was not known to have had any mistress.

Like most French successes, Holmann's had begun in the provinces. In the early years of the nineteenth century three Holmann brothers, bankers at Nancy, had helped to found the cotton industry in France, and then to develop the iron-founding industry. They had interests in nearly all the big undertakings of Nancy, Epinal, Belfort, and the Vosges. For many years they had remained business princes of Lorraine, as the Quesnays and the Pascal-Bouchets were business nobles in Normandy. "France is a kingdom which has a republic for its capital," wrote the most brilliant of English statesmen about 1845. A pregnant epigram. The best prefects under both the Second Empire and the Third Republic acted in direct succession to Louis XIV's *intendants*, and as late as 1900 many provinces still had their own industrial and financial aristocracies, whose members, as they never went to Court, were unknown in Paris, but exercised in a limited territory almost regal powers.

By 1905, thanks to sure judgment, strength of character, and possibly the tremendous activity engendered by a grief which soured any respite or leisure, Prosper Holmann had become the head of even more extensive enterprises. The spinners of the Nord, the Vosges, and Normandy, all wanted to dispense with buying their raw material in the United States and to start large-scale cotton plantations in the French African colonies. To help the pioneer planters, a bank was needed; and for such a bank these spinners were ready to supply the capital. They asked Prosper Holmann to be at its head.

The development of the Comptoir Colonial Français obliged Holmann to shift his place of residence during part of the year. He kept on his house in Nancy, but he also bought a mansion in the Renaissance style in the Rue Alfred de Vigny; it was certainly ugly, but the windows looked out on the trees of the Parc Monceau. Börsch, his attorney, had then become associated with the concern, and the Nancy bank was now Holmann, Börsch and Co. Prosper Holmann soon realized that French colonial cotton would be hard put to it in competing with cotton from Texas and Egypt, and that even if the enterprise succeeded it would not pay for years. Whereupon he insisted that the Comptoir Colonial should take on other business, varied in scope and more immediately remunerative. Encountering opposition to this policy from his board, he bought up shares until he held a majority interest and was the sole head of the concern.

Like Chinese mandarins and Spanish grandees, French financiers are divided into grades. The highest number no more than a score of men, who, by controlling either directly or through their creatures the principal boards of directors, rule banking, trade and industry, create the myth of public opinion, and secretly participate in the deliberations of the Government, which needs them to maintain currency values and the faith of the capitalists.

By 1912 Prosper Holmann had already become one of those men to whom the Premier appeals for advice or support in times of financial panic. After the War, he was one of the first to realize the perils of inflation, and his insistence that a large number of his regional factories should keep their accounts in gold francs saved them from disaster. He himself had put by large reserves, and acquired a practically undisputed authority over the French market. He continued to live in monastic simplicity, up by seven, in bed by ten, and, until his son and daughter-in-law came to live with him, was waited on by only a single manservant.

X

THE qualities which enable a person to amass a great fortune are usually those which also prevent him from deriving from it any enjoyment but the pleasures of power and work. The young clerks who envied Prosper Holmann's success would certainly never have submitted to spending their evenings as that all-powerful man spent his. Every evening after dinner he entered his study, lit by only one lamp, sat down at a large table, and until ten o'clock read files, balance-sheets, and newspapers, occasionally making notes. Denise and her husband sat in two arm-chairs placed on either side of the table so that they could read by the same single lamp. In order not to disturb their father, they kept absolute silence. At ten o'clock Monsieur Holmann would say good night, kiss his daughter-in-law on the forehead, shake his son's hand, and go up to his bedroom.

By her uncomplaining acceptance of this monotonous life Denise had won the old man's heart. He spoke so seldom that his affection had never been expressed in words; and with his son in particular Prosper Holmann had no means of communication. He did not know what to say to him, and was puzzled as to how to make good use of him. Being very masterful, he liked subordinates, but not collaborators. Occasionally Denise hazarded a word of criticism:

"Father, don't you think you might sometimes take

Edmond with you and explain your business to him? He is so eager to understand and to help you, but you intimidate him."

"What do you want me to explain to Edmond, my dear? Business can't be explained. My father never explained anything to me. The only way is by patience, and hard work, and common sense. . . ."

"Yes, but even so one must have a job to do. Edmond feels he is marking time, doing nothing, not getting on. . . ."

"Not getting on? Where? I've put him on two boards. Let him take minutes and make reports. Don't try to make him take up too much at once. I don't like enthusiasm or zeal."

These talks disheartened her. In the plan of life she had drawn up, she had allowed for an apprenticeship; but she had not expected that it would be so empty or so slow. During the first winter she had tried making a trip with Edmond into eastern France, to visit the factories under Holmann control. She was interested in the conditions of the workmen and in welfare organization. The couple came home full of ideas and suggestions. Their father disapproved.

"Never," he said to his son, "never get mixed up with the relations between master and man. It's not your business; you are a banker. You must judge a concern solely through its books and balance-sheets, and know only its management. . . . Nothing else."

Though always very kind to Denise, he did not like to see her calling for Edmond in the evening at the

Comptoir **Colonial.** As she passed through the outer offices, the young clerks would look up from their ledgers, eager and pleased. Even more than the old banker, his partner Börsch found this feminine intrusion irritating. Börsch was about forty. His bushy eyebrows met beneath an invariably frowning forehead. Denise regarded him as intelligent but brutal. Foreseeing that one day Edmond would have to work with Börsch, she had at first sought to enlist him as an ally. But he proved hostile. He had once been a clerk in the Holmann concern, and quite mistakenly imagined that the family despised him. Denise expounded to him her views—acquired from Ménicault—on the political duties of the great banks, and on their potential influence for good in European reconstruction. He replied:

"Madame, allow me to express one hope for our house. . . . It is—that Monsieur Prosper should live to be ninety. . . ."

In the evenings, sitting in that quiet darkened study, its silence broken only by the strokes of Monsieur Holmann's pencil on the margin of a file, Denise would sometimes look up, forget her book, and dream. Was she happy? She was living through a strange period of waiting that seemed to lie outside of time. Sometimes she felt as if she were one of those fairy-tale heroines touched into sleep by a magic wand. The charm worked gently and masked the pain of living. But what would the awakening be like? The obvious adoration of her husband touched her heart. In three years she had had three children: a daughter, Marie-Laure, and two sons, Patrice and Olivier, and the lethargy of pregnancy had helped her to put up with the monotony of her life. She looked after her children with a thoroughness that was studious rather than maternal, but already they seemed to be attached to her. And she still wondered: "Is this happiness?" She knew well that it was not. More than ever she was aware of that "thirst for the infinite" which Mademoiselle Aubert used to talk of. She looked at Edmond and Monsieur Holmann. Why was the son of such a strong father so weak? As ten o'clock drew near, she thought with dismay of the bedroom lined with red damask. There, without desire, without pleasure, she would endure the caresses of an ardent and unskilled husband.

XI

In 1925 the three children had whooping-cough. They spent the summer at Saint-Arnault, a country-house in Normandy which Monsieur Holmann had given his son. For three months life was nothing but paroxysms of coughing. Denise was touched by the sweetness of these little creatures and their amazing ability to forget. As soon as an attack passed, they went back to their games.

In October they had not completely recovered. The

doctor told Denise that she ought to send them south and leave them there until the spring. She passed on the medical opinion to her father-in-law. Any serious question in this household was invariably discussed directly between Denise and the father, with Edmond only an onlooker. Prosper Holmann never shunned these brief talks in which he liked to play the part of the good genie, able with a wave of his hand to annihilate obstacles and make houses and servants spring from the ground. His vast wealth and his daughter-in-law's straightforwardness made the part easy. He listened in reflective silence, and then, with constructive gestures of his broad hand, expounded a course of action. Once he had spoken, the matter in his view was settled, and he would not lightly have allowed Denise to reopen discussion.

"The doctor seems to know what he is talking about," he said. "Very good. . . . Well, I shall make a suggestion which you will dislike at first; but you will see its advantages later on. . . . I think it would be useful if Edmond went over to Africa to inspect our branches there. In connection with staff changes, it is essential that he should get to know our managers and assistant managers, and form an opinion about every one of them. . . . You shall go with the children to the south. My sister Fanny will lend you her villa at Théoule, which she doesn't use. You'll be quite near the Cannes doctors, who are very good. Edmond will see you settled, and then will cross to Algiers, and I can promise he'll be with you for Christmas. . . . I know it's your first separation," he added, as Denise was about to speak, "but it is necessary, and it will be short."

About the end of October "all the Edmond Holmanns" set off for Théoule. They arrived there on a sunny morning. Aunt Fanny's house was a Provençal *mas* with yellowish-pink walls roofed with circular tiles, and so well placed on the ridge of a small headland, that its terrace afforded a view of two bright blue bays lined with rocky creeks. The estate was extensive, and consisted chiefly of pine-woods and olive-trees. Denise was attracted by its wild and natural character. She was intoxicated by the sunshine. The sharp stony contours, the dry pure air, conjured up for this daughter of Normandy a legendary Greece. She wandered with Edmond down paths covered with pine-needles to little beaches, and tried to tell him of her impressions. But he remained depressed and listless. She had often noticed before that neither father nor son had an eye for nature.

They came back and sat down on the terrace. The children had already taken possession of a sandheap and were playing. Denise brooded, and did not speak. She gave Edmond a sidelong glance. He looked tired. She was aware that she had no violent, irresistible love for him, but they had had four peaceful years together never marred by any quarrel. Why shouldn't that state of sentimental peace last for ever? She could no longer imagine life without Edmond. The coming separation frightened her. Might it not break the spell which held her asleep? Was not this frail happiness built on shifting sands? If it were touched, might it not fade, and vanish like a soap-bubble striking an obstacle. The curious thing was that, alongside of this dread, she felt also a surge of hope, as if her coming loneliness were going to give her back herself—a Denise stronger than the old, more grim but more complete. Again she looked at Edmond, and caught his eye. His look seemed to say:

"Yes, I realize that you can't love me, you put up with me and find me dull and tongue-tied in the presence of a fiery power like yourself; but you have a soul of greatness, and what finer thing could you do?"

With a glance she reassured him, and then, leaning back in her arm-chair, she lost herself in the blue sky. . . . With whom would she have liked to be looking up at it? She remembered the varnished stakes and the sandbags of the dug-out into which Robby had led her. Robby? Jacques? Ménicault? Somebody unknown, more nearly perfect than any of these? Edmond's voice drew her from her reverie. He was talking about a cheque-book to be left with her, and then about a doctor for the children. She sat up:

"What were you saying, dearest?"

"I was asking how you thought of passing the time in this house, all alone."

"Oh, I've brought books, and music. . . . And there's the children. . . ."

"I told you I knew the owners of the next villa, the Villiers. . . . He is one of our customers, and my father has an interest in several of the Villier concerns in Morocco. . . . I am sure they'll call."

"I don't want them to. I like being alone. . . . Besides, I've heard your Aunt Fanny talking about Solange Villier; what she says about her is rather unpleasant."

"Yes," said Edmond, "no doubt. Still, if they ask you over, do go, once at least. Aunt Fanny is puritanical, and very likely she exaggerates a lot."

He paused for a moment.

"Only," he said, "do be careful. If any men are staying with the Villiers, don't have them here. The most honest woman may find herself compromised by . . ."

She interrupted him, rather annoyed.

"How unworthy of you, Edmond! Really, you've seen enough of me in the last four years to see how I behave. The only person in the world I want to see is you. If you could make a break in this two months of separation, by running over for a day or two from Oran or Tunis, I should love it."

He said he would try, provided his father approved. The reply annoyed Denise slightly. She disliked the feeling of his childlike obedience. And again she dreamed. Far away, from over by Cannes, came the hum of a seaplane. Already she felt herself alone. She thought of that strange moment when a steamer is not yet under weigh, but all the hawsers have been cast off. She felt at once the anguish and the delight of setting out on a long journey. Looking up into the fathomless sky, she again heard within herself that wondrous, and always interrupted, melody from the "Unfinished Symphony." . . . Two heralding notes, and then that divine gladness spiralling upward. Whither?

The same evening, at the station, Edmond kissed her good-bye, as deeply moved as if he were going off to war.

"Don't forget me, darling; I've nobody but you."

"But come, Edmond, you're ridiculous. *I've* got nobody but *you*."

Having said all they had to say, they remained silent, looking at each other now and then, embarrassed and sad. "Is this happiness?" Denise wondered again. And, barely audible, a voice within her answered: "No." When she got back to the villa in the mild darkness, the wind-stirred pines and cypresses seemed to hold some rendingly mournful beauty.

XII

Denise lay on an extended chair reading a book by Bertrand Schmitt. Behind the characters and the wording she tried to rediscover the man who had been her friend. It was difficult. Some things Denise recognized. Rouen names and remarks of Royer's; but they were enveloped in a richer, more substantial material, which must have been acquired later. Since the War Bertrand had been writing, and he lived in Paris. Several times she had wanted to ask him to the house. And then it had occurred to her that Edmond would not like it and that Bertrand must have forgotten her. She had never come across him again.

The sound of a car made her look up. The *mistral* was bending the tops of the pines, and giving white crests to the short blue waves. A car braked up, scattering the gravel of the drive. She listened, very much surprised. Who could it be? She heard voices, and then Félix appeared and said in a low voice:

"Madame Villier to see you. . . . She says you know. . . ."

"Oh, what a nuisance!" thought Denise.

She sighed and closed her book.

"Say I am coming."

On entering the drawing-room, she was agreeably surprised. She had expected Solange Villier to be very much made-up, and over-dressed for the country. But she found a still pretty little woman, faded, but healthy and strong, wearing a brown jersey and a chestnut-coloured tweed skirt.

"May I introduce myself?" said Solange. "I am your neighbour. Your husband wrote to mine that you were here alone with three sick children. I came to see if I could help you in any way."

Denise thanked her: the children were rather better.

"It's really I who am not very well," she said. "This

climate makes me feverish. . . . Oh, it's nothing, but. . . ."

"You're too much alone," said Solange. "Come over to luncheon or dinner. . . . My place is very cheerful just now, I've some friends staying: Robert Etienne, you know, the man who writes about Morocco, and Dick Managua. D'you know him? He's such fun."

"No. . . . May I be quite frank?" said Denise. "I've really come down here chiefly to rest, and I'm rather afraid. . . ."

Solange leaned towards her.

"May I be frank too? I'm afraid you've heard unpleasant things about me. . . . As chance brings us together, I'd like to have things quite clear. . . ."

The conversation grew very intimate. Solange explained that she and her husband had agreed to be quite free, but remained good friends. Did such an arrangement shock Denise?

"Oh, no, not at all. Every human being is entitled to act as he or she thinks fit, so long as no harm is done to others. All the same I don't understand. . . . Why not get a divorce?"

"And why get a divorce? I'm very fond of my husband, and we have a son."

"Do you think that children's happiness is shielded by not divorcing?" said Denise. "I don't know what your childhood was like, but I myself shall always bear the marks of my parents' failure to get on."

She stopped. It was a subject she could never bring up without pain. "It's very odd," Edmond would say to her; "you are kindhearted, but as soon as it comes to your mother, you turn unfair." This hinted confidence made Solange Villier become very human. She asked for a cigarette and lay back on the divan.

"She's really rather nice, like a big comfortable dog," thought Denise.

"I too," said Solange, "I too bear the marks of my childhood. . . . My mother spoilt me, because I was the youngest. She showed her favouritism so clumsily that my brothers and sisters hated me. They would not let me join in their play. I would feel spited, and tell tales about their naughtinesses. . . . I was 'that horrid Solange,' 'that beastly Solange.' None of them would have anything to do with me. I assure you that even now, as a result, I'm afraid of people not liking me. . . . For instance, when I saw you, I thought I was unwelcome. And my sense of humiliation made me put on a sharp manner to give myself courage. . . ."

"How well you understand!" said Denise. "I have sometimes felt—but in quite another form!—something just like that. . . . But I've never been able to admit it to myself."

"Nor could I, for a long time. . . . And then in Morocco I made friends with a man who compelled me to look right into myself. But you'll meet him— Robert Etienne, who's staying here just now."

"Is he the author of 'La Prière aux Oudaïas'?"

"Yes. . . . He's a civil commissioner near where we are, and controls an almost barbaric territory. . . . It's a splendid job. . . . A king's job. . . . You know, of course, that we spend half the year in Morocco? You can't imagine how good it is for one to lead that straightforward life amongst men of action. I've tried to be a source of strength for the best among them."

"How much I should like to be that for my husband!"

"It's curious," said Solange—she had a funny way of saying, "It's curious," rolling the *r*—"it's curious, we're utterly different and yet we've points in common. Promise you'll come over. . . . You'll see, I'm a very good friend to women. It's no virtue: I'm afraid of them. So you will come? I've heard you're very musical. . . . I have a good piano."

"I haven't touched a piano for six months," said Denise. "Last year I still used to play at sight, but since I've married I have given up practising. Repeating a passage twenty times . . . it bores me."

"Yes," said Solange, rising. "When a woman's sentimental life is not properly balanced, she does nothing. We only work happily for a man. We're poor creatures."

XIII

Denise walked over to the Villiers' for luncheon. A private footpath ran through the pine-wood, joining the grounds of the two houses. She walked slowly, her head down. The bouts of fever she had nearly every night were depressing her. The beauty of the country and the softness of the air both gave her a strange sense of strain.

"It's queer," she thought as she opened the small white gate to the Villiers' grounds, "down here I feel as I do at a concert, or in the theatre, when too keen a pleasure makes me suddenly feel how short life is. . . ."

That morning she had received a letter from Pont-de-l'Eure which had really upset her. Her mother's letters still had a violent effect on her feelings, plunging her back into the poisoned atmosphere of her childhood. Indeed, she always hesitated to open them. When one came, she would leave it on the mantelpiece for a whole morning, sometimes taking the envelope up in her hand as if to weight its content of suffering. Then she would tear it open abruptly, and read very fast, like an invalid swallowing a nasty medicine with his eyes shut. To-day Madame Guérin explained that Jacques Pelletot wished to marry Charlotte, that it was "a desirable marriage from every point of view," and that it could take place all the more easily if Denise would make over to her sister her inheritance from Monsieur Aristide, who had died a few months before. "I know you will agree, my dear. What difference can it make to you? As for Suzanne, she insists on continuing to live in England. It's a queer idea, but in any case she needs this little fortune. And you are so well off. . . . Besides, you owe it to Jacques to do some-

thing for him.   The poor boy was terribly upset, I can
tell you, when he saw you agreeing so quickly to make
a more brilliant match. . . ."   Of course, Denise had
immediately replied that she would sign whatever
Maître Pelletot wished.   But she was disturbed by the
news.   Why had Jacques proposed to Charlotte rather
than any other girl?   Did he expect to find in her sister
something of herself?   Or was it rather that Charlotte,
always in the wake of her elder sister, had wished to
make a conquest of the man who had so long loved
Denise?

Emerging from the path into a fine garden in the
Italian style, she noticed several people near the house.
Men in white trousers were lounging in orange deck-
chairs.   Solange came forward to receive her.

"Good morning, Madame Holmann!   We have been
waiting for you to have cocktails. . . .   Let me introduce my three men. . . .   My husband, Robert
Etienne, and Managua.   Martini, Madame Holmann,
or orangeade?"

"Orangeade, please.   But I've interrupted your talk."

"It was gruesome," said Solange.   "The men were
talking of death. . . .   Robert Etienne has just been
reading a little book on 'the art of dying' and he contends that when men die they say things connected with
their work. . . .   Examples, Robert?"

Robert Etienne was bald and strikingly ugly.   He
tapped each word with a hammer-blow as he uttered
it, as it were contemptuously.

"Oh, countless examples!" he said.   "Napoleon—

'Head . . . Army!'—Father Bouhours, a grammarian —*About* to die, or, *Going* to die: both idiomatic.'— Frederick William I, King of Prussia, when clergymen were singing at his bedside—'Naked came I to this world, Naked shall I leave . . .' they sang; and he retorted: 'Not at all, I'll wear my uniform.'—Heinrich Heine—'God will forgive me; that's His job.' But the best saying by a dying woman is, I think, this of Madame d'Houdetot's—'I regret myself.' "

"No, I don't care for it," said Managua, "it's a miser's saying."

"And you, Madame Holmann," said Solange, "what will you say on your deathbed?"

"I?" said Denise gravely. "I shall say—'At last!' "

"What?" said Managua. "What? With eyes like yours, do you mean to say you don't wake up every morning with the thought, 'How wonderful to be alive?' "

She looked at him more closely. His face was strong and sunburned, the colouring of a man who lives in the sun, his eyes grey and bold.

"No," she said. "I am more likely to sing every morning that lovely air—Monteverde's, I think—'O death, I trust in thee. . . .' "

"Yes, it is by Monteverde," said Robert Etienne. " 'O death, I trust in thee, and in thy dark I hope.' It's admirable."

Managua turned to Solange.

"Quickly, give Madame Holmann a Martini—two

Martinis—three Martinis!   We've got to teach her the delights of being alive!"

Robert Etienne spoke of the Mohammedans' contempt for death.   This time his calm, aloof voice appealed to Denise.   Villier said he also knew a story about a man dying with a professional phrase on his lips, and told the story of a conjuror at a children's party, who announced that he was going to make himself disappear.   He wrapped himself up in a great black cloth, and cried: "Look out!   Hey, presto!   I'm gone!" Thereupon he fell down.   After a couple of minutes the hostess said: "Excuse me, but this is not funny, and doesn't amuse the children."   The man did not stir. He was dead.

"What a gloomy story!" said Solange.   "What's the matter with you all to-day?   Let's go into luncheon."

During the meal the men discussed the financial situation, which was becoming serious in that autumn of 1925.   The franc was being artificially pegged.   Capital was hastening abroad.   Villier blamed the Radical majority in Parliament for causing uneasiness by its incompetence in government.   Supported by Robert Etienne, Denise disagreed with him: on the contrary, for the first time since the War, France's relations with Germany seemed human.   After her long spell of solitude, Denise was unused to weighing her words, and was unconsciously rather violent.

"So you're a woman of the Left, Madame Holmann!" said Villier.

"Yes. . . .   Is that wrong?"

"It is wrong," said Villier; "but anyone so beautiful as you is fully privileged."

She thought him commonplace and unpleasant, and changed the subject. After luncheon Solange suggested a walk. She wanted Denise to see her gardens. Denise soon found herself ahead of the group with Managua. He was lauding Robert Etienne:

"A most remarkable man," he said. "He has completely changed our friend Solange. Before she knew him, she was impulsive, flirtatious, and fickle."

"And she is true to him?"

"Oh, without any effort. . . . She admires him, you know. . . ."

Then he spoke of herself.

"How melancholy you are!"

"I think it must be this part of the world," she said. "In Paris I was all right. . . . I am like old bottles, you know: the lees are at the bottom . . . they mustn't be shaken. . . . That is why I've lost all taste for travel since marriage. . . . Anything beautiful stirs up a sense of anguish, the feeling that I've made a mess of my life. In Rome, during our honeymoon, I said to Edmond—to my husband, 'Take me away; this magnificence makes me want to die.' "

No sooner had she uttered the words than she blamed herself for saying them. It was quite true, but why tell a stranger?

"You don't look after yourself properly," he said. "You certainly can't take enough exercise. Would you care to come sailing with me? I've only got a little 'six-meters,' you know, but it's fun.   Are you a good sailor?"

"I don't know," she said cheerfully.   "I've never tried."

"Come along to-morrow, if the mistral has dropped. . . . Look here, I'll call for you in any case about eleven. . . . If the weather's all right, we'll go out in the boat. If not, we'll play duets at sight: Solange told me you were a good player. . . ."

"Do you play the piano?"

"Yes. . . . You seem quite surprised!"

"I am. You look more like a golfer or a tennis player."

"I can play tennis too. I can do anything, Madame, and everything badly—except make love. . . . Well, shall I call for you to-morrow morning?"

She agreed, not knowing how to refuse, but yet she felt pleased. When she had gone, Managua said to Solange:

"Rather interesting, isn't she?   But damnably neurotic."

"Not much of a marriage," said Solange. "I thought of her for you, Dick. I think you could give her a taste for life."

"Well," said Managua, "I've staked a claim. . . . I'm seeing her to-morrow morning. . . . Only, Winifred is turning up in a week; I haven't much time."

"My dear Dick," said Solange, "you may as well admit that you have never let Winifred cramp your style."

As Denise walked back along the path through the pines, she was reproaching herself. With fond anxiety, Edmond had said at the station: "Don't have any men to see you while you are alone, dearest. . . . The most honest woman. . . ." And she had answered: "How unworthy of you! Really, you've seen enough of me in the last four years to know. . . ." Now, at the first temptation, she had yielded. Then she thought of Managua's sunburned face, and of the sharp slap of the wind in a white sail; and suddenly she felt very cheerful, as on the spring days when she walked through the Luxembourg, her books under her arm.

"Yielded," she said to herself, "but how have I yielded? I've done nothing wrong. . . . How could I have said anything else?"

Nevertheless, she felt dissatisfied with herself. As always, she dined alone, went up to say good night to the children, and went to bed early. Before settling down to sleep she read a few pages. But her mind was elsewhere, on the waves topped with white foam, and she did not know what she was reading: "The black stove, with the coals glowing like red eyes within its cavities, was making the saucepans give out little wisps of steam and a heavenly smell of cabbage soup and beans."

Her hands sank down, and letting the book rest on her knees, she dropped back into the past. She saw Victorine's stove, with its round cast-iron lids which were lifted up with a hook and under which the coals glowed; Monsieur Courteheuse, with his open shirt and

hairy chest and his elbows on the table, singing, *"Pleur'*
pas comm'ça, ma p'tite Suze-e-e-ette; and the Abbé
Guillemin blushing as he said, "Denise, you are like a
flame. . . ."

Out in the garden the dogs were barking. She rose
and opened the window to quieten them. The moon
was at the full. The shadows of the cypresses hemmed
in the house. Farther off, the reeds were rustling in
the mild air. When she fell asleep, the stove became
a demon and its coals were his red eyes. She woke up
several times. At last the dawn cooled her fever.

XIV

Towards the end of November a telegram from
Oran announced that Edmond was coming to spend
three days at Théoule before continuing his trip. The
news filled Denise with terror. For a fortnight she
had been Managua's mistress. From their very first
meeting the man had attracted her. He had taken her
out in his boat and taught her to steer. In his blue,
wide-necked jersey, at one with the wind and the spray,
he had seemed to her like some splendid sea creature.
Once they were clear of the little harbour, he came
and sat beside her, and she had been entertained by his
glittering, superficial culture. He could explain Ein-
stein, but was ignorant of Galileo. He had read Freud

and neglected Plato, discovered Prokofieff and despised
Beethoven, been round the world and forgotten France.
The swiftness of his repartees and the sparkle of his
similes made his cleverly juggled commonplaces pass
momentarily for paradoxes. He knew the latest gossip
of Vienna, London, and Venice, and repeated it all very
amusingly.

"Look out! Push the tiller right over. . . . Keep
your head down—the sail's going to swing over you.
. . . I'll let go and haul on the sheets."

The handling of the boat had brought their bodies
near to each other and made Denise less stiff with her
companion. He put an arm round her waist to guide
her, and brushed his fingers across her breast. After
that she kept him at a distance, but not unkindly.

"No, no . . . I am the quietest, the most sensible
of women. . . ."

He laughed, and made fun of her. He spoke of
love as of a pleasant "technique." On parting, Denise
had refused his offer of another sail for the next day.
Further, against her inclination but because she thought
it wiser, she did not go back to Solange's villa.

It was afterwards that she escaped the restraint of
her will. The picture of that large sun-tanned body
haunted and disturbed her, and then Solange came
again. Solange talked about cowardice, and provoked
Denise's pride.

"You're being absurd," she said to her. "I assure
you. . . . Even my husband, who never notices anything, remarked, 'Madame Holmann is the paragon of

good little girls.' *Your* husband? But he won't know anything about it; what's more, it's a good thing for him that you should know other men. . . . I can't understand an intelligent woman like you refusing to admit that she is attracted by a man with such appeal as Managua. . . . It's so natural. . . . Marriage is an institution no longer suited to our ways. . . . It will evolve. It has evolved already."

In the end Denise had agreed to go to an evening concert in Cannes with the Villier party. Solange ingeniously worked things so that she had to come back alone with Managua in his car. The music and her feverishness had weakened her. Managua had profited by his first rebuff; he changed his tactics, and triumphed. Having taken her home, he did not leave until dawn. In a sleep that bordered on delirium Denise was left in melancholy brooding. How could she have broken, so soon and so quickly, those genuine promises? "I didn't want to," she said aloud, "I didn't want to. . . ." She recalled that night in her room in the inn at Verrières, when she had wondered if she had any right to marry Edmond without loving him. At that time she had sincerely believed that she was renouncing love for ever; now such a renunciation seemed to her a piece of self-righteous pride and unreal. "Words," she thought, "just words. Does anybody who is alive and young ever say good-bye to love?" A little girl lying on her stomach on the carpet, looking at a picture of the Holy Penitents. . . . A great sinner. . . . Was any sin greater than hers? She had sinned not only with the flesh, but with her mind and heart. "I didn't want to," she was repeating to herself, "I didn't want to. . . . That animal woman was not myself. . . ." She was so hot she threw off the bedclothes. Then she told herself that at least she could spare Edmond the cruel pangs of jealousy. As soon as he got back, she would tell him the truth, and later she would marry Managua, whom she loved. Poor Edmond, it would be a dreadful blow! But anything was preferable to a daily degrading lie. "He could make a fresh start," as people said. When morning came she dropped off to sleep, overwhelmed with fatigue, almost soothed, and dreamed of black sea creatures dancing on the waves.

Days of unhappiness followed. She had thought she had found a source of strength in Managua; but as soon as she tried to talk in a serious and virile tone with him, she discovered his real softness. He loved her, in his way; he desired her; he admired her. But his insensibility and flabbiness offered nothing to catch hold of. The chatterbox talked about his "success" to all his friends along the coast, and called them to witness to the importunate simplicity of a woman who regarded love as a tragic passion. Solange came over to give Denise "a talking-to."

"This won't do, you know. . . . You're playing a dangerous game. . . . Dick is nice and patient, but one must not make oneself a nuisance to men. . . . When you have my experience, you will realize how selfish they are. We are only entitled to be ourselves when

we're alone . . . or with other women. A man insists
on her being his particular type, and often a type that
is not really hers. . . . Play the part, or lose our
lovers—that's our fate. . . . One gets used to it."

Denise was resting her head on her hands, with wide-
open eyes. She did not seem to be listening.

"What a man," she kept saying, "such a cow-
ard. . . ."

"But really!" said Solange, losing patience, "what
have you against him? What is his crime?"

"This!" said Denise angrily: "that he has smashed
the idea I had fashioned of myself; he has turned my
life upside down with no desire to devote his own to
me; that he is fickle, talkative, and lacking in moral
courage. . . ."

"I can't make you out," said Solange. "What did
you expect from a fellow like Dick? That he should
divorce his wife and marry you? He'll never do that
. . . I know the family well. His father took his own
life about 1920, after ruining himself. Dick liked a
good time, expensive sport, and women, and up to the
time he married he had been running up debts. Then
he met this girl Winifred over in America, and everything was changed. She brought him a fortune, and
happiness and freedom as well. Even if he didn't
care for her, he owes Winifred a great deal; but as it
happens he's very fond of her. She is slight and fair—
charming. . . . Unfortunately she has wretched
health. Just now she's in Switzerland. But she's due
here in a few days. . . . You'll see her."

Solange had gone on for some time without realizing the effect of her words, and then suddenly, seeing the stricken look on Denise's face, she broke off.

"What's wrong? I assure you I can't see why you take such an ordinary story so tragically."

"Ordinary? I don't think you'd call it that if you realized what my marriage has meant to me. I've had three years of absolute openness, and such a fine, such a true friendship. Poor Edmond! Oh, no! After coming to me so generously when I was unhappy, he doesn't deserve to be treated in this way, and by me."

"But he won't suffer unless you tell him."

"Don't believe it! I know, I've seen what it means to be a man wrapped up in lies, suspecting them, pro-longing them. . . . It's horrible!"

Solange had slipped away, and on reaching home she found Managua lolling in one of the orange canvas chairs. She told him of her talk with Denise. He sighed and raised his arms.

"Oh, no, Solange! Not at all my style. . . . You must get me out of this affair. . . . She is pretty, intelligent, anything you like, but she is off her head. . . . You can't imagine! She weeps. . . . She wants to tell her husband everything, and he'll be here next week. She implores me to get a divorce. Poor Wini-fred! You can picture how she would take it. . . . No, no! I didn't think women like that still existed in 1925!"

"I made a mistake about her," said Solange. "She comes from the provinces, poor soul, and she's had a peculiar childhood. . . . Besides, she's religious at heart. . . . You don't expect it, because to hear her talking politics or science you'd think she was quite emancipated. But once you really get to know her, you realize she has a terrible way of going off on a saintly tack. It's dangerous, because she runs the risk of ramming everybody. . . ."

He lit a cigarette.

"Well, Solange, you've pushed a saint into my arms. . . . But what do you expect me to do with a saint?"

"I feel just as awkward about it as you do, my dear Dick," said Solange.

XV

INSTRUCTED by Solange and lectured by Managua, she had resigned herself to lie to Edmond. However, her lying would not only be base, she felt, but futile too, for Edmond would guess the truth. She had an absurd but invincible feeling that the record of her acts was written on every wall of this accursed house. Alone in the evenings she felt as if Managua were sitting in the arm-chair near the fireplace. She had let him come to the house again and, appalled to find she could not resist him, had again given herself to him. She hated him, clung to him, and frightened him with her tragic silences.

On the eve of Edmond's arrival, it suddenly occurred to her that he would question the servants. She was sure of Lucie, her maid, who adored her, but what about Félix? When he was serving luncheon she had to control herself not to say, "Félix, don't mention to the master about Monsieur Managua's visits here."

"No, no," she said to herself, making an effort to eat. "No, no, Edmond has never been suspicious. He has never had any cause to doubt me. Félix and Lucie are decent sorts."

She met her husband at the station and sadly played her part. Seeing him again after a long absence, she had to show every sign of delight. It was difficult. On the way home, in the car, she felt she was being pursued, hunted. At one moment she fancied that betraying voices were calling from the farmhouses along the road. Long arrows of light, mysteriously shooting from the closed windows, were pointing at her.

"Am I going mad?" she said to herself. "It's the sun glinting on the window-panes."

Edmond did not notice her uneasiness. Happy and talkative, he recounted his journey.

"I must take you to Morocco, Denise. It is so lovely, and with just the loveliness that would appeal to you. . . . And what room for development there! That is the country where the banker with imagination, as you're always saying, might create. . . ."

She did her best to sprinkle his monologue with "really!" and "how interesting!" But she was not listening.

"And what about you?" he said at last. "I'm talking all the time, and you're not telling me anything. You haven't been bored? You've seen something of the Villiers? I wrote to them to keep an eye on you."

"I've told you everything in my letters, darling. The Villiers have been very agreeable. I've lunched and dined at their place two or three times."

The children relieved her by keeping their father busy until luncheon. Seeing from the window that Edmond was giving Marie-Laure a pickaback in the garden, she felt frightened. She recalled a sea-wall, and a cement parapet, and a little girl sitting on it. "Daddy, you know when you're not here, a man comes. . . ."

"But Marie-Laure can scarcely speak," she said to herself.

Later, when she was in the garden, she noticed Edmond talking to Félix. Anxiously she listened.

"If you would like it, Monsieur," Félix was saying, "I could get a *bouillabaisse* prepared for you by Madame Villier's fisherman. . . . Those people are good judges of fish."

It was all so simple and easy. She felt calmer until, about four o'clock, Edmond suggested calling on the Villiers. She tried to raise objections.

"No, Edmond, I don't want to. I've got you only for three days, and I'm going to keep you."

"But that would be rude. I wrote to them. They asked you over. They used to entertain my father in

Morocco. He would be offended if I didn't see them at least once. Besides, they're bound to know I'm here."

"I told them, but I also said you were most unsociable."

"What an odd notion, Denise! I'm not unsociable. In fact, I rather like the idea of seeing people after a month of business travelling, especially as they come from Morocco. We shall have lots to talk about."

He was so insistent that she had to yield, and telephoned to Solange to say that Monsieur and Madame Holmann would come to tea about five. In silence they took the path carpeted with pine-needles leading to the white gate. To Denise that visit was torture. She knew quite well that the party were watching Edmond ironically. She was especially pained by the ostentatious way in which Managua made himself agreeable to her husband.

"One must always be nice to husbands," he had said one day. "In any case, they're so easy-going. . . ."

Managua's cordiality made Edmond stick to him. Sitting beside Solange, Denise saw the two of them walking up and down the terrace, laughing.

"He is absurd," she said to herself. "And it is I who have made this man who loves me absurd."

She could not look at the indolent suppleness of Managua without thinking of his caresses. She almost felt angry with Edmond for suspecting nothing. She wished that her lies had not been believed, that he had seen through everything, and insulted her, and turned her out. But no, there he was, pleased and trusting, and laughing at Managua's stories.

Next day when they were walking together by the sea, she had to ask him not to take the path on the cliff's edge, below which the waves were beating on the rose-coloured rocks. A morbid giddiness was drawing her towards the gulf. Managua turned up in the afternoon and suggested they should both come out in his boat. Edmond gladly agreed, but as soon as they were on the water he became silent and pale. Denise, who was now an expert, had taken the tiller. She was startled by her spontaneous, mischievous delight in the contrast between her husband's impotent weakness and Managua's smart handling of the boat. When the wind was heeling the boat over, Managua, in his open-necked jersey, would fearlessly jump from thwart to thwart.

"You're not comfortable, darling," she said to Edmond with cruel concern. . . .

"I'm all right," he answered. "I like it ever so much." He turned very yellow.

"Look out!" cried Managua. "Put your head down, Holmann. I'm going about."

Screened by the sail, he smiled at Denise, and threw an ironic glance towards the poor man leaning his head forward, and gazing at the waves. Denise reflected with horror that the weaker and more cowardly of these two men was her lover.

XVI

She returned from the station on an evening as balmy as that when she had first given herself to Managua. The moon was full, the reeds rustled in the warm breeze. Giant creatures were gliding over the woods and leaning towards her whispering.

"It's starting again," she thought. "I'm feverish."

She could not sleep. The things she had done in the last three days were those she despised most. She had lied, misled, and betrayed.

"Why didn't I tell Edmond? It would have hurt him, but by now he would be free of me, and at least I should have been loyal. Perhaps I ought to write to him. . . ."

But she knew she would not write. Strong as she was, she felt suddenly devoid of will.

For one instant out in the boat, she had thought of Edmond falling overboard and being drowned. As a wealthy widow, she would have married Managua. She now reproached herself for that swift passing thought as for an actual crime. In the silence of the night she could hear the barking of the fox-terrier and Marie-Laure's fits of coughing. "Marie-Laure is choking. . . . I've killed her."

Not even a strong dose of veronal could bring her sleep. In the morning when her maid Lucie drew the curtains, she said to Denise that the child had been sick all night and that "there was a little blood."

"Heavens!" thought Denise. "She is going to die."

She gave orders for the doctor to be fetched, and then rose to go and see her daughter. Scrambling into her dressing-gown, she caught a small looking-glass, which fell and was smashed.

"I'll sweep up the bits at once," said Lucie. "It brings bad luck. . . ."

"Don't say that!" cried Denise sharply.

Then she felt sure that the accident was an omen, and that she no longer had a right of entry to the nursery.

When Lucie got back to the pantry, she said to Félix:

"I don't know what's wrong with Madame, but surely she can't be well. . . . All at once she turned and looked at me in a very funny way."

The girl was kind and devoted. She had such a strong presentiment of danger that several times during the morning she went in to her mistress on various pretexts. She found her at her dressing-table, her eyes staring, sitting rigidly still. About eleven she was horrified to see Denise holding a revolver. Edmond had given it to her when they were setting out for the Riviera, saying, "I don't think one should be unarmed in a lonely house." Lucie ran to her mistress, who seemed to emerge from her daze, smiled almost naturally, and said:

"Don't be frightened, Lucie, I was cleaning it. . . . What did you think?"

After that, as the reply came from the doctor's that he had already started on his rounds and could not come until the evening, Félix and Lucie conferred and decided to telephone to Madame Villier.

A little later Managua came over. Lucie had been looking out for him at the door, and told him what she had seen.

"In my opinion," she said reproachfully, "it's the shock of seeing Monsieur Holmann again after what has been happening, Monsieur. . . . In any case, ever since Madame came here she has not been very well. . . . The important thing is that you should take away her pistol, sir. . . ."

Then she went upstairs to announce Monsieur Managua. Denise, still seated at her dressing-table, not yet dressed, made a sad and weary gesture. When he entered, Managua was startled to see this woman, who was so modest even in love, receiving him half-naked and apparently unaware of it. He took her in his arms. She let him, and then pushed him savagely away with a few incoherent words. He tried to joke, and after a few minutes her tone seemed more natural again.

"You should go to bed and call in a doctor," he said. "You are a little delirious. It's your fever."

"Why do you say that? Have I been talking nonsense?"

"No, but. . . . Well, I should like it if you would look after yourself."

He called Lucie, made her promise not to leave Madame Holmann, and hastened back to the Villiers'.

"I don't know what's wrong with her," he said to Solange. "She's wandering. . . . What do you suppose? Brain fever? And what can we do? A fine mess!"

"I'll go over after luncheon," said Solange, equally anxious. "Have a cocktail to pick you up, Dick? You're looking like nothing on earth."

She put a record on the gramophone and went out. Villiers was left alone with Managua.

"You've blundered, my dear fellow," he said. "Not that I criticize you for betraying Winifred. . . . We're all free. . . . Only it's so easy to pick a woman who understands life. . . . I took this woman's measure right away—a musician and a fanatic. Music, my dear fellow, is like religion . . . Excellent in its way, but not to the point of fanaticism. . . ."

"Leave him alone," said Solange, who had returned. "It's all my fault. Here, Dick, here's your glass: I've made it strong for you."

After luncheon Solange hurried over to the Holmann villa, and in spite of her coolness felt quite at a loss. Denise did not recognize her. Sitting up in bed, kept there with difficulty by Lucie, she seemed to be watching some dreadful spectacle invisible to all but herself. . . .

"Oh, I'm burning!" she said. "Eyes of hot coals. . . ."

And she kept endlessly repeating:

"The un-for-giv-able sin . . . The un-for-giv-able sin. . . ."

Solange was alarmed. While she was in the bedroom, the doctor came. Dr. Sartoni was a shy little man with a small black pointed beard. He seemed surprised and baffled.

"I must call in a specialist," he said. "There is one at Cannes—Dr. Cazenave. But where is the family?"

He knew Mademoiselle Fanny Holmann, but Solange did not think she ought to be summoned.

"Her husband is away, in Africa," she said. "Should he be sent for?"

The little man seemed scandalized.

"Of course, Madame, of course! This is very serious. Decisions will have to be taken."

Solange hesitated.

"It's a rather delicate situation, doctor. . . . Might I have a word with you privately?"

They went down to the drawing-room and she told him what she knew. He seemed shocked by her cynicism. Yet Solange Villier was feeling remorse. But how could she have foreseen that this woman . . . ?

"Well, doctor, that's agreed—I'll wire to Monsieur Holmann. Meanwhile, you will summon the specialist."

On reaching home, Solange told Managua he had better leave at once. He protested lamely.

"Don't you think it's my duty to remain within call of her?"

"My dear Dick," said Solange, "your being about can only make things more difficult when the husband gets back. . . . Run off and join Winifred. . . . In any case, it will never do for her to come here just now. This business is going to make a stir."

XVII

SUMMONED back from Morocco by an obscure and
alarming telegram, Edmond Holmann had a most dis-
tressing journey. He got as far as Toulouse by air, and
then had to take a rather slow train to Marseilles.
Unable to sleep, he kept wondering, in an agony, what
state he would find his wife in. What was wrong with
her? If it was typhoid, as the word "delirium" in the
wire made it possible to suppose, the dangerous period
was nine days, and he would be with her in time. With
closed eyes he thought of these three years of happiness; life without Denise was unthinkable. He told
himself that if she was dead he would kill himself.
When he got out of the train at Cannes, he found on
the platform a little man with a small black beard, who
introduced himself as Dr. Sartoni.

"Monsieur Holmann? I thought I'd better come
myself to prepare you. . . ." he said.

"What for?" stammered Edmond. "She isn't
dead?"

"Oh, no, not at all. . . . She's not even in danger.
. . . But it is a case of mental confusion which must
be alarming to a layman."

He used the word "layman" to persuade himself that
he was an expert. His eyes were scrutinizing this husband of whom he had been hearing for five days. During the drive, he explained what he had done. He
seemed to be trying to justify himself.

"I've called in my eminent colleague Cazenave from Cannes. . . . I may say he was reassuring. . . . He diagnosed a confusional state with a dream delirium which should normally be reabsorbed in two or three months, perhaps less."

"I beg pardon, I don't understand, doctor. . . . Are her wits wandering? Is she feverish?"

"No, she hasn't much of a temperature. . . . But she is delirious, yes. . . . By fits and starts. Perhaps your arrival will be a happy shock that will hasten her recovery. Three days ago she was asking for you incessantly; and kept saying, 'I want my husband to fetch me. . . . I want my husband to fetch me,' in a monotonous voice, for hours on end. . . . Don't be frightened if she makes absurd remarks. Don't let yourself be upset. . . . I admit I was myself at first. I am a general practitioner, and in general practice these ailments are rare."

"But what can be the cause, doctor? My wife was perfectly intelligent, perfectly clear-minded. . . ."

"Oh, dear, the causes. . . . Dr. Cazenave will explain them better than I can. I've asked him to come over again this afternoon to see you."

The nearer they came to Théoule the more apprehensive Edmond became. What was he to say—or do? The sun lit up the pines and cypresses just as on the day they had arrived. He recalled the mournful sadness of their farewell. The confusion of the hall indicated a house overshadowed by disaster. At the foot of the stairs, Lucie, the little maid, stopped Edmond, her blue eyes full of tears.

"Oh, sir, at last!" she said.   "At last, you are here to save Madame."

"My poor Lucie," he said, "this is dreadful."

"I'll go up first," said the doctor.   "I'll try to make her understand that you're coming."

Lucie, whose anxiety made her behave familiarly, seized Edmond's arm and drew him aside.

"This doctor is no good, Monsieur.   He is doing Madame harm.   She's afraid of him."

"What do you mean—*afraid?*" said Edmond.

But the doctor was calling him.   Denise was in bed, and at first sight of her Edmond felt relief; she had not changed; she could not be very seriously ill.   When he came nearer, he was appalled by her vacant eyes.   It seemed as if a veil of mist had been laid across those clear pupils.

"I must keep calm," he told himself.   "She certainly needs quiet."

He tried to speak in the most natural tone:

"Good morning, my darling.   Here I am, back at last."

She looked at him, seemed surprised, and ran her hand over Edmond's face, as if to assure herself that he was really there.

"It is you?" she said.   "It's true?   It's really you, Edmond?"

"I must be matter-of-fact," he thought, "quite matter-of-fact.   I must say quite exact, concrete things.

. . . Yes, it is I," he went on aloud. "I got to Cannes at five past eleven. I came from Toulouse. I crossed by air."

She caressed his hair fondly.

The doctor signed to Edmond and went out.

"Come quite close to me, darling," she said. "I must tell you. . . . You alone can save me. . . . That doctor is a devil and he wants to burn me."

"Not at all, darling: you've been delirious. . . . Now I am with you, that's all over. This doctor is a local doctor, who has already attended everybody in the house."

"No," she said in the same timid, terrifying voice. "He says that, but he is a devil. He comes here at night and kindles brasiers. . . . He wants to throw me into one, but I struggle, I'm strong. You'll help me, Edmond, won't you? You'll help me? You'll forbid him to come in?"

Patiently and tenderly he tried to reason with her. Sometimes she seemed to understand, and said with a smile:

"Yes, you are quite right, darling. But what does it mean? Have I been mad? Have I had fever?"

Then she would fall to brooding again:

"I wanted to raise up the world," she said, "and I've been beaten."

When Dr. Sartoni came back, she sat up in bed to drive him away.

"Get out! You shan't have me. . . . Yes, I have

committed a great sin, but I didn't want to, you know very well. . . ."

She dropped back on her pillows and for a few minutes kept repeating in a monotonous voice:

"An un-for-giv-able sin. . . . An un-for-giv-able sin. . . . An un-for-giv-able sin. . . ."

Edmond stayed with her for a long time, although she no longer seemed to recognize him. So long as she was alone with him, she remained fairly quiet, but whenever the doctor or one of the servants came in, she became restless, and furious. Edmond tried to understand, and fancied he caught glimpses of some dreadful mystery. Lucie came to tell him that the children wanted to have their meal with him, and that she would take his place at the bedside for an hour. She was the only person whose presence the sick woman would stand. In the afternoon Solange came to ask for news. When Félix told her that Monsieur Holmann had arrived, she did not ask to see him.

XVIII

ALTHOUGH nobody in the house had the cruel temerity to tell Edmond the truth, he could have found it all out during the first hours of his return. In her lucid moments Denise kept shouting it at him, accusing herself, begging his forgiveness.

"Madame!" little Dr. Sartoni would murmur, "Come now, Madame! Remember our understanding. You are not to tell anything to your husband."

The children, their governess, the gardener, and Lucie—they each unintentionally handed Edmond a link in the chain.

"What? Didn't you know, sir? It's all the fault of that Madame Villier. . . . Oh, if only you had been here, sir. . . ."

But like all who are afraid of a too painful truth, Edmond used the materials thus supplied to him to piece together the most innocent version of the affair, and the one most favourable to his wife. A man staying with Solange Villier had courted Denise. She had been imprudent, and perhaps she had loved the scoundrel. Then, unwilling to yield to him, torn by conflicting feelings, she had ended by this collapse.

Dr. Cazenave, the Cannes specialist, came over in the evening. On the occasion of his previous visits, Solange had explained matters to him, and he at once guessed the fiction with which the unfortunate Holmann was consoling himself and took care not to destroy it. Cazenave was an old man with a white beard, with a pleasing expression of quiet serenity. Before going upstairs to the patient he had a talk with Edmond.

"I don't wish to be too optimistic," he said, "but all the chances favour her recovery. At her age, and in her circumstances, it is almost a certainty. . . . All she needs is absolute rest. . . . No excitement, no visitors. She must recover weight and she must sleep, and in a relatively short time she will be just as you knew her before."

"And will the attack leave no traces, doctor? Her intellect was so very clear. . . ."

"Absolutely none. Her present state is analogous to the dream state. . . . Once you wake up, you cease to believe in your dreams. . . . It's the same thing. No doubt the same causes might produce the same effects. But it would be very surprising if. . . ."

"And what are those causes, doctor? I gather she must have had to fight against a strong temptation? Why does she keep repeating, 'The unforgivable sin'? And how can she talk about the devil? She doesn't believe in him."

"You mustn't pay too much attention to what she says. Once again, the state is like dreaming. . . . If you are asleep and have a feeling of fever, you build up on that the dream of being in a hot country or a furnace-room, according to your work or your memories. She had a convent training, so she thinks of the devil and hell to explain a purely subjective fear. If she were a Greek of the time of Sophocles she would fancy herself chased by the Furies."

"But is she really in pain?"

Dr. Cazenave gave the anxious man a pitying look. To him these things were all so simple.

"She suffers as one suffers in a dream. . . . But at the same time she finds a refuge in her delirium. . . . You must understand that such a state is due, on the one hand, to a physical predisposition, and on the other, to a moral conflict. . . . In different degrees, you know, we are all in a state of conflict. We are honest and we deceive the Customs. . . . We honour friendship, and we fall in love with our friend's wife. . . . How are we to escape? Often by sacrificing one of the tendencies. 'Let friendship go hang!' More often still, by a dissociation. One part of us deceives the Customs, the other is convinced of its honesty. In the normal state the dissociations give rise to dialogue between self and self. In the hallucinatory state one of the sacrificed 'selves' becomes a separate personality. It is no longer yourself, but the devil who leads you into doing wrong, or blames you for doing wrong. . . . So long as a human mind can find a means of self-deception, of 'rationalizing' the conflict, that mind remains sane. When it is faced by a conflict so serious that no means of self-forgiveness is visible, it takes refuge in what the public calls by a name which has no precise meaning—madness."

The old doctor's calm in the presence of this hideous drama astonished Edmond, shocking him and reassuring him simultaneously. They went upstairs together to the sick-room. Denise was sitting up in bed, excited and worried. She received Dr. Cazenave with respect. It seemed as if in her delirium little Dr. Sartoni was connected with infernal powers, and Cazenave with the forces of heaven. She murmured very humbly to him:

"My great failing is pride. . . . I wanted to raise up the world. . . . You didn't let me. . . ."

She asked him to come nearer and whispered into his ear:

"He is my husband. I wanted to kill him. Will you ever forgive me?"

The doctor took her hand and tapped on it.

"Why, certainly," he said. "Yes, certainly. . . . You are quite forgiven."

Then he went downstairs again with Holmann.

"She must be isolated for a few weeks," he said; "and it is particularly essential that she should not see you. Your presence is doing her harm. You can have her looked after here by two nurses, or, if you prefer, I have at Cannes a small lodge I can put at your disposal. She would be entirely alone there, and have a private garden. It would enable me to keep in daily touch with her."

When Dr. Cazenave had gone, Edmond remained alone in his wife's room. It was getting dark. The old doctor had persuaded Denise to take some chloral—she would accept nothing at the hands of Sartoni—and she had dozed off. Edmond sat beside her holding her hand. The room grew quite dark. About six o'clock Lucie came in and said she would light "a bit of fire," as the night was going to be chilly. Edmond knew that in the eyes of this pretty girl, of Solange, and of everybody who had seen his return, he was a husband who had been tragically fooled. But he kept his wife's hand in his, watching for the shudders of her sleeping body, and in that utter abnegation, that despairing humility, he found a strange happiness. About midnight she awoke and recognized him:

"Is that you, Edmond?" she said. "Is that you, darling?"

Then she caught sight of the flames dancing in the fireplace and screamed.

XIX

WHEN Edmond returned to Paris he found that everybody had heard the Théoule story. The Villiers entertained a lot; Riviera society is idle and therefore gossipy, and such a drama was too exciting to remain hidden. Monsieur Prosper Holmann alone did not mention it to his son, but he sent him off forthwith on business first to London and then to Holland. Edmond threw himself into his work as never before, and even Börsch recognized that perhaps after all this frail young man was a Holmann. The old ladies of the family tried to bring about a judicial separation, even a divorce. Aunt Fanny, deeply offended by the use that had been made of her villa, was the most insistent of all.

"My poor boy," she said, "after what has taken place, you can never build up a happy married life again. I am no believer in the solitary affair. Once a woman has had a lover, she is bound to have others. It is no good blinking the facts of life."

"Why does Aunt Fanny insist on knowing how I feel better than I do myself?" Edmond would say to his father. "She is always telling me that there are other women besides Denise. But I realize perfectly well that there is only Denise, and that only with her have I been happy. . . ."

Every fortnight he went to Cannes and called on Dr. Cazenave. He was still reassuring. Progress was slow but sure.

"There's much to be said for these fiery temperaments," the old doctor would say. "They have reserves. The apathetic and stupid give me more anxiety."

But he did not allow Edmond to see his wife.

"There must be no relapse," he was still saying after three months. "Next week, however, I shall let her write to you."

Next time he came, Edmond was handed a short note written by Denise. The clumsy distorted handwriting moved him. Her words were rather incoherent. She asked him to forgive her and to come and free her. Dr. Cazenave emphasized her physical improvement.

"She has gained nearly four and a half pounds. She is beginning to use her hands again. She knits. Next time perhaps I shall allow you to see her. She still has some queer notions, but they are vague—imaginary memories which will fade away of their own accord."

A fortnight later he greeted Edmond Holmann quite cheerfully.

"This time, Monsieur Holmann, I have no further fears. I am going to show you a woman who is entirely normal, in so far as the word 'normal' means anything."

He took Edmond along to the little lodge in his car. Along one of the garden paths, lined with great brown jars full of flowers, Denise was strolling on a nurse's arm. She did not seem changed. At the sight of her husband she gave a little cry, and ran up and kissed him.

"At last!" she said. "How I've longed for this day!"

He looked at her. Only her eyes had still something strange about them.

"Are you going to take me away, Edmond?" she said, full of hope.

He looked nervously at the doctor.

"Not to-day," said the latter. "I'll allow a short walk, but you must be back this evening. . . . In another fortnight, if all goes well, I'll let you go."

Edmond went off to find a car. He returned to find Denise wearing a hat and very cheerful, looking just like the Denise of old times. Dr. Cazenave escorted them as far as the gate. Spring was beginning, and the air was extremely mild. The chauffeur drove them inland. Denise asked for news of her father-in-law and of the children.

"Oh," said Edmond, "how glad my father will be to see you again! He's the only person who has not tried to part us."

She looked down.

"But are you certain, darling, that you want me back? Certain you have forgiven me?"

Without replying, he took her hand and pressed it. Then, after a long silence, he said:

"And you? Are you sure you don't want anything different? Can you put up with that monotonous life?"

"If you only knew," she said, "how often, since my fever ended, I have vowed every day and every minute to see nobody but you, nobody at all!"

"I don't want to feel you tied by a vow. . . ." said Edmond.

"You're so kind, darling. . . . Such an easy vow to keep!"

As the car was on its way back to the town, she said:

"Where are you staying, Edmond? I'd like to see your room?"

He hesitated for a minute. Was it sensible? What would Dr. Cazenave have said? But he was powerless beside her. When she was in his room, she stood clasping him tightly.

"Keep me," she said, in a serious, almost sensuous, voice that he did not know.

Towards evening a nurse from the lodge came to tell Dr. Cazenave that Monsieur Holmann had telephoned to say that his wife would be staying at the hotel with him. The doctor looked up from his writing.

"I never imagined she would come back," he said.

The nurse smiled.

Next day the Holmanns returned to Paris.

PART III

I

In April 1931, Marc de Lauterie, an important official in the Ministry of Finance, returned from a fortnight's mission in Russia. He was a young man who had risen rapidly. He had played an important part in several financial conferences and in the formation of the Bank of International Settlements. The business world respected him, and he was offered seats on the most picked boards of directors. There was considerable excitement when it became known that he had been quite favourably impressed by the U.S.S.R., and that in his view the Five-Year Plan had elements of success.

Reactions were varied. Young Communist writers were exultant. A wave of apprehension passed through the Bourse and the political world. For ten years past bankers and politicians had been embroidering the reassuring theme that as Communism was contrary to human nature, it could not succeed. Yet here was an orthodox economist, one of the hopes of French finance, impressed and almost admiring. The leading newspapers published interviews with Lauterie. "If capitalism intended to put up a fight," he said, "the time had come to organize itself. The situation was not desperate, but there would have to be more intelligence." For a week he had the approval of the leader-writers.

Then came the next move. It was said that Lauterie was not so competent a man as had been supposed. The law of the line of least resistance was coming into play: it seemed easier to alter one man's reputation than the methods of Europe.

Baroness Choin, who, every Tuesday for thirty years, had been giving the finest dinners in Paris, conceived the idea of giving one in honour of Lauterie. Her custom was to group her guests round a central "star," selecting them to ensure a varied and consistent conversation. To Madame Choin any event was merely the occasion for a dinner-party. She had given a dinner for America's entrance into the War and another for the Armistice. Since the Revolution, however, she had not had a Russian dinner. It was neither from fear nor from inability. She could not very well have the Soviet Ambassador at her table, for she had been a friend of the poor Grand-Duke Paul. In any case, would the Ambassador have accepted? But a dinner for Lauterie would not be a Soviet dinner. It would strike just the note she sought—original, daring, yet not shocking. Whom should she ask?

The Baroness Choin's dinners, like those exotic soups which are kept endlessly cooking and are enriched from time to time with a piece of meat, some vegetables, and some fresh water, had both a fixed basis and variable ingredients. The fixed element consisted of Admiral Garnier, who had been presiding opposite her ever since the Baron's death; the Abbé Cénival; and her cousin Théorat, an intolerable bore, but useful for filling up a place when neighbours were touchy. The variable part had formerly consisted of from eighteen to twenty people. After her seventieth year, however, Madame Choin was quite glad to reduce it to six or seven picked guests. "Twelve is a good number," she would say, much as a great painter might declare, "In my old age I shall paint only in three colours." She would add, "I may even come to giving dinners for eight, or even six."

Arranging a Lauterie dinner was child's-play in her experienced hands.

"Let's see," she reflected, "the talk must be about finance and Russia. . . . One of the men should disagree with Lauterie; I shall ask the Saint-Astiers; with the Admiral and Théorat, that will be enough for that generation. . . . Now I need a young financier, who can stand up for Lauterie. . . . Well, Edmond Holmann; yes, certainly, Edmond Holmann: high finance, rather wild in his ideas, and a pleasant wife. . . . A minister? Thianges and his wife. . . . A young deputy? Monteix. . . . A diplomatist? Brodski. . . . He's a Pole, but he must understand the Russians. . . . A writer and his wife? The Schmitts, of course. . . ."

Three years earlier Bertrand Schmitt, the novelist and playwright, had married Isabelle Marcenat, the widow of one of Madame Choin's nephews. Madame Choin ticked off the names she had written down.

"Fourteen. . . . With a surplus of men. . . . I'll try to get Béatrice de Vaulges and Solange Villier—

they go out without their husbands. . . . Sixteen. That'll be capital. . . ."

She summoned her chef.

II

At the head of the staircase a footman held out to Bertrand Schmitt a salver spread with folded cards. In that year 1931 there were ten million unemployed in Europe and seven million in America; the Reichsbank and the Bank of England were in danger; Spain was in revolution, China at war. At Madame Choin's, when dinner was announced, the men had to give their arms to the women and form a long winding procession to the dining-room.

"Madame Edmond Holmann," he read on his card without interest. "Isabelle, who is Madame Edmond Holmann?"

"It must be the banker's wife. . . . I knew the old Monsieur Holmann, the one with the big moustaches, who died four or five years ago. . . . But I've never met the young ones. . . ."

"Well, that's cheerful," he said. "What shall I talk to her about? Really, the old lady is quite impossible. . . . She knows I don't like strange women. . . ."

As he took his cloak-room ticket, he murmured further:

"No! I'll never come here again."

The door opened. Madame Choin left an already large group, to come forward and greet them. Long experience had taught her never to begin in her own drawing-room a sentence which could not be instantaneously broken off.

"Ah, how delightful!" she said. "It's not easy to get both of you! See, Isabelle, my dear, your admirer Brodski is over there. . . . You know everybody?" she asked Bertrand.

"I'm afraid I don't! I have to take in Madame"— he glanced at the card—"Madame Edmond Holmann —and I've never set eyes on her."

"What?" said Madame Choin. "But she asked to be put next to you. She said you were childhood friends or school-fellows . . . I forget. . . . Look, this is Madame Holmann," she continued, leading him up to a young woman who was talking to Maurice de Thianges.

Bertrand Schmitt could never link faces with names. His first glance at this woman told him that he knew her. Certainly, he had often seen those lovely fevered eyes, that look of an impassioned young student with the shingled black hair. Unconsciously holding Madame Holmann's hand in his, he looked steadily at her. She smiled, and suddenly the smile conjured up a grey-padded railway compartment, a trumpet or a whistle sounding, lines of poplars, a landscape of the Seine.

"Denise Herpain!" he exclaimed with delight.

"Oh, how nice!" she said.   "After fourteen years.
. . . For he hasn't seen me since nineteen-seventeen,"
she added for Madame Choin's benefit.

"Come, come!" said Madame Choin.   "You're only
a child. . . . If I were your age. . . ."

Quite smoothly she broke off her sentence in the
middle.

"Ah, my dear Abbé!"

The Abbé Cénival had come in, fingering his low
collar.

"So *you* are Madame Holmann," said Bertrand.
"How did I never hear that?"

"Because you never made any inquiries!" she
laughed.   "I, of course, have known all the time that
Bertrand Schmitt the writer was my Bertrand of the
Rouen train.   I've read all your books, and often recognized memories of ours. . . . In 'Interférences,' the
orderly little student is Jacques Pelletot, isn't he?   Several times I almost wrote to you. . . .   And then I
said to myself, 'I don't want to bother him.' "

"And you?" he said.   "Would you have recognized
me?   I've grown much older."

"No, Bertrand, you've turned a little grey, but
you've kept that inquiring look of yours. . . .   Tell
me, isn't Madame de Thianges, over there, also from
our part of the world?"

"Of course, she's Hélène Pascal-Bouchet. . . .   Her
husband is Minister or Under-Secretary of I forget
what. . . .   She has a salon. . . .   You know them?"

"I was at the Saint-Jean Convent with her. . . . It's very far away."

Bertrand Schmitt introduced her to the Thianges. They were pleasant. Thianges talked to Bertrand about the presidential election, which was near.

"Well," said Bertrand, "is Briand going to stand?"

Two currents of opinion met, and a froth of words bubbled up. The drawing-room was at once divided into Briandists and Anti-Briandists. Bertrand observed with amusement how vigorously Denise, who was for Briand, scolded the Admiral, who was against him. Maurice de Thianges came in on her side.

"People in society," he said, "do not understand Briand. Briand is neither a fiend nor a saint. . . . He is a poet. . . ."

Bertrand touched Madame Holmann on the arm. She was leaning forward, listening.

"And your pretty mother?" he said.

"Mamma? She's still pretty. . . . You know she married again? Dr. Guérin. . . . Papa died in 1918. . . . Had you heard?"

"Oh, yes, I did. In fact I wrote to you. . . . But I had forgotten. My life has altered so much. That Normandy period now seems like a dream. The doctrine of reincarnation is true, only it's not in different existences, it's in the course of one single existence that we're different beings."

"And who *is* this Madame Holmann?" Isabelle asked Hélène de Thianges, who was beside her.

"Don't you know her? Oh, it's very odd. . . . She

was at the same convent with us, and Mamma wouldn't let us play with her because her mother was—well, rather gay. . . . It seems incredible, but we were very strict in the provinces then. . . . It seems, by the way, that the daughter is not a paragon of virtue herself. . . . She has a fine head. Look, the husband is that thin man talking to Brodski by the fireplace. Maurice says he's a wonderful financier."

They turned back to the main group, where Briand was still under discussion.

"And if he stands," said Isabelle, "will he be elected?"

"The secret ballot," said Bertrand Schmitt, "is very interesting, because it is a truthful expression of Parliament's subconscious. It gives results quite different from those of the public ballot, in which a man must be true to his type. In the secret ballot a candidate votes for himself. In the secret ballot personal grievances play a much greater part than abstract principles. In the secret ballot the desire to catch a train is put before the salvation of Europe. . . ."

"Hard sayings, but true," said Thianges.

Isabelle was watching her husband, who was talking with unusual animation. For the tenth time Madame Choin reckoned up her guests with her eye. Fourteen! Two still to come. They were the Saint-Astiers. They were intolerable. The little *soufflés* would be hard and burned. The men were talking disarmment.

"Everyone," said the Admiral, "is entitled to defend himself as he thinks best."

The door opened, and the Saint-Astiers appeared. She was thin and shackled with pearls, he, lofty and affable.

"Madame the Baroness, dinner is served," said the butler.

III

MADAME CHOIN could perceive only the æsthetic values in conversation. To her it was not an exchange of ideas, working to bring both talkers and listeners to some true or useful conclusion; conversation was a symphony made up of various, and often clashing themes, and ending sometimes with a dazzling resolving of chords, or sometimes on a few soft and pleasant notes. She herself hardly joined in; but like the conductor of an orchestra, she kept her eye on all the performers, who in turn watched her intently, on the alert for the nod, the wave of the hand, or the low utterance of a name, which would call forth their discreet drumtap, or their solo on oboe or flute.

She felt it was vulgar and clumsy to "present" the guest of honour so early as the soup, except for a single remark, just as Beethoven sometimes displays a theme at the opening of a symphony, and then disports himself for a while with lighter melodies. Thus, after a few points of proper and fitting concord had been reached, Madame Choin would allow private conversations to be resumed until she considered the time had come when everyone should dutifully listen to the anecdotes or paradoxes which formed the crowning dish of the dinner, and next day would make all Paris say, "It seems to have been very interesting last night at Baroness Choin's."

That evening she allowed Lauterie to talk to Hélène de Thianges, and Bertrand Schmitt to Denise Holmann, until the *bœuf Stroganoff*, whilst two minor instruments—Admiral Garnier and the young deputy, Monteix—were opposed in quite a spirited duet.

"What," said the Admiral. "D'you mean that we've got to allow England and America to force a certain class of battleship on us because it suits their convenience. Nonsense! What I say is this, 'If I want to build submarines, I shall build submarines.' And mark my words, I have no trust in the future of the submarine. With the advance in naval flying, it's quite on the cards that submarines will soon be obsolete. But it's a matter of principle. We pay the piper, and we can call the tune."

"What is so nice about these little *soufflés*," said Madame Choin to Brodski, "is that they only need five minutes to prepare."

"And how did you meet Holmann?" Bertrand was asking Denise.

"We were students together. . . . Oh, our story is rather queer. I'll tell you about it if you come to see me."

"Of course I'll come to see you. . . . And are you happy?"

"What does 'happy' mean?" said Denise. "My husband couldn't be nicer to me. My children. . . ."

The admirable butler was launching the sturgeon and its escort of horse-radish sauce at four different points of the table.

"My dear cousin," Théorat was saying to Solange Villier at the foot of the table, "wanted his dinner to be quite Russian. It's most amusing."

Solange was listening without interest. Théorat was plain, malicious, and sententious. She wished she had been put next to Monteix. He had the head of an athletic Robespierre. Théorat meditated between two mouthfuls of sturgeon. "A dinner like this," he said, "runs to two thousand francs."

"Counting the wines and the flowers?" protested the expert Solange. "Three thousand at least."

To a small group at the centre of the table, Lauterie was beginning to talk about Russia.

"I don't claim," he said, "that the Communist system is superior to the capitalist system. . . . That's not the point. What I do say is that an economic dictatorship, made possible by a mystical faith, is enabling the Soviet to organize production and avoid unemployment. . . . That is a fact."

"Come!" cried Madame Choin to Théorat and Solange. "Come, you must listen. This is most interesting!"

"My dear fellow," said Saint-Astier sadly and

severely—"my dear fellow, you're doing a lot of harm by talking in that way. . . . The reason why there is no unemployment in Russia is very simple, and has nothing to do with the Communist system. . . . The Soviets have had—in fact, they still have to industrialize a country which has hitherto been almost agricultural. They do so under easy conditions, because they are utilizing centuries of capitalist experience in the form of American and German engineers; and their costs are low because they pay their workmen badly. . . . That's the whole secret. . . . But do you imagine that Communism would bring the slightest relief, say, to England's troubles? Communism, my dear fellow, would mean the end of England. England only lives on the income drawn by her capitalists from abroad. The only cure for unemployment in England —let me tell you—is the cutting of wages directly or by inflation."

Denise Holmann was leaning forward excitedly, trying to catch her husband's attention.

"I want him to say something," she said to Bertrand. "He has such very just ideas about wages. He's just had an argument with Saint-Astier on the subject at a board meeting. . . . I don't like Saint-Astier. . . . Do you?"

"I find him unattractive and sensible," said Bertrand.

Madame Choin glanced reproachfully at this pair of undisciplined instrumentalists.

"You must listen!" she called to them. "It's most

interesting. . . . Monsieur de Lauterie is saying that we shall all be turned into Bolsheviks."

She seemed lively and pleased. The butler gave the signal for four ice-puddings to start off on the round, and they were followed by fresh cream in silver jugs.

"I'm not saying any such thing!" Lauterie protested. He had become quite flushed. "I say that, if the bourgeoisie insists on believing what it would like to be true, instead of facing what actually is, it is bound to disappear. . . . But it will be its own fault. . . . It's my belief that now, in April 1931, the bourgeoisie is vastly stronger than the Third International. But if it persists in a policy of nationalist and individualist economics, in competition with a policy of planned economics, then the position might easily be transformed."

Saint-Astier declined cream brusquely.

"My dear fellow," he said, "if you want to know what planned economics lead to, look at Germany. . . . The fact is, men can no more control world economics than a pilot can control the waves of the ocean. These are forces beyond us. . . . Don't you agree, Admiral?"

To show his powerlessness against the waves, the Admiral dropped his spoon. For some minutes Holmann had been trying without success to get a hearing. At last Madame Choin noticed him, and she gave him the floor rather distrustfully.

"It is too easy," he said, turning towards Saint-Astier as to an opponent, "to condemn every attempt at organization because Germany is in difficulties. . . . German industry organized production without considering distribution. I don't call that an excess, but a lack, of organization. The sole remaining chance of salvation is the organization of Europe."

"How can one try to organize Europe?" interrupted Brodski, the diplomatist, in a tone of mock despair. "My dear Monsieur Holmann . . . that is a most visionary and dangerous notion! The only wise course is to attempt no organization, and let Europe take her own course. Everything comes right of its own accord after a century or two, just as running water will level mountains in the end."

"That is fatalism," said Holmann. "We've heard that before. . . . But there is such a thing as building dams and embankments. . . . You don't really mean to tell me that a general plan, drawn up by genuine statesmen. . . ."

"That's the greatest nonsense of all!" said Brodski. "For ten years now my work has taken me to all the conferences of European statesmen. . . . I have yet to see any decision of theirs carried out, or even one truly creative idea put forward."

"I can say the same of Cabinet councils," said Maurice de Thianges.

Holmann, rather overwhelmed, looked at his wife.

"You may be right," he began, "if you are referring to general policy, but still, meetings of technical experts like the Wheat Conference. . . ."

"I have also attended economic conferences," said Brodski. "I'll tell you what happens. There is a large table, usually oval and covered with green baize. Round this table sit a dozen or twenty most imposing gentlemen, ministers or ambassadors, representing the great European countries. These Knights of the Green Table know absolutely nothing—nothing whatever. They are helpless, but harmless. Behind them, on ordinary chairs, sit groups of four or six men. These are called the Experts. They know all about potassium, or steel, or cereals. They are admirably versed in the problems at issue. Unfortunately—they never can agree. They all have the specialist's vanity, which is the worst form of human vanity, and if it were not for the honest ignoramuses of the Green Table, who for the sake of suffering humanity always accompany them, every economic conference would end in a war. But after long argument the Twelve Incompetencies intervene, deliver pacifying and vague remarks, silence the Experts, and finally agree on a meaningless formula, which just lets nature take its course. There, my dear Monsieur Holmann, there you have the economic organization of Europe."

Madame Choin wished to round off the dinner on a less severe note. She questioned Lauterie about married life and love in Russia. He spoke of the rooms in Moscow which have each to hold a complete family.

"The bourgeoisie is not going to disappear," Bertrand was saying to Denise, "it has disappeared already. . . . It has become proletarian by taking to soft collars and repairing its own cars, just as the nobility became bourgeois by wearing black coats, and as the King ceased to be King by attending the Opera without an escort. A class disowns itself by renouncing an irksome ceremonial or boring privileges."

"What you say is so true!" said Denise. "Clothes make the man. When I walk out in the morning in a raincoat. . . ."

"But you must listen!" called the Baroness imperiously. "Monsieur de Lauterie is saying that twenty people would be made to sleep in my dining-room. . . . It's most interesting."

Béatrice de Vaulges, a dark woman with sensual, Oriental eyes, said that a revolution would probably make human beings happier by freeing them from restraints.

"Everybody," she said, "longs to leave a family or a social group. Weakness or habit restrains us. A revolution sets each person free. Don't you suppose that in 1791 many of the *emigrés* were much happier?"

Isabelle Schmitt interrupted with outraged hostility:

"What an idea! I'm sure that most women do not in the least want to leave their homes or their families."

"It seems to me," said Lauterie, "that in Russia women are reacting against sexual liberty, as something that has lessened their prestige."

Respectful footmen were handing round dishes of chocolates and *marrons glacés*. Watching for the final chord, Madame Choin was gathering up her gold handbag, her feather fan, and her little box of digestive tablets.

IV

In the drawing-room the guests broke up into fresh groups shaped by stronger forces of affinity. It was a time of political and financial anxiety, and the men tended to keep together. Madame Choin had much difficulty in achieving that mingling of the sexes which she deemed necessary for the success of a party. Denise brought her neighbour Bertrand over to Edmond.

"You must talk to my husband," she had said. "You'll see how intelligent he is."

Bertrand took careful stock of Holmann. He had delicate features and tired eyes; he seemed a care-laden, serious man, and crushed as if by a weight too heavy for that slight frame.

"My dear," said Denise, "this is Bertrand Schmitt. . . . You know he's one of my childhood friends. I told you how we used to travel together in the train to and from Rouen."

As she came up to her husband, she looked at him as a rather worried mother looks at a shy and delicate son in a children's party, wondering if he is enjoying himself. She said, "Are you all right, dear? Enjoying it?" She smiled to the two men as she moved away.

"I was struck by the few words you said at dinner," said Bertrand. "I didn't think that great bankers were so liberal, so bold."

"Let's sit down, shall we?" said Holmann. He took out a cigarette and rubbed it between his fingers without lighting it. "It would not do to judge the attitude of the big bankers by my own. To men like Saint-Astier, I seem a dangerous visionary. . . . Nevertheless, I feel that in intellectual circles the business world is not fairly judged. To most of us, the idea of profit is far from being the only one that dictates our actions. After all, a man's personal needs are quite easily satisfied. No, our mainspring of action is a personal pride, the desire to maintain the prestige of our concerns, political prejudices, and even, within the limits compatible with human selfishness, the desire to be useful, to help in keeping the world at peace or in keeping it well balanced."

Next to them somebody was saying:

"Briand will get five hundred votes. I've seen the list showing the estimated votes."

"I don't know if you realize," Holmann went on, "what the political part played by a banker may be. . . . Take this Franco-Italian agreement which is about to be signed; it has been preceded by a bankers' agreement. . . . Obviously there is still a lot to be done. . . . We ought to help Germany; so far as I am concerned, I am trying to do so. . . . We can lend support to Eastern Europe. Why should loans cost thirty or forty per cent in Rumania, and next to nothing in France? There is no lack either of capital or of the need for capital. What is wanting is confidence. . . . It is for us to create it, and to level up these dangerous dif- ferences. . . ."

"You probably feel," said Bertrand, "that the man of

letters is more of a conservative than the banker. But do you really believe that confidence can be created? You talk of loans to European countries. How would they be guaranteed? It seems to me that any security in a foreign country must lose its value in the event of revolution or war."

"True. But what security keeps its value in the event of revolution or war? Bolshevism—well, bolshevism is being fostered and encouraged by Saint-Astier's banking methods. . . . For my own part, I try to stem it. I think capitalism still has life in it, but there must be a desire to save it. . . . You see, Monsieur Schmitt . . ."

Denise returned, bringing Monteix. The two men rose.

"My dear," she said, "excuse me interrupting your talk, but Monsieur Monteix has been telling me such interesting things that I thought you should hear them —and you too, Bertrand."

She laid her hand on Bertrand's sleeve. He thought the gesture unconventional and charming. "So natural, she is!" he thought. Holmann looked at the hand without saying anything.

"Now, Monsieur Monteix, expound what you were telling me. . . . Why, in your opinion, it is too late to save our civilization."

"It is very simple, Madame. . . . The reason is that in most European countries disorder has gone beyond the point at which it can possibly be controlled. . . . Oh, not in France, of course! France has won-

derful equilibrium.   You have only to see my con-
stituents in the Dordogne, farmers who live altogether
on their land, and whose exchanges with the outside
world amount only to six hundred francs' worth of
groceries a year, which they settle for by selling a few
sacks of wheat, and you will realize that no upheaval
can affect them seriously. . . .   The other day I
travelled from Paris to Marseilles.   Men were drink-
ing, smoking, and discussing their local papers. . . .
No, at present France is certainly not a revolutionary
country, but she will be drawn along.   A dozen
European countries are at the mercy of a smash—Spain,
Italy, Germany, even England. . . .   Don't forget that
revolution, like war, is always unpredictable. . . .
Only after the event can the historian discern the causes
neatly and pigeon-hole them.   A taxicab-driver scuffling
with a policeman, a little bloodshed, the surge of a
crowd, a spell of financial uneasiness—that is how the
great storms break. . . .   It might begin to-morrow."

"Anything is possible," said Bertrand, "but as Monsieur Holmann was saying just now, nothing is fixed by
fate.   A revolution can be foreseen and prevented."

"Why prevent it?" said Monteix.   "You can only
make room for the new by destroying the old.   And to
build afresh would be glorious!   I can't help it. . . .
I'm a young deputy of twenty-eight, and the temptation
is strong.   I feel like an architect who is told, 'You can
demolish a whole district of Paris and have a free hand
in the rebuilding.'   It's splendid!"

"I am very suspicious of similes," said Bertrand.

"They are delusive. . . . Building a house and reconstructing a civilization are tasks with no common measure. The process of building houses is known and well established. But who is to refashion the work of centuries? Certainly not you, Monsieur Monteix, for you won't even be called in as architect. What are you? A socialist?"

"A radical-socialist."

"You haven't the ghost of a chance. . . . You will be one of the Girondins. . . . The actual architect will be your successor's successor. Perhaps. . . ."

"What matter?" said Monteix. "Would you be prouder of being Stalin than Lenin?"

"I am not the man to ask," said Bertrand. "I dislike the idea of revolution. Don't imagine that I think our societies perfect, or that I regard them as immutable. On the contrary, I hope they will be transformed, but I should like that to happen without needless suffering. To destroy what men have so painfully erected, peace and laws, seems to be absurd. . . . And to what end? To return to the starting-point, after twenty years of horrible wretchedness during which all those we care for will have died. . . . No, thank you!"

Denise removed her hand from his arm.

"I can't believe it's you, Bertrand," she said. "In the old days you were not so timorous. I confess I agree with Monsieur Monteix: I think it would be wonderful to build all over again, to find suddenly that you belonged to a generation of pioneers, after imagining for thirty years that they were custodians of ruins."

"But what is achieved by revolutions?" said Bertrand with a trace of irritation. (He disliked her siding with the younger man.) "What was achieved by the men of 1789? After forty years of proscription and war, they ended by setting up in France the constitutional monarchy which the English had had since Magna Charta."

"All the same, you won't tell me that the Russians have not been innovators?"

"Russia?" said Holmann. "At present Russia is discovering America. In a hundred years' time she will invent capitalism."

"Still, you must admit," said Monteix, "that the present system, which condemns millions of people to be out of work must either be transformed or give way to something else? You agree? Very good. . . . Have you ever seen just and moderate politicians succeed in effecting big reforms? I can recall very few instances. . . . The truth is that big things are only achieved by the brute. Napoleon was a brute. Capitalists will learn nothing until brutes compel them to abdicate. . . ."

Holmann protested in his gentle tones:

"You must not run away with an idea like that. The capitalist world has altered a great deal. . . . A banker like myself considers himself an official, a trustee of the country. He is ready to accept State control. In actual fact, he does accept it."

"You, Edmond, yes," said Denise, "but not Saint-Astier, not the others. . . . You can't expect me to believe that; every time you come home from a board meeting, you complain of your fellow-directors' obstinacy."

He looked at her sadly. Why was she deserting him in the midst of the fray? He looked at his watch with annoyance.

"Denise," he said, "I think it is time we were going."

"Oh, already, dear? And it's been so interesting. . . . I am disgusted."

Isabelle Schmitt too was coming up.

"Bertrand, I think. . . ."

"Well, is that a promise—that you'll ring me up?" said Denise to Bertrand Schmitt.

Standing near the door of the drawing-room, Madame Choin was dispensing sweet drinks. The Schmitts left with the Saint-Astiers.

"Do you know that fellow Holmann?" said Saint-Astier to Bertrand.

"No, I used to know his wife very well. . . . But it was fifteen years ago. . . . He is intelligent."

"A misguided intelligence," said Saint-Astier. "He's rash. I think he's on the wrong road. . . . Two of his African concerns will collapse one of these days; what's more, I know he is heavily committed in Germany."

"The wife is off her head," said Madame de Saint-Astier in a piercing voice.

"Cécile," said Saint-Astier, "you mustn't shout on the stairs. They might be just behind us."

V

"And then?" said Bertrand. "Did you keep your vow?"

Since their meeting at the dinner-party, he had been habitually calling on Denise Holmann, nearly every afternoon. He would find her lying on a divan. Through the windows one could see the trees in the Parc Monceau. Beside her was a low table piled with books. Bertrand had been glancing over the titles. Some were novels he himself had suggested to her, but she also read books on special subjects. It must surely have been Lauterie who had given her "Economic Life in Soviet Russia," and Brodski that manual of Byzantine art. The contribution of Monteix must be that "Bachelier" by Vallès, or perhaps that treatise on foreign policy. Was one or the other her lover? Bertrand did not know. During the previous fortnight she had gradually told him a great deal of her past; glad to find liberation in the telling. Of the present she hardly spoke. Many men were her close friends. They called on her freely, and she went out with them. When Holmann found some of them there upon his return from the bank in the evening, he would greet them in a friendly way. Bertrand was observing this shifting topsoil; its deep sub-soil he could not quite understand.

"Did you keep the vow?" he repeated.

She shook her head.

"Why do you ask?" she said. "You know."

"I know nothing at all. . . . Nothing exact at least. . . . People say you have many lovers."

"Yourself among them, for the last fortnight."

"Exactly. . . . As it isn't true in my case, I refrain from believing in the others."

She raised herself on one elbow and looked at the flowers.

"You are right," she said, "in not believing. . . . No, these men I see all the time, who fill my life, whose names, as you say, are linked with mine—they are merely my friends."

She paused for a moment, and then went on with an effort:

"But I have had lovers. . . . And yet . . . Look here, Bertrand, I'd like to tell you about it. . . . I'd like you really to know me. . . . I need so much to talk about these things. . . . And I can only do so with the Abbé, or with a man like you who is almost professionally an observer of other people's lives. . . . But I'm so afraid of distorting everything by expressing it. Don't you think words misrepresent everything? They are so much more fixed and solid than our feelings. . . . My real thoughts are not to be put into language. They're like a stream into which a splash of petrol has dropped, flashing and changing every moment. . . . If I tell you I had no love for my mother, I am being superficial and inaccurate. I had no love for her, it is true, but I admired her, I frantically wanted to love her. It's just the same with my conduct these past five years. It must seem monstrous to you; but I know its inner workings. . . . How can I point them out to you?"

She half-closed her eyes, like a student trying to recall the process of a demonstration, and held out her hand to Bertrand. He took it. It was a long hand, very white, and extraordinarily gentle.

"Here is what I find within me," she went on, "when I try to understand myself. . . . A woman you know well, Solange Villier, told me once that she had retained from her childhood a sense of humiliation, and all her life she had tried to compensate and deaden that pain. . . . Well, that is even more true of me than of her. . . . In my case the humiliation was due to the notion I conceived of my mother's unworthiness. . . . Now, last year I had several talks with a very intelligent doctor, Dr. Bias, who told me things about myself which at first made me indignant because they were so true; but later I saw how right he was. He claimed that for a child to be mentally balanced and contented, it must be brought up by parents whose relations are normal, that is, it must have a strong-minded father, who commands and is obeyed, and a loving mother, who does her duty and submits to the father. If, as in my case, the daughter is disappointed by the father, if she finds feminine rivalry, and later jealousy, if her parents are criticized or laughed at by the people round her, she acquires a sense of guilt."

"Why guilt?"

"Well, because she assumes towards herself, and

towards her parents, the attitude of 'other people.' . . .
Don't interrupt, Bertrand—it's very hard. . . . I am
trying my best to probe to the bottom of the wound.
. . . Well then, being disappointed in the father, in
the male, she herself becomes the masculine element.
She withstands her mother—such was my case. She
wants to rule her in turn. For instance, although I care
nothing for money, I was delighted when my marriage
made me far richer than my mother. . . . She takes
up masculine studies, she has a man's pride and also a
man's qualities—courage and loyalty. . . . For a long
time I thought I was seeking for a strong man who
would rule me and whom I could love. But the fact
is that, whenever I met such a man, I ran away from
him—or fought him. Actually, I was seeking a weak
man through whom I myself could be strong. And that
probably, though I was unaware of it at the time, is
why I married Edmond. . . . That's why I shall
never be in love with you, Bertrand. You are too well
balanced, your art gives you a freedom of mind which
makes me feel you don't need me. When I met you
again at Madame Choin's, I realized there was a danger
—we had common memories of childhood, and work
interested me. . . . So instantly I made that impossible. . . . I could have played the part of a lover for
you; instead, I'm telling you all the things which can
hold you from me. . . . I am depreciating myself in
your eyes. I offer you the key, because I know you
won't take it. If I felt you were putting out a hand to
take it, I should withdraw it. And probably I should

turn against you. I should destroy you within myself.
Do you follow?"

He sat wondering.

"I think it is more complicated than that," he said.
"All the same . . ."

"One moment. I'll ring for tea."

VI

"ALL the same," Bertrand went on, "if you have not
been satisfied with a husband who has given you security, who has adored you, and whom even now you
are so obviously fond of, it must be because, consciously
or unconsciously, you have been following up a real
love."

"No, Bertrand! Physical love. . . . True love I
know I shall never find. . . . I know it, because true
love for a woman means to minister, to minister gladly,
and I am so made that I cannot minister. . . . Two
or three times I've felt that I was becoming enslaved,
that the touch of a man was melting me, making me
feel all hot—and then I ran away."

"Why? He that humbleth himself shall be exalted."

"You are telling me just what a priest I was very
fond of used to tell me when I was eight. . . . But
the fact is, I cannot humble myself. . . . It's awful
—I'm stripping myself bare in front of you. . . . Do
I displease you?"

"Not at all! I admire your clear-headedness and frankness. But somehow I can't very well picture your life. . . . If the lovers you speak of are none of those you are said to have had, who were they?"

"What can it matter to you, Bertrand?"

She fell into a reverie. He was careful not to interrupt it.

"The first," she said at last, "was a man I met in the south, at Solange Villier's, as it happens. What a wretched story! I was alone; I was bored; I had been through three horribly dull years. . . . This man appeared. He was handsome, alive, and cheerful. He brought me everything I lacked: freedom, youth, and the love of nature. He took me out in his boat. He could talk interestingly about the sea. I thought I loved him. . . . When I realized he wanted to make me his mistress, I tried to escape him. Then the whole Villier gang made fun of me. . . . Solange said I was 'the paragon of the good little girl.' I had my pride, I would not stand being ridiculed. I remember an evening at Cannes when Solange literally pushed me into this fellow's car, against my will. . . . Afterwards I went mad. . . . I wanted to kill myself. . . . The man was certainly not worth it. He was a cad, married to a rich woman, and all he worried about was not compromising himself. However, I don't know why I am telling you about him. I never think of him. . . . It's queer."

Darkness was falling. An arc-lamp in the Parc cast the only light in the already shadowy boudoir—a strange, swaying glow. Denise straightened some tulips in a vase.

"And since then?" Bertrand asked after a long pause.

"I've had short affairs," she said. "I was not going to allow any affair to become a scandal under my own roof. . . . A lover who became one of the family would remind me of my mother and disgust me. The others . . ."

"But those whom you chose thus, Denise—did you always break free from them . . . immediately?"

"Yes, nearly always."

"And the poor wretches didn't put up a fight?"

"Oh yes. That Abbé I was telling you about just now used also to say to me, 'Denise, you are like fire. You burn everything you touch.' It's still true . . . I am one of the damned."

"You weren't a believer in the days when I knew you, were you?"

"I don't know. . . . I was very religious as a child, and then I wanted to free myself in reaction against a family and surroundings. Now, I can't tell. . . . This is a most extraordinary world if it leads to nothing. . . . How can you yourself work when the thought of death comes to you?"

"It never comes to me. . . . We shall not know we are dead, therefore death is not an idea. . . ."

"Words, my poor Bertrand, words. . . . We see ourselves dying; we know we shall die. . . . But what I want to know, Bertrand, is what idea *you* have of the meaning of life. In our old days together, you were always the one who talked; now you do all the listening. It's not fair."

"May I tell you about a play I should like to write? It comes to my mind because it expresses something of my view of life."

"Do . . . please. I love being told stories."

"Oh, it's not a story: it's a metaphysical play. . . . In the prologue there will be the Showman of Marionettes, a gigantic character with a white beard. He will take his puppets out of their box, and while he gets them ready he will explain what he intends to do with them. There will be the lover, the jealous man, the ambitious man, the poor man, the rich man, the revolutionary, the conservative, the judge, and the criminal. In the first act, the marionettes will be impersonated by real actors, and they will take the stage and perform the play promised in the prologue by the Showman, who will be visible on an upper stage spangled with stars, from which he pulls the puppet-strings."

"And the actors will have strings to their arms and legs?"

"Yes, of course; and they will play that first act with the stiff, staccato movements of marionettes. The second act will begin in the same style. . . . Suddenly a character will stop dead, in such an attitude that the strings will no longer control his movements. Having thus freed himself, he will explain the play to the others, and the follies they are all about to commit, and how to escape them. From that moment the marionettes will no longer perform the Showman's play, but another play which they will make up themselves."

"It will be the Robots' revolt against their maker?"

"Just so, and what I aim at showing is that we are God's Robots. . . ."

"It's a fine idea, Bertrand. You must write the play."

"I'm working on it. . . . I have written the first act. I even have a title: 'The Marionettes have understood the Play.' "

"And how will it end?"

"I don't know yet. I think the Showman will win in the end, by smashing the rebellious marionettes. . . . For after all, the strings are there."

"You might even say they are terribly tight. But you're right: some of them can be slackened. There is no doubt that for a long time I looked upon myself as 'one of the damned,' as I told you just now, and that since I had the courage to examine myself frankly, I have felt I am beginning to vanquish that relentless destiny."

A little girl ran in and stopped shyly at the sight of the stranger.

"Say how-do-you-do, Marie-Laure. . . . What do you want?"

"Mummy, it's Grandma from Pont-de-l'Eure. She is in the schoolroom and wants to see you."

Denise shook her head, instantaneously vexed.

"All right. Tell her I'll be there in five minutes."

She threw back her fur rug, sighed, and rose with a groan. Bertrand smiled.

"One of the strings remains very obvious. . . . You are still obsessed by your mother. . . . I've been struck with that from the beginning of your story, and it seems to me rather unfair.   I remember her; she was a charming woman. . . . She was in the wrong?   No doubt, but which of us . . ."

"Oh, yes, Bertrand, I know. . . . What I blame her for is not that she was selfish and unfaithful, but that she hid it all behind a mask of virtue. . . . Do I make you laugh?   Really what I can't forgive the older generation is its hypocrisy.   I must show you some of Mamma's letters.   Don't move: I'll read you something from her last one. . . . It was wonderful. . . . One moment.   Ah, here we are: 'My great consolation is that, in my life, I have given far more than I have received.'   Don't you think that's splendid?"

"The marionette has not quite understood the play," said Bertrand.   "Your mother is waiting for you.   I must go."

"No, no, Bertrand, it's only six.   I am entitled to another hour.   I'll go and see her. . . . Find a book. . . . I shan't be long."

VII

DENISE found her mother in animated conversation with the governess in the school-room.   They both stopped when she came in.   Standing at the table,

Marie-Laure was pretending to stick stamps in her album, but her downcast eyes and uncomfortable air indicated that she had heard remarks which upset her. Patrice was sitting on the carpet winding up a toy motor-car.

"Ah, here's Mummy!" said Madame Guérin. "How are you, my dear? The servant said you had a caller, a gentleman. I didn't like to disturb you."

"You might just as well have come in," said Denise. "There's nothing mysterious about the 'gentleman.' It's Bertrand Schmitt. You know him."

"Oh, indeed! So you're in touch with him? How did you come across him again? We read his books. . . . Georges says they're interesting, but rather neutral."

"How is Georges?"

Madame Guérin brightened. Denise thought to herself: "How she loves him! Mention his name and she looks ten years younger. . . . In any case, she *is* amazingly young."

"Georges is very well, thank you. . . . He asked to be remembered to you. . . . Your sisters say he has a weakness for you. . . . You saw he had sent a paper to the Academy of Medicine? No? But the Paris papers mentioned it. . . . A remarkable paper on infant mortality. You know he's managed to reduce it among the working-class population of Pont-de-l'Eure from nineteen to twelve per cent. That's an achievement. Monsieur de Thianges says he ought to get the

Legion of Honour. . . . The Prefect is seeing about it."

"And Jacques? And Lolotte?"

"They're all right. . . . *Their* Denise is splendid. . . . Jacques is still in love with you."

Denise held up her finger and indicated the children. Madame Guérin gave a slight shrug of her shoulders.

"At their age! It's impossible, they can't understand. I brought them some little cakes from Belgiati's. They always say the Pont-de-l'Eure *madeleines* are better than the Paris ones, don't you, my dears?"

"Yes, Grandma," murmured Marie-Laure with an indifferent, far-away air.

Madame Guérin rose and took Denise by the arm. "Could I have a word with you?"

"Of course . . . let's go into my room."

Following her along the passage, Denise again found herself admiring that youthful bearing. Her mother's light-coloured dress was in the best of taste. She closed the door of her bedroom and waited. Madame Guérin settled into an armchair.

"Well, here is what I have to say. . . . You know how I hate interfering with what doesn't concern me, but I've been having a talk with Mademoiselle. . . . Now, I don't want you to think that she speaks ill of you behind your back! On the contrary, she adores you. . . . But underneath what she actually said, I grasped quite a number of things. . . . You go out too much, my dear, you see too many people, and you don't give enough time to the children. Mademoiselle does her best, but there are some things which only a mother can settle. Marie-Laure has no nice clothes for the summer. Patrice is very musical, but he makes no progress, because he hasn't got the right teacher. These children are not fully looked after. I assure you they are suffering from it. You don't realize, because you and your sisters were spoiled. . . ."

Denise stood there amazed. She was on the point of a cruel retort. But she was keeping Bertrand waiting, and a discussion about the past would go on interminably.

"Mademoiselle has only to tell me what is wanted," was all she said. "I'll attend to it."

"You will find it a bother," said Madame Guérin. "You will find you'll have to give up a few outings with your admirers, but, believe me, one never regrets the sacrifices one makes for one's children. . . . You can't tell how proud I feel when I hear that you are one of the queens of Paris!"

"What rubbish, Mamma, I am nothing. I try to do as little harm as possible; and that's not easy."

Madame Guérin became serious.

"No, not very easy, unless one has a husband like Georges, and then everything is easy. He is wonderful, and not only in medicine, you know. . . . For instance, now that we are in for a slump, it turns out that he has made no bad investments. . . . How is business with Edmond?"

"All right, I believe. . . ."

Madame Guérin became very affectionate.

"How nice you look, my dear! But you seem a little tired. You ought to come and have a few days' rest at Pont-de-l'Eure. Everybody would be so pleased to see you. . . . I'd enjoy hearing you at the piano. Georges and I were saying only the other day, 'Nobody can play Chopin like Denise.' And look, I wanted to ask you if you need those pretty embroidered table-cloths of yours just now. On Monday we are giving a dinner for eighteen for the opening of the *crèche*. The Préfet is coming. It would be absurd to buy a table-cloth just for once."

"I'll turn you over to Félix, Mamma, and he'll lend you whatever you like. Now, I hope you'll excuse me, because poor Bertrand has been waiting for half an hour alone in the boudoir."

They kissed.

VIII

"Ouf!" she said, lying down again. "Hand me the rug, Bertrand, will you? What have you been doing with yourself all this time? Were you looking at Edmond's portrait?"

He came and sat beside her again.

"Yes, I was wondering. . . . I'm terribly indiscreet, Denise . . ."

"Not at all . . . I am very glad you should speak of Edmond. . . . People understand us so badly. It would pain me if you thought my husband's attitude weak, when really he is so noble and generous-hearted. . . . Do you know, in the ten years we've lived together I've never seen him doing one mean act? The truth is, Bertrand, that Edmond knows nothing about me—at least nothing definite. . . . Of course, you may guess, he has been jealous over and over again of the men in my intimacy, whom I constantly see—of yourself, for instance."

"Jealous of me?"

"Men are funny. Each one imagines his case unique and his coming quite natural. Your case is also Lauterie's, and that of Monteix too. More than once, after being jealous over a friend of mine, Edmond has had to admit that he was wrong, that there was nothing in it . . . which was true. He welcomes these reassuring signs avidly, and to prove my innocence to himself he brings the same determination that other husbands show in proving an infidelity. I think he has a rooted idea now that I am a free-and-easy, bold, adventurous woman, but incapable of love. . . . He's not so wide of the mark."

"Before he settled down to that, he must have suffered."

"I'm afraid so. But he never said a word. Yes, sometimes, just a remark. . . . Some time after my recovery, I thought I was going to be ill again. One night I had a nightmare, almost a hallucination. Edmond, who was sleeping in the adjoining room, heard me scream. He came in. I said, 'It's horrible, I've seen that fire again. . . .' He took me in his arms and said, 'Perhaps I don't know how to love you, but I'll always be there to protect you.' "

"And what occupies his life?"

"I think he has mistresses; I used to be jealous, but I had no need to be: they hardly count for him. What really matters is his business. He has actually become what I hoped he would: a leading man of action. Since his father died he has been head of the board of the Holmann Bank, and he is the managing director of the Comptoir Colonial. . . . I've encouraged him to take a share in European reconstruction, and he has founded a special organization to assist the farmers of Central Europe. You can't imagine how astounded all the people at the bank were when they saw how, although in his father's day he had been so shy, amateurish, and self-effacing, he at once came forward and took charge, organizing, ordering. . . . You see what I mean?"

"Very clearly. . . . In short, he has escaped from himself into business, as an unhappy poet does into his dramatic poem, or a novelist into his novel. I find that extremely interesting, because the theory that a man of action is first and foremost a poet is becoming one of my favourite theories."

" 'One of my favourite theories!' How like the old Bertrand! The Bertrand of the Rouen train! Bertrand, I like you, that is to say, I shall never be in love with you. . . . But let me return to Edmond. When I realized that he had the stuff of a great business organizer in him, I was delighted, and I've helped him as much as I could. I've stood by him in all his battles, and he's had some pretty tough ones. To begin with, he had an opponent in his own bank. Börsch, his father's partner, a remarkable fellow, imagined that Edmond could not possibly have any future as a financier, and he alone would control the business when my father-in-law died. Edmond and I used to call him the 'Tyrant.' We got the better of him. . . . He withdrew from the bank. But he has gone for us with all his might and main, helped by that man Saint-Astier you met the other day, whom we have to be careful with because he has a big parcel of shares in the Comptoir Colonial."

Bertrand rose and leaned against the mantelpiece.

"What an expert you are in business!"

"I've worked. I'm still the prize pupil. I prepare Edmond's board meetings with him. I try to gather round him men who will be useful. I don't say this to give you an exaggerated idea of my importance, but so that you may understand that my husband and I are very close allies, very fond of each other, inseparable. . . . You see what I mean?"

"Yes. . . . In short, you too are trying to substitute a life of action for your emotional life."

"Not at all."

"Oh, yes, you are. Hullo, you have Pilniak's book about the Volga. I found it exceptionally good."

"It was Monteix who gave me that."

"What is he to you—Monteix?"

"No more than you are. He interests me very much,

partly because he reminds me of a friend I had once, Ménicault, a lad with genius who foundered, nobody knows why; besides, although he looks like a Terrorist, he is very human at heart."

The telephone rang.

"Hand me the telephone, will you, Bertrand? Hullo! Is that you, darling? Well, and how is the Bourse?"

Bertrand Schmitt turned over the pages of a book.

" 'A man is but an observation-post lost in the storm,' " he read at random.

"And the Ubangi affair?" said Denise. "Who? Börsch? Oh, just like him. . . ."

Bertrand picked up another book.

" 'Where are you,' " he read, " 'when you are not present to yourself? And what will it avail to have tormented your body and mind if you have yet failed to watch over yourself?' "

"He seemed embarrassed?" said Denise. "All the better. . . . Yes, that's only what he deserves. . . . You should be glad. . . . And now you're coming home?—It was Edmond," she said, putting down the receiver.

IX

It was a lovely May. The Holmanns opened Saint-Arnoult again, their house in Normandy, in the Auge district. Denise loved that enclosed valley. Far off a wooded hill closed the horizon with its long, high, tufted line. In the foreground, on the left, an orchard dropped down to the bed of the valley; on the right, a bare meadow sloped in a symmetrical curve emphasized by a strip of firs. Seen from the terrace, these two beautiful lines met almost in the centre of the view; and the simplicity, the broad features, the silence, broken only by the creak of a cart or the croaking of frogs, all combined to give the unspoilt landscape a singularly soothing character.

On the first Sunday in May the Holmanns asked out a few friends to Saint-Arnoult—the Schmitts, Monteix, Lauterie, Dr. Bias, the Abbé Cénival, and two minor financiers and their wives. The Schmitts and the Abbé were to stay for three days; the others wished to get back to Paris the same night.

The evening was fine and mild. On the terrace at Saint-Arnoult the guests paired off in the moonlight. The air smelled of honeysuckle and mint. Bertrand Schmitt went up to Abbé Cénival, whom he liked.

"Can you recall for me," he asked him, "that beautiful sentence from Chateaubriand which you repeat so well? You know—'The moon. . . .'"

The Abbé raised his arms delightedly, and repeated with loving articulation:

" 'And soon, over all the woods, she spread that great secret of melancholy which she tells so lovingly to the immemorial oaks and the ancient shores of Ocean. . . .'

Ah, so you like Chateaubriand, Monsieur Schmitt? Are you too in quest of the Sylphide?"

"I have sought her for a long time. . . . Now I am getting old. Like Stendhal, I might write on my trouser strap: '*I'm about to enter the forties.*' "

"Stendhal spoke of entering the fifties, Monsieur Schmitt. . . . The forties are youth. In any case, old age does not find peace. Think of Chateaubriand himself, and Anatole France, and Goethe. . . . The devil is old, Monsieur Schmitt; and you had better grow old before understanding him."

"The saints too are old."

"Not at all, not at all. . . . On the contrary, I should rather maintain that there is more saintliness in the young."

So crystalline was the silence in the valley that one could hear the murmur of the stream, flowing sinuously in the bed of the shadowed slopes. In the sky a dazzling moon, almost at the full, climbed among the constellations.

"I cannot grasp," the Abbé said, "why Goethe liked watching the stars yet did not learn the taste for the infinite. He had neither the fear of death nor the sense of sin. . . . It is curious."

"Why so? I admit that I think as he did. How can I fear what I cannot understand? In questions of metaphysics, to affirm and to deny seem to me equally impossible."

"The Church prefers the agnostic to the atheist,"

said the Abbé, "and even to the heretic. . . . The agnostic has respect, but he lacks the sense of the infinite. . . . You haven't the sense of the infinite, Monsieur Schmitt. In that you are like women, who scarcely have any."

"Except a few. . . . Our hostess . . ."

"Our hostess is a very intelligent woman, but she has never found a true balance. . . . She too is in quest of a Sylph, and is afraid of finding him. . . . A spoilt life. . . . Nearly all lives are spoilt, Monsieur Schmitt, and that is why you writers shape imaginary destinies. You are quite right. . . . I too sometimes compose novels; I don't write them, but I live them. . . . Often, for instance, when I have a few minutes for day-dreaming, I become the third private chaplain to the Empress Josephine at Malmaison. . . . An easy job. . . . On Sundays, Mass for the servants. . . . But I see the Emperor from a distance. . . . One day he spoke to me. 'Monsieur l'Abbé, last night I read the Gospels.'—'Ah, Sire?'—And at once, I take notes. . . . When the smash comes and the Emperor goes into exile, I am the faithful priest, the Abbé Bertrand. . . . Yes, I have been Abbé Bertrand, the chaplain on St. Helena. There he talked to me a lot. . . . I had religious conversations with Napoleon. . . The 'Celestial Memoir'—what a journal! Of course, when I get back to France, I am badly treated by the Restoration clergy. . . . I am given a tiny country parish and left there until I die. . . . But what matter? I had a noble destiny."

"That's charming. . . . I'm glad you liked Napoleon."

"Ah, yes, but unfortunately it's all just a novel. . . . Everything is spoilt in this world below, Monsieur Schmitt, everything is spoilt. . . ."

"No, not everything. . . . Remember your Chateaubriand, 'Those days of charm, days of enchantment, and frenzy . . .'"

Denise, coming up silently in the dark, joined them and took Bertrand's arm.

"Who's talking of enchantments and frenzies?" she said.

"Monsieur Schmitt and Chateaubriand, Madame. . . . But they are both victims of an illusion. . . . The enchanting days do not last; there are two, or three, or fifteen of them. . . . And the awakening is dreadful. . . . When I have to save the young from dangerous desires, I sometimes say to them, 'Suppose that what you are so eager for has come about, then imagine what happens next. You say, "I have her. . . . Good. . . . She is beautiful." A week later— "She's not so pretty as I thought. . . ." A month later—"She telephones, insists on letters, wastes my time." After two months—"She's always saying the same thing. . . . She bores me. . . . She writes, and writes badly."'"

"Yes, but one can't imagine these things in the days of frenzy. . . ."

"Ah, Monsieur Schmitt, you unbelievers are like the

may-flies dancing in the sun, never thinking they'll be dead by the evening."

"Exactly! Being a may-fly, I have the peaceful thoughts of a may-fly!"

"I envy you," said Denise. "I am like the Abbé, I think about death."

"That shows you are a better Christian than you admit, Madame," said the Abbé. "You have no right to be happy, Monsieur Schmitt. Both religion and art need unhappiness."

"You are a Romantic, Monsieur l'Abbé."

"A twofold Romantic, my dear sir: as a priest, and as a friend of Chateaubriand."

A shooting star slanted across the gold-studded sky.

"Quick! Wish a wish!" said Bertrand to Denise.

With a serious air she answered:

"I have wished, or rather I've made an old wish anew, for I made it already on New Year's Day."

"What is your wish, Denise?"

She hesitated.

"It'll greatly surprise you. . . . I've wished to die within the year. Yes, there you are. . . . I am still quite young, I haven't done any irreparable harm, but I'm afraid I might. . . ."

She dropped Bertrand's arm suddenly and said abruptly:

"Monsieur l'Abbé, I should like a word with you about my daughter."

Bertrand left them, and sought in the darkness for someone else to talk to. Isabelle and Monteix had taken two chairs beneath the terrace. He overheard Monteix talking about the presidential election, and a deputation to Briand the day before.

"He received us very affably, but sceptically. . . . We said to him, 'The country is asking for you.'— 'Let's have no exaggeration. . . .' Briand replied. For my own part, I have a deep affection for him; he is such a simple man."

Going farther along the balustrade, Bertrand came upon Dr. Bias, who was coming the other way.

"Is that you, Monsieur Schmitt?" said Bias. "Are you alone?"

"I have been for a minute, doctor. I was with the Abbé."

"And what was the Abbé saying?"

"Let me see, what was he saying? That I have no right to be happy."

"He is right. . . . He is right. Suffering alone produces genius."

"Oh, every man suffers, doctor. You should know that better than anyone."

"True. But I should say that a writer ought to foster his sufferings, and press on the sensitive spots. It is when he makes himself cry out with pain, when he touches his sensitive chords, that he liberates the best that is in him. . . . I myself have a theory, and I tell it you bluntly, that the modern writer no longer appeals to the masses because he no longer knows what misery is. The pain of the poor—there is the great tragedy, and it finds no place in your novels. It is in

'Les Misérables' and sometimes in Balzac and Dostoev-
sky. . . ."

"It was in Julien Sorel, doctor, and he is not a popu-
lar hero."

"And for a good reason—Julien Sorel was not one
of the real poor."

"Dr. Bias!" a voice shouted. "It seems I'm giving
you a lift back to Paris."

The scattered guests turned back towards the light.

X

THE bedroom was in the conventional country-house
style—Jouy hangings, Directoire beds—but pleasing.
Isabelle closed the door carefully.

"Bertrand, kiss me."

"Delighted! What's the matter, Isabelle? Why?
you're crying!"

"No, no, it's all right. . . . I am so glad to be
alone with you, glad to love only you, glad to feel I
am safe. . . ."

"Nobody is ever really safe. . . ."

"Of course, there is always death. . . . But I meant
safe inside."

He did not reply. Standing at the window, he was
looking out at the starry sky. Isabelle felt that he was
in a bad humour, and undressed in silence. But he was

not in bad humour; he was worried. He was thinking
of what Dr. Bias had said about the danger of happiness to an artist. Denise too had said to him once,
"What you need, Bertrand, is a drama. . . ."

"I've seen too many dramas. . . ." he had replied.
"Don't you know that profound saying, 'Poetry is emotion recollected in tranquillity'? There is a tragic stage
which is youth, and a stage of meditation on the tragic,
which is maturity." Where did the truth lie? Isabelle
was brushing her hair.

"Why did you say that, Isabelle?"

"What?"

"What you said just now—that you were glad to find
you were safe. . . . What made you think of that?"

She reflected.

"Oh, it's the evening we've spent—the contrast between the apparent peacefulness of the countryside and
the house, and the hidden dramas that one can feel
going on in them. . . . Your friend, Denise, unstable
and flirtatious amongst all her men. And Lauterie
glowering if she strolls with Monteix. . . . I had a
long talk with Monteix; he is attractive and brilliant,
but madly in love with that woman, who can only bring
him to harm. . . . Those two other couples, on the
brink of divorce. . . . And Bias, moving about among
all these invalids, observing their reactions with an air
of competence. . . . It made me think that to me, life
is much more simple; there is you and only you, as
before there had been Philippe and only Philippe. . . .
And it's better so. . . . That's all. . . ."

He too began undressing.

"Yes, that's a good thing. . . ." he said. "All the same, I wish you could see more clearly the nobility, quite different but quite real, of the life of a woman like Denise. You call her a coquette. But she's not a coquette. . . . She is sensual and unsatisfied, which is quite different. . . . But in friendship she is capable of loyalty, faithfulness, and devotion, to a point extremely rare in women. Let me give you an instance. I found out the other day, quite by chance, that she knew an old college friend of mine—Ménicault, a fellow who in youth was a kind of genius but who, goodness knows why, has failed in life. . . . I've tried over and over again to do something for him, to get something of his published; it has been quite impossible, because he never gets anything finished. Well, although nobody knows about it, Denise Holmann goes to see him three times a week, and it is certainly because of her that he has not committed suicide. I tell you, there's something of the saint in Denise."

"Perhaps. . . . But there's something else too."

"There was something else too in the saints. . . . They bartered earthly virtues and earthly resignation for eternal happiness: it was a good investment. . . . What I like in Denise is that she tries so hard to be disinterestedly sincere. . . . She has faults and failings, no doubt, but no hypocrisy. It is restful, after other women."

Isabelle was now in bed.

"I am not sure," she said, "that hypocrisy did not

have excellent results. . . . And I'm certain that we suffer nowadays from an inverted hypocrisy. Lots of our own friends really want nothing but a quiet life, and vex their existence only to satisfy desires which they don't really feel. . . . Besides, there are the children. . . . You can't chase elusive happiness and also make your children happy. . . . I've had confidences from young women. All those whose mothers were too free-and-easy have been the worse for it."

"In the old days, Isabelle; but that is less and less true. . . . Nowadays there is a companionship between many mothers and daughters that almost makes them fellow-conspirators. . . . For instance, an Englishwoman told me lately how she had been left a young widow with a little daughter, and how she sacrificed all her chances of a fresh love for the child's sake; and then, when the girl was sixteen, she said one day, 'Mother, am I my father's daughter?'—'Of course you are! Why?'—'Oh, it would be such fun to be somebody else's daughter.' "

"Oh, such a girl must belong to a very 'sophisticated' circle. I don't believe myself that children have altered. . . . Now, I was watching the children here this afternoon. . . . Little Patrice is terribly jealous of the men who are always surrounding his mother."

"You exaggerate. . . ."

"Not at all, Bertrand. . . . Amours and nurseries can't be combined. . . . In any case, I can't feel any pity for these women who claim at once the security of marriage and the freedom of celibacy; I can't take them seriously. . . . One has to make one's choice."

Bertrand went in his pyjamas to the window. He gazed at the moon-white trees.

" 'And soon, over all the woods,' " he thought, " 'she was spreading that deep secret of melancholy. . . .' I shall never remember how it goes."

He turned round.

"I'm not playing fair, Isabelle. At bottom I agree with you. . . . I believe in the stability of institutions, and I believe that only from that stability can true freedom come, even to an artist—provided the artist has known what suffering is. . . . Actually, Tolstoy, Flaubert, and even Proust, all the great novelists, have led lives with very little romance in them. . . . Why do you laugh?"

"Because you lead back every question to yourself. . . . I do the same, for that matter. . . . Everybody. . . ."

He laughed in turn, and put out the lamp. A gleam of moonlight lit up the room. Presently Bertrand spoke again in the darkness:

"What about Holmann, Isabelle? Do you find him intelligent?"

"He is nice, but visionary and cloudy."

Bertrand did not reply. Soon he was dreaming that Dr. Bias was sitting on his chest, anl refusing to get off. Isabelle could not sleep. A happy couple, she reflected, were like the people on a raft—when the sea was smooth.

XI

For a fortnight the presidential election of 1931 sundered, if not France, at least the five thousand who, "because they go to bed late, imagine that they run the world." The rift was almost as deep as that of the Dreyfus Affair. The Thianges were in Briand's camp, and drew in their political and writing friends. The Saint-Astiers and their circle fought on the other side. Denise Holmann was passionately Briandist, and cried her faith aloud, with aggressive bravery, in the orthodox drawing-rooms. Her husband showed less ardour. Business anxieties made him fear any disturbing force.

"I have nothing against Briand," he would say, "but I don't believe the Elysée is the place for him. He would be a prisoner there, quite impotent."

On the evening of the election, Monteix, a leader of the caucus, scolded him.

"If you spent your time in the Chamber," he said, "you would see that the President of the Republic is far from powerless. Doumergue has been the real controller of French policy for seven years. . . . Ask any of your friends who have been ministers; they will all tell you how a President goes back on a Cabinet between two meetings, and puts his own interpretation on a crisis or an election. . . . Suppose the next elections give a majority to the 'Left' bloc. . . . A hostile President can break it up, and form a ministry of centre groups; a friendly President, on the other hand, can

cement it by parleying with the Socialist leaders. . . .
The President has just the same powers and function as
the King of England. These are far from being non-
existent."

"I agree with Monteix absolutely," said Denise excitedly.

"There's another point of view," said Holmann with
kindly firmness. "Briand is a tired man, who has to
live under doctor's orders. You'll kill him by making
him open exhibitions of painting every morning."

"There is no reason why he should open exhibitions
of painting," said Monteix sharply. "Formerly the
Presidents did nothing of the kind. They had more
leisure and more prestige. It's the same with the ministers' travelling. In the early days of the Republic it
was a great event when a minister came to visit some
town. Now the ministry is a football team, going off
as a body every Sunday morning. But that is not in
the Constitution."

Holmann sighed and shook his head.

"Well," he said, "let's admit that basically you are
right. In point of fact, and in the present state of
public opinion, Briand's election is undesirable because
it would split France into two. The President should
be a moderating influence, a brake, a guiding-wheel, not
a subject of controversy. Suppose you get Briand
elected to-morrow . . . what will his return to Paris
be like? There will be hostile demonstrations."

"All the better," said Monteix. "I'd like to see the

Avenue des Champs-Elysées condescending to demonstrate against Briand; next Sunday, my friends and I would bring along the working-class districts and the suburbs. . . . It's high time this country was roused a little. . . ."

"I'll certainly come and demonstrate with you, Monteix," said Denise.

"I shall be greatly honoured, Madame. . . ."

"And I shall be extremely anxious," said Holmann.

Monteix asked if she would come to Versailles next day. Baroness Choin had invited her, but she had not accepted. Luncheon with the Saint-Astiers and the Admiral? No, she preferred to await the result in Paris. Monteix arranged that he would telephone to her from Versailles after the election, and that they would go together to see the new President drive back.

Next day she spent quietly, shopping on foot in Paris. The chestnuts were in flower. She got home about five. Monteix telephoned earlier than she had expected.

"It's shameful," he said. "We're beaten. . . . Yes. . . . Four hundred votes. . . . Yes, I'm staying on for the second ballot, but Briand is not even a candidate this time. . . . The Thianges will give me a lift back. Shall we meet at eight at the corner of the Avenue du Bois and the Avenue Bugeaud? No, I shan't have had dinner. We can go somewhere or other. . . ."

"All right. . . . I'll be there. . . . Oh, one moment, Monteix! Edmond has not come in. . . . I don't know where I can reach him. . . . Oh, well, it doesn't matter; I'll leave a note for him."

"But you're coming alone?"

"Of course."

She found Monteix waiting as arranged. He took her arm in a familiar, companionable way, and led her off.

"There's quite a decent little restaurant at the Gare Maillot. . . . We've plenty of time. Doumer can't get back before nine. I'll tell you about the Assembly over soup and fruit."

Through the adjoining streets, all along the avenue, troops were arriving. The hoofs of horses rang on the roadway. Regiments of policemen, their capes on their arm, deployed like sharp-shooters along the deserted pavements.

"This Third Republic of ours is pretty sturdy," said Monteix. "Somebody told me what the Prefect of Police said. 'I'll answer for keeping order in any case. Only, if it's the one, I'll need two thousand men; if it's the other, six thousand. That's all.'" They took a taxi. The driver turned round to them.

"Well, who is it?" he asked.

"Doumer," said Monteix.

"Ah! Where does he come from? If he comes from the south, it's all right."

"The greybeards in the Senate," sighed Monteix, "understand this country better than we do."

Over dinner he described the session.

"It was doleful. . . . The corridors stank of treachery and bad air. . . . As soon as the result of the first ballot was known, Briand was left standing in a hideous void. . . . There was that bent old man, suddenly deserted alone in the centre of the Hall of Mirrors—it was Shakespearian. . . . I went up to him. With forced cheerfulness he said to me: 'What do you expect? They voted for their President.' " [1]

"The Saint-Astiers must have been exultant!"

"Yes, her voice drowned everything. . . . She was screeching at the Trianon Palace Hotel. . . ."

They went back on foot to the Avenue du Bois. The crowd was growing along the pavements. Monteix got hold of two chairs and made Denise climb up on one of them. Her other neighbour, a fat man in spectacles, did not leave her enough room, and she leaned against Monteix. He became silent and tender. Backed by such a woman, he felt he would be equal to anything. Then he recalled the days when he was a poor student, and how once he had come over to this part of Paris to fan the flame of his hatred of the rich, watching women just like the one beside him giving languid orders to their chauffeurs. . . . Police officers, wearing even more and more stripes, passed up and down the deserted roadway. There was a distant hubbub. A small carriage appeared, bearing two men anxiously looking to right and left. Denise leaned forward, supported by Monteix, who had put an arm round her; in the distance she saw a wave of horses, the flashing of

[1] M. Doumer was President of the Senate when he was elected President of the Republic.—(Trans.)

sabres and a blue cloud of cavalrymen. The carriage was so heavily surrounded that they could see no face. Round them men were baring their heads. Waving his hat, the man with round spectacles shouted unintelligible words. It was all over. The flood of taxis poured in behind the procession. Monteix stood for a moment longer on his chair, for the pleasure of holding Denise close to him a few seconds. The man with round spectacles turned to them.

"And who was it, after all?" he said.

Denise burst out laughing. For the rest of the evening that remark kept on amusing them. They had no wish to part. It was a fine warm night.

"Let's go round the lakes," said Denise.

As they walked, Monteix spoke more frankly than he had ever done of his hatreds, his hesitations and his hopes. She felt very fond of him, and sincerely anxious to cheer him up and hearten him. These mingled feelings looked like love. When they came back to Paris, late at night, he tried to kiss her. She let him, and then pushed him gently away.

"No," she said, "you mustn't. . . . I should make you so wretched. . . ."

Edmond was waiting for her.

"You're mad . . ." he said. "What have you been doing? I was terribly anxious. I was just going to ring up the police. For the last hour I've been at the door, watching every car that stopped."

She found ready excuses. The truth was, that during those few hours she had completely forgotten him.

He could not sleep, and complained of pains under the ribs which made his breathing difficult. Denise looked after him, but she felt that he was complaining chiefly in order to compel her to make a fuss of him.

XII

Once a month Denise Holmann gave a musical evening at the Rue Alfred de Vigny. She did not like society and devised this way of entertaining, as sparing her the kind of conversation she found boring. Her evenings were famous in Paris for two things—the quality of the performers, and the severe discipline Denise Holmann enforced. That of June 29, 1931, proved supremely attractive, not to the musical—though Denise had secured for the evening an admirable Viennese soprano—but to financial people and to society people with no artistic pretensions. The reason was this: most of them knew that the Holmann Bank would not meet its monthly obligations on the following day. Many were curious to see if the pair would face the storm bravely, others felt pity and wished to show their sympathy, and a few wanted to score points in anticipation of the day of Holmann's come-back.

His failure was due to very varied causes. It was bound up with the all-pervading slump, which jeopardized every kind of business. But Holmann himself had been rash. His partner, Börsch, at the time of their spectacular split in 1926, had foretold the crash.

"Young Holmann will fall," he had said, "as surely as the sun will set. Firstly, he takes on too many things at once. I don't know what ails the fellow, but he goes in for business as some people go in for speeding. A man who drives too fast and not very carefully runs into the landscape. Secondly, he has a false notion of the banking profession. He confuses the banker with the pioneer. He thinks that a bank can establish plantations and factories. . . . That's false!" (Börsch would shout emphatically the word "false.") "A banker is there to lend a hand in developing some enterprise already started by an individual specialist, not to turn himself into a creative expert. Thirdly, having shouldered more concerns than he can finance by his own means, he has been obliged to appeal to the public for money to put into new concerns, still uncertain, which have not yet had the distemper. Old Monsieur Holmann—he was a real banker—made it an absolute principle never to expose enterprises whose returns were not yet certain to the nerviness of the small capitalist. When a concern is still in the hands of a few men, it can easily be put on the shelf and left for better times. But for those in which the public has invested, any unpleasant rumour, any year without dividends, means a panic, refusal of credit, stormy shareholders' meetings. To hold up the shares, one risks short-term deposits; and then, at the slightest jolt of the market, one founders. Fourthly, Holmann's sugar refineries, his rubber, his cotton, his metals, have left him no longer a banker, but a producer of raw material, and so he has been left at the mercy of an economic slump. But that's his look-out. He will do what he wants. For my own part, I'm leaving the ship."

He had resigned, and as early as 1929 was a "bear" on all Holmann stocks. He brought down the Comptoir Colonial shares—"a knife in their ribs," he would say—from 2,200 to 215 francs. The game won him a vast fortune.

Börsch's diagnosis was sound. Like many men who entered business about 1922, Edmond Holmann imagined he was a great swimmer because a tidal wave was carrying him along. He was diffident to start with, but came to believe in the success of all that he undertook. By 1927 he had become as powerless to arrest the development of his concerns as Napoleon was in 1812 to limit his conquests. When the European rout began, he tried, partly to please Denise, some sort of international salvage. He lent large sums in Central and Eastern Europe. The failure of the Credit-Anstalt of Vienna and the fresh fall of the mark finished him. For a moment he hoped that the Hoover moratorium would save him by restoring a measure of confidence to the markets. "The injection of camphorated oil," Börsch called it.

To those guests aware of this situation, that party in the Rue Alfred de Vigny was a spectacle full of hidden interest. Holmann was pale but determined, and more lively than usual. Denise looked beautiful and forthright, swathed in a long black silk dress, a cascade of diamonds falling from her neck, and was calmly seating her guests. Friends of the family, Bertrand Schmitt, Lauterie, and Monteix, watched her with anxiety. Guests from the other camp, such as the Saint-Astiers, clustered in corners for whispered backbiting.

"Six thousand francs for a singer, on the eve of bankruptcy—it's a scandal!" screeched Madame de Saint-Astier.

"Cécile!" said Saint-Astier, signing to her to lower her voice. Quite a number of people had overheard. Some agreed with the complaint: "The Holmanns should have cancelled this party. . . ." Others again thought they were showing pluck. A few thousand francs more or less would not affect a balance-sheet involving several hundred millions, and anyhow, was the failure certain? Many eyes were on Lauterie, who, as a leading official of the Ministry of Finance, was bound to know the situation.

Bertrand Schmitt manœuvred to get to Denise, and then he led her off towards the piano.

"Is it true?" he said.

"Yes, short of a miracle, and you don't believe in miracles."

"What will become of you?"

She waved a welcome to a couple coming in, and replied in a low voice:

"We give up everything, to our last franc—these diamonds, all this furniture; we leave this house, and we work."

"You're brave. I always thought so; but it's fine of you all the same."

"I don't deserve praise," she said. "I don't care about these things. . . . I have owned them; they have never owned me. Don't go on talking to me, Bertrand; people are looking at us. . . . But do help me to get them seated. . . . They're awful."

And certainly she was powerless that evening to maintain the celebrated discipline of the Holmann drawing-room. Whole rows, already seated and settled, would rise to listen to whispered news from some late arrival.

"You know that she's his mistress?" one young woman was saying, indicating Denise and Monteix.

At the other end of the drawing-room Lauterie and Saint-Astier engaged in vehement discussion.

"All the same it's scandalous," Saint-Astier was saying, "that Hoover should confront France with an accomplished fact, when it means her giving up her rights. Sheer blackmail."

"My dear fellow," said Lauterie, "you're distorting facts. . . . France has been kept posted. . . . Do you know what I regret? That we didn't put forward the proposal ourselves. Four months ago, Wladimir d'Ormesson was advising exactly what you're now agreeing to. You cried out as if he had committed a crime. Result—we've lost the initiative. Thanks to people like you, we are always lagging in our surrenders. We keep on haggling, and in the end, without saving the situation or making ourselves liked, we surrender the very thing which, had we suggested it ourselves at the right time, would have restored confidence."

"Whose confidence?" said Saint-Astier. "After all, we can't tolerate Frenchmen being treated as fools, or that debts, which are really war expenditure, should be put on the same footing as reparations, which are the cost of all the damage done on our territory. For my own part, I refuse . . ."

"Come along, Lauterie," cried Denise, standing at the end of the row. "Do please sit down and make the others sit. . . ."

The singer came in. There was silence. Madame Holmann announced:

"Richard Strauss's 'Morgen.' "

For a while the music soothed the turmoil of feeling. Once or twice there were whisperings; immediately heads turned indignantly. The full, flowing voice of the singer gave out that sense of splendid ease which gives an audience assurance and heightens the enjoyment. There was much applause. Denise half rose, and turned to announce:

"Bach's 'Bist du mit mir.' "

It was a slow, calm, moving air. This time every murmur ceased. Resting his tired face on his hand, Holmann took in the words avidly:

> *"Bist du mit mir, geh' ich mit Freuden*
> *Zum Sterben und zu meiner Ruh' . . ."*

"Yes," he thought, his eyes on his wife's delicate profile. "I shall go fearlessly to ruin and death, if you keep beside me—if you never leave me. . . ."

Denise, too, was applying the words to herself and Edmond. She knew well what Edmond must be feeling at that moment.

"Misfortune raises our stature," she thought. "I feel more satisfied with myself than I have for a long time."

"Ach, wie vergnügt wär', so mein Ende,
Es drückten deine schonen Hände
Mir die getreuen Augen zu!"

"With thee beside me, I can go with joy . . . To death and to my last repost. . . ." The air was ending. Denise turned to glance at Edmond. He looked overcome. She smiled at him. Bertrand Schmitt was watching them both, and he caught the smile. "She is the stronger partner," he said to himself. During the next item, Mozart's "Il Re pastore," he reflected on that strange blend of womanly charm and manly strength.

When the hour's music was over, the guests crowded to the buffet. Madame de Saint-Astier was indignantly counting the little iced cakes, ranging them for some vengeful statement of account like so many millions lifted from the shareholders of the Comptoir Colonial.

XIII

HUMAN malice, no small thing, is largely made up of jealousy and fear. It is disarmed by misfortune, and for that reason people who suffer from lack of love derive a tart satisfaction in the private or public disasters which befall them and, in humbling them, grant them a kind of social absolution. When the news spread through Paris, on June 30, that the Holmanns were ruined, that Holmann had called together his creditors and placed at their disposal all he possessed, and even the jewels and the small fortune of his wife, and that the latter was asking her friends to find her a job to earn her own living, a wave of sympathy surged up, and those persons who, like Saint-Astier, had helped to break them, began to worry about means of rescue for them.

Industrial civilization has, for a century past, known many cyclical depressions; but the one which began in 1929 was exceptional, and stood out from the common run in several respects. One was its political character, and the constant intervention of governments, which were far from socialistic, to refloat or to buoy up private concerns. In the case of the Comptoir Colonial and the Holmann Bank, the interventions of politicians were persistent. They used strong arguments. Why should the numerous manufacturers in eastern France with accounts in the Holmann Bank be ruined by its collapse? Should the colonial depositors, many of whom were natives, be allowed to question the soundness of French credit? The Ministry of Finance favoured a collective effort by the great banks and advised the Bank of France to act with them.

Monteix had concerned himself with the matter from the first, with the aggressive energy he put into everything he tackled, and won the support of several deputies belonging to his group, hostile though they were at first. Others criticized him. His friendship with Madame Holmann was known. "Drawing-rooms and women have been the ruin of more than one young radical who, like you, entered Paris incorruptible," old Ferraz, a deputy for the Ain, told him sternly. He respected Ferraz, and the reproaches pained him.

After trying to see what could be done at the Ministry, he called on Denise. He found her calm and told her what he had learned.

"Things are not going well. The Ministry is not to blame. The officials, like the Minister himself, are well disposed, but the banks are humming and hawing. Lauterie called together the big concerns this morning. He has just told me that never before in such a case had he met with such resistance."

"Why is that? Edmond is very much liked."

"Yes . . . I made Lauterie talk, and got the impression that behind all this lack of goodwill there is one steady influence at work."

"Börsch?"

"Precisely! You see, Börsch is very powerful. He has manœuvred the dropping markets in a wonderful way. He now has a vast fortune, and he also owns several financial newspapers. . . . If he goes ahead unswervingly and savagely as a bear with Holmann stocks, as he has done so far, no refloating can succeed. . . . That is what the banks have told Lauterie: 'A futile sacrifice. We shall throw two or three hundred millions into the breach, and in three months the position will be the same again.' So 'No,' they say, 'If Monsieur Börsch is with us, we are quite willing; but if his honour is staked on smashing the Holmann interests, he's big enough to do it, and anything we might do would be vain.' "

"Well?"

"After they had gone, Lauterie telephoned to Börsch asking him to come to see him. Börsch sent word that he was ill, which Lauterie knows to be untrue. . . . So he's obviously against us. . . . I have come to make a proposal to you: would you like me to go and see Börsch? I don't know whether I shall be able to prevail with him. . . . But, I've heard from common friends that he was interested in my recent speeches in the Chamber."

She reflected for a long time.

"Really, it's very nice of you, Monteix. . . . But I have another scheme. . . . Suppose I went to see Börsch myself?"

"Very risky. . . . And also, your husband would object."

"If I go, I shan't tell Edmond. The advantage, as I see it, is that if I, a woman, go to see him of my own accord, my action is of no importance; it can be disowned if the future shows it to be foolish. . . . If you go, as a deputy, it will compromise you in the eyes of a man who may one day be useful to you. . . . Let me take my own risk."

He thought for a moment.

"All right. But you must act quickly. There are only two days left before the balance-sheet is filed. After that, everything will be much more difficult."

"I'll go this evening."

Monteix lit a cigarette and became very silent. Through the window came the shouts of children playing in the Parc. He rose. Denise saw that he was moved and struggling to hide his emotion.

"As soon as you've seen Börsch," he said coldly, "telephone me the result of the interview."

"I will. . . . Thank you, Monteix."

In the afternoon she joined Holmann at the Comptoir Colonial. The tall bronze doors, with their reliefs of palm-tree designs, were closed. Entry was through the porter's lodge. She found her husband in unusually friendly converse with Saint-Astier.

"Denise," he said, "I'd like you to tell Saint-Astier, as I have done, how deeply we're touched by the line he's taking."

"My dear fellow," said Saint-Astier, "we must all hang together."

While the two men went on talking Denise looked up *Tout-Paris.* "B—Ba—Bo—Börsch (Alfred), avenue Hoche, 44, (VIIIe), Telephone: Carnot 13-95."

"But it's quite near here," she thought. "I'll go over at once, and if he isn't in I'll ask for an appointment . . . Edmond," she said aloud, "I don't want to break up your talk. I've a little shopping to do before I go home. . . . I'll see you again when you get back. Good-bye, Monsieur. . . . Please give my regards to Madame de Saint-Astier."

It was drizzling. She turned up the collar of her waterproof, and set off on foot, her hands in her pockets. She was dressed that day like a student, because she liked it, and though she didn't know exactly why, she felt free and strong. The invisible sun fringed the black clouds with rims of fire. What would she say to Börsch, supposing she found him in? She had not seen him for five or six years; she recalled his bushy eyebrows meeting above his nose, and his loud voice. She passed the Beaujon Hospital. A man with trembling hands was reading the contents of the board —"Consultation for Nervous Diseases." What would she say? It reminded her of her exams. She must let him put questions and keep cool. Most likely Börsch would be very hard. The thought of him was already making her feel mulish. "Dog Clinic." A stout lady with a little Pekingese on a lead was ringing the bell. In her ears were huge pearls. She had the worried look of a mother whose child is being operated on. Life was really so simple. To the onlookers this disaster must appear tragic. But actually what did it amount to? To a few interviews, a walk. "Give my regards to Madame de Saint-Astier." A toyshop reminded her that Marie-Laure's birthday was approaching. What kind of a present should she get? She looked into the shop-window at a kitchen-set, a tea-service, a handbag. How much longer would she be able to buy her children toys? She turned into the Avenue Hoche, where the concierges, now the rain had stopped, were coming out on the wet pavements like slugs on the footpaths in the woods. Börsch lived in a big house in the style of 1880; Corinthian columns upheld the porch over the entrance. On the staircase of chocolate-coloured marble the blue and yellow carpet, with its branching pattern blended perfectly with the out-of-date painted windows. An ascetic sense made her go up on foot, and when she rang she was out of breath. The servant who came to the door seemed evasive. He did not know if Monsieur Börsch was in; he would go and see. She handed him her card.

XIV

A LEATHER-COVERED door opened. She saw the Börsch eye-brows, meeting in the middle. He was polite, but surprised. Feeling suddenly quite at ease, she explained her call.

"You must be rather surprised to see me. . . . I realize it. . . . And whatever the upshot, I want you to keep this call a secret, because my husband doesn't

know I am here. What I want to say is this. . . .
Everybody we have been seeing in the last few days,
financiers or politicians alike, seem to think that it is for
the general interest that my husband's concerns should
be kept going. At the same time, they all insist that
without your support, or at least without your neutral-
ity, those concerns cannot be refloated—that is their
expression, I think. I thought it simpler, as I knew
you, to come and ask you yourself what you intend
to do."

Börsch assumed the sad, severe, wise look of rich
men when they are asked for money.

"Madame," he said, "I appreciate your frankness. I
like it. I shall be quite as frank. You say that all the
financiers you have seen consider that Monsieur Holmann's concerns should be kept going. My view, however, is the opposite."

"Still. . . ." she said.

He pressed on the table with his large stubby hand.

"Allow me, Madame. I am aware that you are very
intelligent, but I have some little experience and I can
enlighten you somewhat on this matter. Why is there
a depression? Because money has been lent too easily
and prices have been kept at an artificial level; as a
result, production has been allowed to grow far in excess
of needs. What can end the depression? The weeding-
out of the excess producers, that is to say, those least
fitted for the struggle. All previous depressions have
ended in that way. There comes a time when the
market is as it were 'purged,' and the lusty organisms

which have survived the epidemic can again breathe freely. . . . Good. . . . Well, what do your friends propose? What have people been doing for the last two years? They have been keeping alive something not really fit to live. Imagine a forestry inspector who would never agree to cut down a tree. . . . Nowadays, whenever some gentleman makes a fool of himself, somebody calls on the Premier and says, 'Couldn't the State do something?' What is the result? That the depression goes on. . . . What will be the sequel? That men will become altogether incapable of looking after their concerns and investments for themselves. . . . Why should they take care? There are no longer any penalties. . . . It's exactly like a man with a bad liver being provided by his doctor with a remedy which prevented him from suffering from his attacks. . . . What would happen? He would gorge on all the horrible rich things he liked. . . . And then one day— that would be the end of him. . . . Well, Madame, my position is this—I find myself on board the ship Capitalism, and I have no wish to see her go to the bottom."

She had listened, as always, like a model student.

"I'm incorrigible," she thought. "As soon as I am being lectured, I am vanquished." "I see your position very well," she said aloud, "but my husband's concerns. . . ."

Again the heavy hand fell on the table.

"Your husband, Madame—forgive me if I put it brutally . . . I know him very well. He is an honest man, and a hard worker, but he cannot say 'No.' He's a man who cannot look at a debit account and say, 'Not another penny.' He hasn't got a clear mind; his brain complicates a simple matter with hundreds of grandiose and impossible schemes. . . . He is a visionary who has filled Africa with plantations that have no trees, hotels with no visitors, refineries with no sugar-cane, and unworkable mines, because it excited him to think he was taking over a native mine. . . . Only, a mineral deposit good enough for slave labour will not keep a modern factory fed. I have nothing against your husband, Madame, but he is not a business man: he is an artist. And also, allow me to say it, Madame, he is your husband. That is a fine thing for him because you are charming, but it is also a very unfortunate thing because you have ideas political and otherwise. You have done him some very bad turns. . . . Credits to Germany, loans to Eastern Europe. . . . I can remember the beginnings of that, I was still in the firm then—it was your idea."

"Certainly, yes. But was I absolutely wrong, Monsieur Börsch? Hadn't something got to be done? How would it have helped if we had kept France a relatively undisturbed island, and been swamped and submerged by a universal catastrophe? If the rest collapses, do you think we can keep upright?"

"Madame," said Börsch, "I don't care for discussing such questions with a woman. But if you want my opinion—no, we should have done nothing, at least nothing in the economic domain, because in that domain all the big schemes fail. Nothing can take the place of the individual attitude and the work of individuals. America and England have done Germany a sorry service in giving her the illusion of credit. . . . That Germany should rise again is important; of course it is. . . . I should like to see it come about. But it can only be brought about by the Germans themselves. Apart from that, there can be no salvation."

He looked at the time.

"I was wrong to speak of that aspect of Edmond's affairs," she said. "It is not the one you are interested in. The question I wanted to ask you here is much simpler. In the case of the Holmann Bank, if the Ministry attempts to 'refloat,' would you be prepared to remain neutral?"

He softened, pleased at having expressed his dogmatic standpoint to the woman who had once been his adversary.

"You can well imagine," he said, "that it gives me no satisfaction to see the collapse of that old firm which once bore my name. And, incidentally, there is a point about which you are right. There will be much more to be got out of a liquidation if it is arranged in a private, friendly way. . . . I've seen the assets; they include many industrial claims. Now, an industry, a factory, an equipment is worth x. If you bring it to a standstill, it becomes old iron. It is worth $\dfrac{x}{10}$ or $\dfrac{x}{100}$."

She felt that she must say nothing and wait. Again

he brought down his hand, and again looked at the time.

"Now," he said, "tell Lauterie I'll come and see him to-morrow morning. Perhaps there is some way of arranging things."

On leaving Börsch's house, she walked round the Parc Monceau. Old men on benches were reading the papers. Children were playing at horses. The smaller ones were building sand castles. She thought of the Solférino Gardens at Rouen, where she used to pass on her way home to the Rue Damiette from the *lycée*. The world was going its way. She looked at her watch. There were two hours before dinner-time. She hailed a taxi and drove to Ménicault's. She was his mistress.

XV

THE Holmann Bank was saved. Every one of the surviving big banks, willingly or unwillingly, put up the required millions. An official statement issued by the Ministry of Finance congratulated them on "their spontaneous display of solidarity." Edmond Holmann's private fortune was practically wiped out by the indispensable reduction in capital, but as he had behaved so well, his creditors themselves insisted that he should continue to be managing director of several concerns; and as his household's mode of life had always been relatively modest, it was able to remain much the same.

A cold wet July made Paris gloomy and wintry. Unemployment was growing. Following the mark, sterling worried the financiers. Heavy storms covered the walks of the Bois with hard white hailstones. Denise Holmann asked Bertrand Schmitt to take her to the cinema. They went to see an American film. Nocturnal rum-lorries rushed along a New York avenue under the columns of the Elevated. Huge gates slid open or shut at prison entrances. Faint, sharp revolver shots hardly broke the rhythm of the jazz. There were roundabouts, waves breaking on a beach, aeroplanes roaring. Gangsters in dinner-jackets turned machine-guns on girls from the windows of shiny limousines. In the interval Denise and Bertrand chatted.

"You can't realize," she said, "how weary I feel. Whilst the fight was on I had a moment's hope that something big was coming into my life. . . . Believe me, it's true—I was wonderfully happy taking my stand with my husband. I should almost have welcomed complete ruin, so that my children and I would have been forced into the natural rough and tumble of life. And then nothing happened. Nothing ever happens. As that man Börsch put it, 'Nowadays everything is rescued.' The failure itself is half and half, and circumscribed. I am still asked out to dinner. Börsch sends me flowers. Edmond is resigned to being shelved. He's glad to find himself brought nearer to me by defeat as he used to be by illness. But I—I feel like running away: I want to act, to live. Carry me off, Bertrand."

"I should like to," he said. "But it would only last a fortnight."

"Why?"

"Because you're not in love with me, because I love Isabelle, because. . . ."

"You see, you too calculate, you too weigh the odds. . . . And, as it happens, you're quite right."

Behind them a man and a woman were talking in low tones of jealousy.

"One imagines one is being betrayed," the woman was saying, "one finds one is not; one grows confident, and then it's that confidence which is deceptive."

Bertrand looked round. The woman was pretty.

"The truth is," said Denise, "nothing could satisfy me. I am a tool that's been damaged—ever since childhood. Shall I ever get rid of that inward oscillation? Shall I ever find an equilibrium? I feel like a spring vibrating under a blow, never stopping. . . ."

Advertising films came on the screen. Bottles of wine talked. Magic liquids cleaned cars. Pills swept out colossal intestines.

"What shook me first?" said Denise. "I suppose I've forgotten. . . . The first shock I remember was this. We were all three with my mother at Beuzeval. . . . One night I heard her singing; I went to the window, and I saw a stranger beside her, the man who is now her husband. It is from that day that I ceased to be a happy child."

Next to Bertrand a man said:

"Unemployed? My dear fellow, France has them like other countries. Only in France they're called *rentiers*. It's more ingenious."

"My last great disappointment," Denise was saying, "has been Edmond's financial failure. . . . I had faith in him. I thought him bold and large-minded. . . . So he was, but I had compelled him to demand a part for which he wasn't fitted. Oh, I've a lot to answer for in that affair!"

"My dear Denise," said Bertrand, "you're rather inconsistent. You married him because he was weak and could be your instrument. You must not blame him for your choice of him."

"Yes, that's quite true. That's what I tell you— oscillation, no balance. . . . It's all beyond remedy. . . . I do harm to those I love because by making them do things, I try to satisfy a burning thirst within myself. . . . Do you remember, Bertrand, my wish one evening on the terrace at Saint-Arnoult, when I was talking to you and the Abbé? I was right. . . . I ought to have died there and then."

"Not at all," said Bertrand. "Things are much less complicated than you imagine. You are in search of love; you don't know what it is; you mistake for love a thousand and one other things that you chase after; when you catch hold of one of them, you discover your mistake. There's your whole story."

"Do you think so?"

The cinema grew dark again. A lion roared in a

ring. Horses trotted along a road in the Pyrenees. There was the sound of a mallet striking a ball on a polo-ground in the Argentine. Aeroplanes shrouded the American fleet in a white impenetrable mist. A minister shouted. A bird sang. A globe revolved.

XVI

THE Holmanns usually went to Saint-Arnoult as early as June. In 1931 they had sent their children there, but financial troubles and the bad weather had kept the parents in Paris. Even by the end of July they only got away with great difficulty. All their friends, like themselves, seemed to be fastened to Paris by an insuperable force. It seemed as if, amid this vast confusion of a civilization, human beings were aware of the danger threatening the species, and felt in need of each other. The Schmitts had stayed in town; so had the Thianges. Denise telephoned to her children every evening. Marie-Laure was complaining:

"Mummy, you never come any more. Promise you'll be there on August 2nd for my birthday."

"That's a Sunday," Denise said to her husband. "This time we must make up our minds. I hate disappointing the children. Let's go down to Saint-Arnoult on the Saturday, and if you still have work to do, you can come back to Paris on the Monday."

When they arrived, they found little Olivier in bed with a slight cold, but Marie-Laure and Patrice were delighted to see them. They were cheerful and natural. Patrice was fully absorbed with a puppy, Miquette, which the gardener Ferrand had just given him.

"Miquette's been ill, Mummy. It's her own fault. Do you know what she does? She eats filthy things, the insides of animals . . . you know, Daddy, she goes out hunting at night. She kills rabbits with her teeth. Ferrand has seen her. Ferrand has given us each a little garden. . . ."

"Yes," said Marie-Laure, "but we haven't done anything to them and they're full of weeds. Mummy, have you remembered my birthday cake and my nine candles?"

Denise had remembered. She had also brought Marie-Laure's present. She was determined that, even in that year of disaster, her daughter's birthday should be a happy memory for the child. The weather was fine. In the sun-filled meadows the brown and white cows were seeking the shade of the trees in the hedges. Denise enjoyed sitting on the terrace, but the children's prattle soon tired her. She envied women like Helene de Thianges, who could play children's games all day long and enjoy themselves. The governesses would say: "She doesn't love her children." It wasn't true. She would have done anything for them, but in their company she felt a stranger and restless.

"You know, Marie-Laure," she said, "Monsieur Schmitt and Monsieur de Lauterie are coming this evening.　They will be at your birthday luncheon.　Have you ordered it yet?"

It was the custom for the three children to be allowed to order a meal on their birthdays.

From the open window a mechanical voice spread out over the terrace.

"New York Stock Market. . . . Opening dull. Price list of Messrs. . . ."

"Daddy has turned on the wireless," said Patrice.

"Edmond!" cried Denise.　"No, no!　Don't let yourself be pestered here. . . . Hand me my book, will you?"

He switched off the set, brought out the book, and, picking up a newspaper, sat down beside her.　Alone at Saint-Arnoult with Denise and the children, he was happy.　She tried to read:

"The actions of a few men have for thousands of men consequences comparable to those which the disturbances and changes of their surroundings have for all living beings."

Patrice called his dog.

"Miquette!　Miquette, don't touch that!　Miquette, dirty, dirty!　Here, Miquette!"

"Every being must play the tyrant to another," Denise thought to herself.　She read on: "As natural causes produce hail, typhoons, rainbows, and epidemics, so intelligent causes act upon millions of men, the majority of whom suffer them as they suffer the uncontrollable behaviour of the heavens, the sea, and the earth's crust.　Intelligence and will. . . ."

A bell rang in the drawing-room.

"The telephone," she said with annoyance. "Paris is determined not to leave us in peace. See what it is, Edmond."

He went in to the house, and came out again at once.

"It's for you," he said coldly. "A man's voice."

"Lauterie or Schmitt to say they can't come."

She rose and went to the telephone. In one corner of the drawing-room Marie-Laure lay stretched on her stomach looking at old illustrated papers. Denise picked up the receiver. It was Monteix. She was surprised. The Chamber had adjourned.

"Hullo! Yes, I see," she said. "I thought you were in Périgord."

"No, I'm in Paris for twenty-four hours. I simply must see you. I'm in a very serious mess. An evening with you would be so good for me."

"I am terribly sorry," she said, "it's impossible. The children would be too disappointed."

She looked at Marie-Laure, silently absorbed in her papers. The child had not raised her head.

"Look here, Monteix," she went on, "it's quite simple. You just push on as far as here. We are having friends of yours, Lauterie and the Schmitts."

"No, no," he said. "That wouldn't be the same thing at all. . . . I'm in no state for general conversation. It's you I want. I beg you, do come back, even if it's only for one evening."

"I can't."

"I thought you were more kind-hearted. You've got all the holidays in which to see your children."

Already she was weakening.

"But it's your own fault," she said. "Why do you pick on this day? You know very well that on Saturdays we're nearly always at Saint-Arnoult."

"No. In your last letter you said, 'We can't make up our minds to leave Paris.' I've come from the recesses of the Dordogne to see you. Picture my disappointment when your concierge said you had gone away. . . . I beg you. . . . Only one evening."

"But the house is shut up."

"Go to a hotel."

"No, I can't do that."

She glanced outside. Edmond seemed to be reading, but undoubtedly he was listening. There was a hum of insects. A red-necked bird had dropped on to the lawn and was pecking. In the silence of the countryside, a cart could be heard creaking its way up to some farm. Denise pictured the emaciated face of Monteix, creased with yearning and anguish.

"Well, then . . . Hullo! You hear me? This evening is quite impossible; I'm expecting Lauterie and the Schmitts; and for me to go away would be rude and inexplicable. But to-morrow I'll leave after the children's tea and I'll spend the evening with you. Pleased? Where do I meet you? Where? All right. . . . Well then, about eight. . . . No, I'll come by train. . . . Yes. . . . Of course. . . . Till to-morrow!"

She hung up and went out to explain things to her husband. Already he had got up.

"I imagine I must have misunderstood," he said. "You can't have told Monteix you would go to Paris to-morrow afternoon?"

She had intended to be skilful and affectionate, but this sudden attack put her in turn on the defensive.

"Why not?" she said shortly.

"Because it's absolutely impossible. We've just got here; we've got friends over the week-end. . . ."

"You'll be with them."

"Denise, really, you're off your head! You don't suppose I am going to let you spend a night alone in Paris."

"You don't suppose I'm going to ask your permission?"

"In that case I'll go with you."

"That would be ridiculous, and it's impossible. You can't leave our guests here alone. And anyhow, I'm going to Paris to see Monteix; he's unhappy, in some mess, and he wants to see me—me, not you. . . ."

"Look here, Denise, think what you're doing. Do you imagine I will tolerate your going off to that fellow?"

She was now quite out of hand.

"Yes, I do imagine it. I shan't be doing any harm. Monteix has been a wonderfully good friend to both of us. You know that as well as I do. This time it is he who is in a mess. I'm not the sort to fail my friends when they need me.　Whether you like it or not, I'm going, and I'll go alone."

"Where will you sleep?"

"At an hotel.　Or in the Rue Alfred de Vigny."

"It's shut up."

"It isn't very difficult for the concierge to make up a bed."

Little Patrice ran up howling.

"Mummy, Miquette has been sick all over my hands."

"You swear to me you'll go to the Rue Alfred de Vigny?" said Holmann.

She saw the two children standing before her. Marie-Laure was pale.　Denise signed to Edmond to be silent.

"Please stop this. . . . The children are listening," she said.　"What were you saying, Patrice?"

"Miquette has been sick all over my hands."

"Whose fault is that?" said his sister.　"You give it meat four times a day, and Ferrand told you not to."

"It's not true!　It's not true!　I'll tell you wot she's been doing.　She's been rummaging in the dustbin."

"That's enough!　Enough!" said Denise.　"Go and ask Mademoiselle to wash your hands with eau-de-Cologne. . . .　And you must not say: 'I'll tell you *wot* she's been doing.'　Say: 'I'll tell you *what* she's been doing.'　Do you hear?"

XVII

To cut short any argument with Edmond, she went upstairs with the children, and as she went through the linen-room she said to Lucie:

"Pack my bag for to-morrow afternoon. I'll drive over to Evreux and catch the six-thirty-nine. Just put in my rose-coloured wrap, pyjamas, and some other jewellery. . . . No, no dresses. I shall be back on Monday."

She stopped short, because she had just caught sight of Marie-Laure in the little mirror hanging on the wall. The child was standing behind her with downcast head, listening.

"What are you doing there, Marie-Laure?"

"Waiting for Patrice, Mummy. . . . He's washing his hands."

"Go and wait for him downstairs. . . . Or go and keep Olivier company."

"Yes, Mummy. Is it true that you're going away?"

"Only for a night, darling, and not before to-morrow."

"But to-morrow is my birthday."

"That's why I shan't go till late. I want to be at your birthday dinner."

Marie-Laure grew sulky.

"It's my birthday late as well," she said.

Then she called to her brother.

"Pat, when you're ready, get your bike; we'll go down to the bottom of the avenue."

She went out without looking at her mother.

It proved an uncomfortable day. The children had disappeared; they were not seen again until tea-time. Edmond, pale and taciturn, said nothing except to complain of the pain in his chest. For three months he had been thinking he was ill, and would refer to an aneurism and angina pectoris. The doctors had said there was no lesion in his heart, and that his symptoms were due to nerves. The Schmitts and Lauterie, arriving together about six, realized at once that they had penetrated into a danger-zone and must advance with extreme caution. At dinner-time the children came to say good night. Denise was even more affectionate than usual with them, but they kissed her very formally, and their " 'Night, Mummy," was barely audible.

It was growing dark. Twilight at Saint-Arnoult was like twilight by the sea. A ring of fiery clouds circled the hills. A star came out. The scent of honeysuckle spread over the terrace. Denise put the "Pea Nut Vendor" record on the gramophone; it was the song of the year, and she liked it. The men were smoking in silence. Isabelle, inquisitive and ironical, strove to solve the mystery of the evening's tension. Bertrand said:

"I think I'll take a little walk. Coming, Denise?"

"If you go out, take a coat," said Holmann, "or your Spanish shawl."

Lauterie went into the house to stop the record. Isabelle remained alone with Holmann. They talked about bringing up children. Isabelle said that her son Alain did not care for reading. Patrice was like him. The new generation was a generation of mechanics. Then Holmann, hesitatingly, tried to prepare Isabelle for the coming departure of Denise.

That night the Schmitts discussed the situation in their room.

"It's past belief," said Isabelle. "She's off to-morrow at five, leaving us alone with her husband. . . . It's too much of a good thing. . . ."

"She has explained everything to me," said Bertrand. "She has reasons which I fully understand."

"What are they?"

"I can't betray a confidence."

Next morning when the maid came to open Denise's bedroom shutters, she first made sure that Monsieur Holmann was in the bath-room, at the far end of the passage, and came close up to the bed and said:

"Madame, there's been an accident. But it's nothing to do with me. It's not my fault."

Denise sat up in terror.

"What's happened?"

"Madame, you told me last night to pack pyjamas and your rose-coloured wrap. So as not to get behind-hand to-day, with the extra work for the guests, I ironed them after my dinner, folded them in tissue paper, and everything. . . . This morning I opened your bag to put in your toilet set—and what a sight! Just one great smear! Somebody has poured a bottle of ink right into the bag."

"Ink! But who can have been so wicked . . . ?"

"Oh, I can tell you, Madame. There's no doubt about it. It was the children. Because it's black ink, and they are the only ones who use black ink. . . . You and the master, and everybody in the kitchen, all use blue ink. . . . What's more, I was talking to Mademoiselle about it, and she said she could see very well yesterday afternoon that the children were plotting."

Denise had gone dead white. She jumped out of bed.

"Mademoiselle might have warned me," she said. "I hope she hasn't spoken to the children about this affair."

"No, Madame, because they're still asleep. But they won't lose anything by waiting; she will punish them."

"Tell her that I forbid her to mention it to them," said Denise. "No. Wait. I'll go myself."

"Well, what am I to pack for your journey, Madame?"

Denise reflected, went to the window, and pulled back the curtains. It promised to be a fine summer's day.

"I don't know at all, Lucie. . . . I think I shan't go. . . . Get through to the Hôtel du Quai Voltaire in Paris for me. Or rather, no. . . . Can one send telegrams on a Sunday?"

"Yes, Madame, by telephoning them before midday."

"All right, hand me the telephone. And go and turn on my bath."

Once she was alone, she dictated a telegram.

" 'Mon-teix.' No, no, Mademoiselle. . . . 'Mon-teix.' X for Xavier. 'Hotel du Quai Voltaire, Paris. Despite strong desire come am detained here by unavoidable obstacle.' No, cross out the last three words. Just put: 'Am detained here. Forgive me. Sincerely.' Sign D.' Yes, D for Denise. That's all. Will you read it over?"

Sunday proved even more gloomy than the Saturday. The children were mysterious and hostile, expecting a question which never came. Twice Denise was called to the telephone.

"Madame, there's a Paris call for you."

She had the call put through to her room, and went up to speak out of earshot of the inquisitive. At eleven she took the children to church. Isabelle went with her. The *curé* of Saint-Arnoult preached a sermon on the duties of husband and wife. Marie-Laure listened attentively. Patrice played with his cap and looked at a little baby who wanted to cry and was restrained with great difficulty.

Lauterie and Schmitt, who had remained on the terrace, were discussing the state of the world.

"Are we witnessing the bankruptcy of capitalism?" Lauterie was saying. "Perhaps to historians of the future our era of swollen credits will seem like a curious madness on men's part. Perhaps they will regard it as we regard John Law's system. Or will our notion of

securing currency with gold seem half-witted in years
to come?"

"I think it more likely," said Bertrand, "that we are
witnessing the bankruptcy of democracy. Governments
are as old as their finances, as men are as old as their
arteries. Absolute monarchy was vulnerable through
the prince's personal expenditure and through its weak
fiscal capacity. Democracy is still more vulnerable because it becomes demagogic and dissipates a country's
reserves to win votes. It is paralysed because it cannot
act quickly. The United States Congress is certainly
the most ridiculous and unwieldy institution imaginable
for a business nation. And even here in France. . . ."

Holmann joined them and asked if they had slept
well. He seemed cheerful and soothed.

"You've heard Denise is not going after all," he said.
"The sunshine and her friends have kept her."

"Splendid!" said Lauterie. "That's good news. . . .
I don't altogether agree," he continued, addressing
Bertrand. "It is not so much democracy, as a certain
type of parliamentary democracy, that has failed. I
think the corporative industries will play an ever greater
part in the state. Inside every such industry, strict
control will be essential. The stock exchange brokers
exercise it. Banks. . . ."

"Oh, if you're going to bring up the banks," said
Holmann, "I'll go and meet the children."

He took the little path that led to the church.

"Was it Monteix who asked her to come to Paris?"
Lauterie murmured. "Did she tell you?"

"Yes," said Bertrand. "I don't know why she dropped it. . . . I'm almost sorry. That whole-hearted conception of friendship. . . ."

They stopped talking because the group of women and children had appeared round the corner of the terrace. Patrice was running ahead, calling his dog.

"Miquette!"

Marie-Laure, very cheerful, came and said good morning to Bertrand Schmitt, who was a friend of hers.

"Good morning, you lazy men," said Denise. "You're sure you've had everything you needed? Lauterie, may I take Bertrand away from you for five minutes? I want a word with him."

She led Bertrand Schmitt into the rose garden.

"I want to talk to you," she said. "It's more than I can stand. . . . Has Edmond told you I've decided not to go? Monteix has telephoned three times this morning. He reproaches me violently, says I've behaved like a silly flirt, and that I have every kind of bourgeois cowardice. Edmond doesn't understand what has happened, and assumes the air of a conqueror, which infuriates me. And on top of it all there are the children. . . ."

She told him about the ink bottle.

"You realize, I'm terrified of making my children suffer as I suffered myself. . . . It's an obsession. . . . Yes, I know all about your theory that modern children don't worry about such things. . . . Perhaps it's true when they're older, adolescent, and even then I'm not certain. . . . But it is certainly not true when they're quite small. Oh, not at all. I've seen the look in Marie-Laure's eyes sometimes. . . . That child is beginning to size me up. . . . So altogether, what with her, my husband, and Monteix, I've had enough— believe me, more than enough."

"Well, go away," he said. "When things are all wrong, a change of scene nearly always acts like a charm."

"Yes, but where could I go? If I go to Versailles or to Tamaris, Edmond will now feel that I'm going off to Monteix. Do you know where I would go if I hadn't such painful memories of the place? To Pont-de-l'Eure. My mother always sends me a pressing invitation in her letters."

"Why, certainly!" he said. "Go to Pont-de-l'Eure. It will probably do you far more good than you imagine. Nothing is more unhealthy for a nervous person than to persist in the fear of some house or some person. Phantoms must be dissolved by going straight for them. Treat your body like a horse which won't take a jump. Use the whip!"

She pushed aside a branch obstructing the path.

"Mind your eyes, Bertrand. . . . There's a good deal of truth in what you say. . . . Yes, if I can bring myself to do it, I'll go to Pont-de-l'Eure. Say what you like, this business with the children makes me ill. . . . I took such precautions against that danger. That is why I left them in the country nearly all the year round. . . . You remember, Bertrand? 'The Marionette has understood the Play!' Yes, but what's the good of her having understood, poor wretch? She goes on acting God's play."

"Partly at least. Did I tell you that I've got an epilogue for my play?"

"No. . . . What is it?"

"The marionettes have heroically staged their own play and their leaps or listlessness have more or less freed them from the Showman's strings. The curtain falls. When it rises again, the Showman is seen once more on the lower stage, quite unmoved. He carefully stows away the puppets in their box and announces his next play. . . . Don't you think that's good?"

"It's a sad ending."

"Why sad? It's natural. . . . We shall all be beaten by death, but we shall have made a noble or base use of our existence according to our courage. However, my play is not quite true to life. In real life the strings are invisible and the Showman does not care. It's easier."

"I like your optimism, Bertrand. There's something despairing in it which appeals to me. . . . You leap into the abyss saying, 'All's well.' Sometimes I think that I'm going to follow your example, live for the moment, leap. . . ."

They were passing a little pond with ducks on it. Bertrand gazed at the double wake left behind each bird, a liquid angle forking wider and wider till the tipples touched the bank. He stopped, picked up a stone, and threw it into the water. Circular eddies, started by the splash, spread wider and wider as far as the eye could follow them, and streaked the reflections of the trees with horizontal strokes. The pond became smooth again. Denise had followed Bertrand's action and his thought. She met his glance and smiled.

XVIII

THE familiar journey from Paris to Pont-de-l'Eure passed quickly. A bald, fat man tried to get into conversation with Denise. He told her that he was an orchestral conductor, on his way to England from Egypt. His wife was much younger than he. He had a little boy. He didn't like leaving them. Denise listened inattentively but sympathetically. Strings of barges were gliding between the rows of poplars. Alone in this narrow box with a stranger, she felt wonderfully free. How little it needed to escape one's destinies! A little courage, a few hours in a train. Through the doorway of the corridor she caught scraps of conversation:

"He only opens his mouth five or six times in a year, and always to announce a disaster. . . ."

She tried to get on with her book. . . . It was a study of Chekhov:

"How strange the destiny of these heroes of Chekhov's! They strain their inward forces to the utmost, but with no outward result. They all stir our pity.

One woman takes snuff, dresses anyhow, neglects her hair, and lets herself go; another man is irritable and grumbling, a drunkard who wears out the patience of those around him. They all speak and act irrelevantly. They do not know how, if indeed they ever wish, to adapt the external world to their needs."

In the corridor the same voice went on:

"He has two thousand seven hundred and twenty-five hours' flying to his credit. . . . From that standpoint, he is attractive. But his father and his younger brother don't get on with him. He looks on them as idiots. He doesn't try to hide it."

She amused herself by picturing a family involved in some drama; then she continued reading:

"It is impossible to reflect calmly and try to foresee the future. One can only run one's head against a wall, interminably. What will it lead to? In the long run, will it lead to anything?, Is it the end or the beginning? Is it a new form of creation, or non-human creation, *ex nihilo?* 'I can't tell,' replies the old professor to his ward Katia, who is shaking with sobs. 'I can't tell,' Chekhov replies to all who weep, all who are tortured. It is with these words, solely with these words, that a study of Chekhov must end—'Resign thyself, O my heart, sleep on as the brute beast sleeps.' "

She closed the book and wondered.

"Why, 'the brute beast'?" she asked herself. "Bertrand too would say 'I can't tell'; but he would add, 'still, I am trying to know something.' 'Resign thyself, O my heart, and sleep on as the brute beast sleeps. . . .'

Yes, sometimes, one has to sleep like that to forget, to let the brute beast be reborn. But are there no awakenings? No victories?"

She looked out at the hills near Pont-de-l'Eure, at the chalky cliffs and grassy humps where she knew every footpath, and felt as if she were on the verge of some such awakening, and reaching one of those peaks from which, after years of climbing and struggle and disappointment, the spirit discovers a great truth.

"What truth?" she asked herself, surprised at her own cheerfulness.

The din of the wheels became louder. The train was crossing the bridge just before Pont-de-l'Eure. Denise got up, put her book away in her bag, and looked out of the window. She knew every farm and every house hereabouts by name. The braked wheels screeched.

"Pont-de-l'Eure!"

Madame Guérin was on the platform, smiling and animated.

"What a lovely surprise!" she said. "You can't imagine how delighted we were to get your wire! Give your bag to the chauffeur . . . I've hired a car from Monsieur Bouctot . . . Georges needed his. . . . Monsieur Bouctot, take Madame Holmann's bag. . . . You know, Georges is terribly busy," she said, as Denise was looking for her ticket to give up to the collector. (It was no longer the fat man who used to say "Fine day to you, lady and gents!") "He is now the chief medical officer at the hospital. Monsieur de Thianges expects he will be promoted an officer of the Legion of Honour in the Fourteenth of July List. . . . Now, your friend Monteix might do something about it. . . . Do you still see him? We read his speech about Geneva. Georges said it was good, but rather vague. . . . Will you get in? We're going to the Rue Carnot, Monsieur Bouctot."

The town was dead. A few dogs wandered from one refuse-heap to the next. The car took the street running alongside the wall of the Quesnay factories. On the pavement a very old gentleman went hurrying by, his elbows pressed in, a freshly cut flower in his buttonhole. It was Monsieur Lesage-Maille. Where was he off to? Down a gutter a wide yellow stream poured like a torrent. The factory chimneys were giving out smoke. The dull thump of the looms vibrated the warm air.

"The factories aren't very busy," said Madame Guérin. "It's this depression. . . . But Georges says we haven't much to complain about. I've asked the young Bernard Quesnays for this evening to see you, and of course Jacques and Lolotte as well."

"Are you on good terms with the Quesnays?"

"What a question, Denise! I am on good terms with everybody. Madame Pelletot says I am the town's Providence. They've asked me to preside over the Maternity Clinic Committee. By the way, may I put you down as a donation member?"

"And Victorine and Eugénie are still with you?"

"Of course. . . . You heard that Eugénie married

Georges's manservant?　Just now he is at the Rue de la Convention, at Georges's consulting-room."

"Where is the Rue de la Convention?　I've forgotten."

"It must be new to you: it used to be the Rue Saint-Etienne. . . .　This Municipal Council, you know. . . .　We have kept on both houses.　The Rue Carnot was not convenient for Georges.　There was no way of fitting up an operating-room.　Ultra-violet rays, radiography—all that is available in the Rue de la Convention."

The car was stopping at the corner of the Rue Carnot. The brick house looked asleep and uninviting.　Opposite, outside the café-tobacconist's, a workman in a cap turned round.　Eugénie was on the pavement.　She had grown grey, but was wearing the same blouse as in the old days, with an upright collar with a white border. A threaded needle was stuck over her bosom.

"Ah, here's Mademoiselle!　It's very nice to be seeing Mademoiselle Denise."

"What do you mean—*Mademoiselle* Denise?" said Madame Guérin gaily.　"I've given you your old room, you know.　I thought you would like that."

Followed by Eugénie, carrying the bag, they went up the narrow twisting staircase.　The plaster showed a scratch made by Monsieur Herpain's coffin.

"She is right," thought Denise, as she detected an almost imperceptible smell of carbolic acid.　"I'm glad to think I shall sleep to-night in my room.　It's queer.

. . . I used to be so unhappy in this house. . . . Perhaps it is just because I used to be so unhappy."

Her mother came into the room with her.

"Look, I'll unpack your bag. . . . What's this you've got? Pyjamas? So you sleep in pyjamas? Don't you think it's not very womanly?"

Outside a train whistled. For a brief moment Denise felt as she had when a child—she longed for this woman to leave the room, longed to be alone. Then the scene struck her as unreal and comical.

"I told you Jacques and Lolotte are coming to dinner? They'll be ever so pleased to see you . . . Jacques and Georges get on together very well, especially since Georges pulled Jacques through his pneumonia. I'll put your books on the table by the bed. What have you got? 'Une Femme à sa fenêtre' . . . 'Point Counterpoint.' . . . Do you think that sort of thing is all right? Georges, you know, has come to like your Proust, and got me to like him too. He reads aloud to me on evenings when he isn't disturbed. . . . It's appalling how often he's called out—even other doctors want to consult him. Yet heaven knows what jealousy there is among doctors! You didn't hear the sound of a car? I think it must be he. I'll go down; if it is, I'll call."

She vanished.

"How she loves him!" thought Denise again. . . .

Then she lay down on the bed of her girlhood. Six o'clock struck. The carillon of the École Bossuet played "Le Carnaval de Venise." Between two phrases it paused so long that one wondered if it would ever go on.

XIX

WITH his fresh, pink complexion, and his rather long, curling white locks, like those of a certain British statesman, Guérin had an imposing look. He greeted Denise with an admirably compounded mixture of assurance, reserve, fondness, and gallantry.

"You are very welcome," he said.

Pressing Denise's hand between both of his, he examined her features with a clinical eye as if looking for symptoms or making sure that a recovery was complete.

"Had an interesting day?" Madame Guérin asked him.

"Very. . . . I operated at the hospital for an intestinal occlusion, and I think I've saved my man. Then I had a consultation at Louviers for the little Bellouin girl. . . . Leucocæmia—nothing to be done."

The three of them had entered the drawing-room, and the doctor had taken the big arm-chair.

"Poor Papa," thought Denise, "he never had that easy manner, or such authority, such strength. . . ."

About seven Jacques and Charlotte arrived for dinner. The Guérins were faithful to the provincial times for meals. Denise and Charlotte kissed. Denise was looking at Jacques in astonishment. He had become quite stout; she hardly recognized him.

"Is that the man who was my first lover?" she said to herself.

The idea, like the fear of her mother just now, seemed alien to her own life. Jacques was embarrassed and sought to hide it under an assumed gaiety. Denise felt that Charlotte was watching them. Then she decided she was mistaken. Jacques had certainly never told. "He was a sensible fellow," she reminded herself.

The arrival of the Bernard Quesnays broke the family circle, and relieved a tension that had become almost painful. Bernard had matured very differently from Jacques. He was spare and bronzed, but hints of future wrinkles marked out the lines of his face. His wife, Yvonne, on the contrary, had grown thin and almost pretty. The two young couples, the Pelletots and the Quesnays, engaged in a conversation of local interest: they arranged a bridge-party for next day and agreed to go together on Sunday to the Rouen golf club. Denise welcomed the announcement of dinner.

"Victorine insisted on combining all your favourite dishes," said Madame Guérin. "It will make rather an odd meal, and I apologize; but she was so keen on it. . . . You're going to have your famous chocolate cake."

"Alas! Mamma, my liver doesn't allow me to touch chocolate."

"Oh, you'll have to eat a little; poor Victorine would

be so upset otherwise. It won't be defying doctor's orders?" she added, turning to her husband.

"Not at all," he said. "Happy memories are the best thing for the digestion."

His manservant was waiting at table, assisted by Eugénie. Yvonne Quesnay spoke of her boy; she was asked if she intended to make a manufacturer of him, and if he already had the abrupt ways of Monsieur Achille and Bernard?

"I don't know," said Bernard, "whether the trade is hereditary."

"Not at all," said the doctor. "People have the most ridiculous notions about heredity. No characteristics acquired during life are hereditable. You may both go and live naked under the African sun, make yourselves as dark as negroes—your children will be born white just the same."

"Yes," said Jacques very quickly, "that is Weismann's theory, but nevertheless. . . ."

"Jacques wants to show me that his brain isn't rusty," thought Denise.

"Nevertheless," he continued, "chickens have learned in two generations to get out of the way of cars."

"No," said the doctor, "each generation of chickens learns from the previous generations, just as Bernard has been given an oral tradition and an example by his grandfather."

"Are you as hard as your grandfather, Bernard?" said Madame Guérin. "Poor Louis was awfully afraid of him."

"Bernard?" said his wife. "Oh, yes he's appallingly 'Quesnay.'"

"Denise, do you notice? *Your* macaroni mould . . . ." said Madame Guérin with a fond look.

"Why *appallingly?*" said Bernard, a little vexed. "I've realized that one can't run a big factory without subjecting oneself to a strict personal discipline. . . . A simple life, immense reserves, limitations of production . . . otherwise one founders in a slump. . . . There was once a great economist—Joseph, Joseph of the Bible, who interpreted the dream of the fat and the lean kine. . . . But most men forget that the lean years are bound to follow the years of plenty."

Denise was watching him with approval. She liked his strong head, his rather domineering voice.

"But don't you think, Bernard," she said, "that if we were better organized, society could join up the fat kine?"

He shook his head contemptuously.

"What are you trying to suggest? I've learned one thing, and it was just as true during the War as in my own business. In action there are no rules, no unvarying doctrine. One has to devise the means whenever one comes to an obstruction. . . . Always. . . . And it will always be true. Humanity will never be able to go to sleep in a capitalist or a Bolshevist paradise, saying, 'This time we've hit on the right way.' And I add, 'All the better, for it would be damned boring.'"

The doctor agreed.

"Quite true, Bernard; and it's true also in medicine, which is a form of action. Certain diseases are cured; other diseases rise up. . . . Vaccines are invented; germs become harder to kill. . . . Man's struggle with the world will never end. . . . And there is something fine in that."

"Denise," said Madame Guérin, "*your* chicken with olives. . . ."

A bell rang insistently. Eugénie came and murmured to Madame Guérin that Madame Holmann was wanted on the telephone. Denise went to the instrument. It was her husband. He told her how the children were getting on. Marie-Laure was running a temperature, 100: nothing serious, but he hoped Denise would come home soon. The Bourse? Bad, depressed. And herself? Was she enjoying her visit?

"Yes, very much. I must say I'm having quite a good time. . . . I find the people in Pont-de-l'Eure very interesting. Their talk is worthy of old Madame de Choin's. No, no, I shan't stay long . . . I'll see you soon, darling."

She rang off.

XX

THE conversation after dinner was lively. Denise talked a good deal with Bernard Quesnay, and invited him to come and see her in Paris. Then she made an effort to recover intimacy with Charlotte, but the two sisters soon dropped into artificialities. Their common ground was dead. About nine o'clock the doctor suggested a little music.

"I should like you to see what astonishing progress your mother has made," he said to Denise. "We play nearly every evening. . . . You'll be surprised."

Madame Guérin stood up eagerly and brought the music-stand and the violin. Then, standing motionless in front of the music cabinet, she said, almost respectfully:

"What shall we play, Georges?"

"Whatever you like. Why not the Franck sonata in *A* major? You accompanied it very well last Sunday."

She looked through a pile of scores for the sonata. In a respectful gloom the audience settled themselves in arm-chairs. Bernard Quesnay immediately flew in thought to his factory; his lips moved; his finger tapped the arm of his chair, counting off bales of wool, or wages. Yvonne, leaning forward and resting her chin on her hand, gazed at Denise, trying to imagine a life reputed to be romantic. Jacques too kept his gaze on Denise, and seemed to want to catch her eye. What did he want? Approval? Regret? Was he thinking of that young body which he had been the first to win? Of that murmur of protest or pleasure that she gave so gently after their love-making? Charlotte was watching her husband. Denise gazed with admiring curiosity at her mother and step-father: what a fine pair they made! Standing alert, with his bow poised, the white-haired doctor was a picture of restrained strength and fine intellect. Madame Guérin, whom Denise could see only in profile, was radiant with fond submissiveness. She raised her eyes to her husband, smiled, and then, leaning over the keyboard, began.

"What sureness!" thought Denise after the first bars. "Obviously a man's mind has given order to her playing—and her mind!"

Caught up by the music, she listened delightedly to the dialogue of piano and violin. Helping one another, tossing the theme to each other like twin jugglers, catching it together and raising it, lifting it higher every time, ever higher, the two instruments seemed partners in a common and sublime task.

"How beautiful!" thought Denise.

To her, that sonata seemed to mirror love as she had dreamed it—understanding, harmony, dialogue, a brave effort to raise two united lives to heroic peaks. "How they understand each other!" she thought again, as piano and violin rose entwined, soaring with a strength that took one's breath away. She compared her mother's life with her own. Why had she been so unsparing in her blame? "How harsh we were, my sisters and I! And she's forgotten it all! 'You were so spoiled,' she says. . . ."

Denise saw the three young savages barring a door with their thin arms against that kindly, earnest woman who was leaning like a dutiful schoolgirl over her keyboard. "What was her crime?" she thought. "She loved this man; he was strong and brilliant and worthy of love. She did not love my father, who was good but weak." She pictured Monsieur Herpain standing beside that same piano, his head on one side, and singing the *cavatina* from "Faust" in his timid voice, and a stab of pain shot through her, as if the bow had been drawn over some sensitive string inside her. "Poor Papa. . . . She ought not to have hurt him. . . . But don't I hurt Edmond?"

Edmond, pale and anxious, waiting for her on the evening when she had gone out with Monteix. . . . Edmond at Saint-Arnoult, in despair. . . . The dark looks of Marie-Laure. . . . Remorse. . . . The music swept them all away. . . . "How strange!" she thought. "I've suffered so much in this house, on account of this man and this woman, and to-night, after fifteen years, I am watching them with indifference and even sympathy. . . . Those memories were so long tragic and unbearable, and now they are detached from me, and harmless. . . . A painful and living present has become a dead past. . . . The sins that drove me nearly mad with shame and pain . . . a dead past. . . . And doubtless this present which I have just fled, difficult and bewildering as it is, will one day become unreal, like a long-past dream. And Edmond will be an elderly husband, not too faithful, and I shall look after him kindly. And then there will be other difficulties that will seem dreadful and surmountable. . . .

And these in turn will be quelled by death." An extraordinary peace came over her. The crest was conquered, the plain lay open below. The piano and violin bore her away with them into a world of tranquillity where all conflicts were resolved. She was surprised when the music stopped. Her stepfather and her mother had turned to her, awaiting her comment.

She spoke, but without knowing what she said. Her emotion was too strong. Carefully, with his clever, surgeon's fingers, the doctor put the violin back in its case.

"And now," he said to his wife, "you *must* sing."

"What an idea, Georges! An old woman. . . . I haven't sung for at least three years. . . . Since my bronchitis."

"I know your voice hasn't altered," said Georges. "It's a mere inhibition. . . . And this evening is a unique chance for overcoming it. . . . Come, Denise, help me!"

"Well, all right, I will sing," said Madame Guérin fondly, "but on one condition—that my little daughter accompanies me—as she used to."

Denise protested: she never played at all now; she couldn't. The others gathered round and pressed her. Suddenly she felt that she wanted to. "One must make oneself suffer," Dr. Bias had said. . . . "Press on the sensitive points," Dr. Bias had said. . . .

"Yes, I will," she said to her mother, "but on one condition too—that you sing Duparc's 'Vie antérieure.' "

"The 'Vie antérieure'?" said Madame Guérin in surprise. "Yes. . . . But why?"

Denise anxiously scanned her mother's face. Clearly, the title recalled nothing to her. The doctor too seemed surprised, but indulgent and indifferent. Madame Guérin was a long time looking for the music; at last she came back, triumphant: she had found it. Denise slipped off her rings and sat down at the piano.

"Can you see all right?" asked Madame Guérin. "Take off the shade, will you; I can't make out the words."

The pages of the song, forgotten in a damp cupboard for twenty years, were yellow and spotted.

"How very like her mother Denise is!" murmured the doctor, leaning over to Bernard.

The powerful voice rose up:

"*. . . sous de vastes portiques.*"

Denise conjured up a smell of earth and rotted geraniums, a little girl in a nightdress too long for her, the thick, ruddy neck of the seated man, the waves breaking softly on the sand with a sound of rustling paper. But the quiet beat of her heart, the calm, skilful movements of her hands over the keys, told her that the wound was drained of its poison, that the scar was closed.

"*Les houles, en roulant les images des cieux . . .*"

As she followed that voice, now bearing it up, now striving with it in strength and beauty, she felt a bodily pleasure, an acute sense of joy.

"How she can sing!" she thought.

A train whistled.